MURDER GOES TO MARKET

Published 2020 by Seventh Street Books®

Inquiries should be addressed to
Start Science Fiction
221 River Street, 9th Floor
Hoboken, NJ 07030
Phone: 212-431-5455
www.seventhstreetbooks.com

10 9 8 7 6 5 4 3 2 1
ISBN: 978-1-64506-012-3 (paperback)
ISBN: 978-1-64506-027-7 (ebook)

Printed in the United States of America

MURDER GOES TO MARKET

DAISY BATEMAN

For Cameron

CHAPTER ONE

It is a truth insufficiently acknowledged that a person in possession of a business must at some point want to yell at someone. Claudia Simcoe took a breath and looked down at the stack of paper in her hand. There was nothing for it; it had to be done.

"Lori, do you have a minute?"

Lori Roth, the eponymous proprietor of Lori's Handmade Creations, didn't look up from the pile of tie-dyed placemats she was sorting. "I'm busy right now. Can it wait?"

"Not really." Claudia laid down one of the sheets where the other woman could see it. "This is kind of important."

The page was a printout from the website of a large wholesale importer. The printer that had produced it was not top quality, and almost out of yellow ink, but the images were clear enough to identify the products, next to their wholesale prices and volume discounts, and match them up exactly to the "handmade creations" Lori was selling, at what Claudia now knew was up to a five-hundred percent markup.

"Where did you get that?" Lori asked.

It wasn't the response Claudia had been hoping for. Rather than embarrassed or ashamed, Lori seemed suspicious. Irritated, Claudia pressed on.

"I don't think that's the most important thing right now," she said. "Are these your products?"

"Would you believe me if I said no?"

"No." It was occurring to Claudia that she didn't know much about the other woman. Lori was the newest vendor in the marketplace Claudia ran, a home for independent businesses that were only supposed to sell things that fell into the local and/or artisanal categories. And while Claudia supposed you could make the argument that the machine operators in the overseas factories were artisans in their own way, it wasn't what the customers expected.

Lori herself certainly fit the brief, with her long hair, loose skirts, and coarsely-knitted cardigans, all in an undifferentiated mass of earth tones. Claudia had been surprised to learn, from the driver's license she provided with her application, that Lori was younger than she looked, only a few years older than Claudia's own thirty-four.

Right now she was looking like a sulky child, caught with her fingers in the definitely-not-handmade cookie jar.

"Well? What do you want me to do about it?"

Claudia tried not to let the strain show in her face. This was the part she had been preparing herself for. "I'm afraid I'm going to have to terminate your lease. If you look at the contract, you'll see the criteria for vendors are very clear, and you're well outside of them. You can have a couple of days to clear out your stuff, but I can't allow you to make any more sales from this space."

Mentally, Claudia was crossing her fingers and hoping that the real estate lawyer she had found on Yelp had done a good enough job on the contract, because she suspected Lori wasn't going to take this lying down.

She suspected right.

"Oh, come on!" Lori said, her petulance exploding into anger. "The idiots who come browsing through here just want something they can take home and show off to the other hicks, because it came from California, and believe me, they would never pay what it would actually cost to make this crap. Nobody actually cares who made it."

"Well, I do. And this is my business, so you can go ahead and pack up the crap, as you call it, and take it elsewhere."

Lori was fully enraged now. She came out of the glorified booth that until recently had been her shop and pointed accusingly at the produce market at the other end of the hall.

"Oh, so now you're all high and mighty with your purity? Where was all this when Orlan wanted to bring in the artichokes?"

"Castroville is a lot closer than Bangladesh," Claudia said through clenched teeth. "And Orlan never lied to me, or tried to cheat anyone. Look, I'm sorry, but it's my house and they're my rules. You knew what they were when you signed the lease, so you can be as mad at me as you want, but you and your store have to go."

Claudia braced herself for another outburst, but none came. Instead, Lori started wandering around the empty market, like she was looking for inspiration in the jars of pickles or wheels of cheese. It was an hour after closing, and though people usually hung around for a while, Claudia was glad that everyone else had left. At least, she thought they had, but a flicker of motion in her peripheral vision had her worried. The last thing she needed right now was for the gossip mill to fire up before Lori was even out of the building.

Inside she was kicking herself. When she had opened the market hall she had had a clear vision of only hosting local food vendors, to offer residents and visitors a literal taste of the work of the people and land around them. But one of the booths didn't have power for a refrigerator, and when Lori had turned up with her samples and her rent check, Claudia had ignored her misgivings and welcomed her with open arms and a needy bank account. Even then it had felt like a bad idea, and now she knew why.

Lori passed in front of the cheese shop for the second time, then seemed to come to a decision.

"Please," she said, the anger slipping off her face like a mask. "Please, just a couple more weeks. I just need the space for a little while longer—I'll take all the 'handmade' signs down, lower my prices. It's really important. You've got to let me stay."

"I'm sorry," Claudia repeated. "But this is my business, and I've got to enforce some standards. The whole point of people coming here is so they can get something local and authentic. If we don't have that, we have nothing."

"But I only need a little more time." Lori was pleading now, almost whining. "You have to."

Claudia shook her head. "Three days. And no sales."

Claudia escorted Lori to the door and locked it behind her. Not that it would make much of a difference; all of the vendors had keys, and most of them made copies. The best she could do was to watch until Lori's car was out of the parking lot and hope her erstwhile tenant wasn't about to try anything more stupid than she already had. Claudia made a mental note to call a locksmith in the morning.

She was about to leave when she remembered the impression she had had of someone else being in the building. She wasn't terribly worried about break-ins—aside from the fact that they were in the snooziest coastal town that ever lost its fishing fleet, there was nothing to steal besides various food items and some inauthentic textiles—but a raccoon had snuck inside a few months back and raised havoc among the salamis. So she thought she had better go back and check.

The market didn't have a lot of enclosed spaces; it was just a large rectangular building with a corridor down the middle and nooks for the shops around the sides, separated by low partitions to let as much light as possible in from the windows, so it didn't take long for Claudia to confirm that there was no one, human or otherwise, hanging out behind the cheese fridge or in the compost bin. (She did find evidence that a large percentage of the customers didn't know water bottles weren't compostable, but she knew that already.) Satisfied, Claudia locked up again and headed for home.

She didn't have far to go. When people asked her what she liked best about her new life, her joking response was "the commute," and it wasn't entirely untrue. The market building had come with the neighboring piece of land and two vacation cottages included in the sale, and together they made up her entire living and working space.

As empires went, it wasn't much, but it was a start.

The market was set on the side of a hill, overlooking the bay and the ocean beyond. A narrow road ran up from the town, passing the market, then vanishing over a low shoulder in the hill to where the cottages were, before winding its way up to dead-end at the hilltop, where a large house sat in lonely splendor, the only other building on the road.

On one side of the marketplace were a couple of picnic tables and a small, roughly paved, parking lot with space for about thirty cars, if they weren't too big and people parked carefully. (At least that was what Claudia estimated; so far the lot had never been that full.) On the other side there was an awkwardly shaped wedge of land that ran over the shoulder in the hillside to the cottages. One of the tiny buildings had been gutted by the previous owner, but the other was pretty much livable, so Claudia lived there.

The cottage wasn't exactly luxurious, but most of the lights worked and the roof probably had at least a couple more years on it. Someday, maybe, Claudia would have enough money to finish the renovations, or at least buy a dishwasher she didn't have to roll across the kitchen and attach to the sink, but those sorts of extravagances were beyond her for the moment.

Claudia crunched her way across the hillside, through the dry grass of a California summer, reminding herself for the umpteenth time that she really needed to do something about having it cut.

August on the Sonoma coast meant alternating periods of wind and fog, with infrequent shocks of heat. This night was shaping up to be a windy one, with gusts so strong they made her stumble, and Claudia pulled her fleece jacket more tightly around her shoulders as she crossed the field to her home. In the distance, she could hear the waves crashing on the rocks mingled with the sounds of the ongoing arguments of the local sea lion colony.

It was just past sunset but there was still some light in the sky, so navigating the path back to the cottage wasn't a problem. Claudia had taken to using a somewhat indirect route, because the lot was also home to a pair of large and highly territorial geese, who lived in what looked like a converted doghouse that sat between the cottage and the market. Nobody seemed to know who they belonged to or how they got there, but offers to help move them were equally scarce, and the geese clearly had no intention of going anywhere on their own.

She was almost home when she caught a movement in her peripheral vision. Chiding herself for being so nervy, she was about to put it down to the wind when she noticed the silhouette of a pair of triangular ears in the gloom. A dog, part German shepherd but mostly not, was sitting in the middle of the field, looking at her. There was nothing threatening about it, but it wasn't a small dog, and Claudia made her way past it as quickly as she thought was reasonable, hoping she didn't smell like fear, or sausages.

Finally home, Claudia tossed her jacket on the chair by the door that had been demoted to that purpose and collapsed onto the couch (which, due to the size constraints of a 600-square-foot house, was actually a loveseat).

Considering that almost none of her furniture would have fit, moving in had been easy. The front half of the cottage was her living room, kitchen, dining room, office, and overflow storage, and aside from the loveseat all it had room for was a makeshift desk, a couple of chairs, a barstool she had found by the side of the road, and a small table. Past the kitchen there was a hallway that was too short to really deserve the name, with the bedroom on one side and the bathroom on the other, and just enough space left to fit a miniature bookcase against the back wall. Claudia had meant to finally get around to organizing it that night, but even as she thought about it, she became aware that she barely had the energy to stand up, much less decide on an alphabetical versus theme-based ordering scheme. If it wasn't for gravity, she wasn't sure she would even have had the strength to stay on the couch.

Until that moment, she hadn't realized how much the conversation with Lori had drained her. She had known coming in that running the business wasn't going to be all biodynamic wine and locally grown roses, but this was the first major personnel problem she had run into. She turned around to put her feet up, deliberately avoiding looking in the mirror next to the door. Intended to make the room look bigger, it mostly just served to remind Claudia that she needed a haircut and possibly an entirely different wardrobe.

Even in her previous, marginally more professional life, Claudia had never been much of a fashion plate—she had always felt that one of the best things about a tech career was that no one had a problem if you dressed for comfort over style—but even by her standards, the jeans she was wearing were on their last legs, literally and figuratively, and there was probably a limit to the number of consecutive days a person could wear humorous T-shirts and still expect to be taken seriously as a business owner.

In that area, Claudia probably needed all the help she could get. With her short stature, heart-shaped face, and large eyes, she had always looked young for her age, and she still occasionally got carded, and not just by people who thought they were being cute.

Some of that she couldn't help, but Claudia had to admit there was probably more she could do. Like getting her hair cut so that it was something other than random waves taking routes of their choosing from her scalp to her shoulders, or deciding on a color for it other than "mostly brown, except for the parts that used to be highlights."

She held up a lock of it in front of her eyes, seeking the line where the highlights ended. That would have been about two years ago, when she was still doing that sort of thing, until the round of bad luck that had gotten her here in the first place. She had been living in San Francisco, a software engineer at an idealistic startup out to change the world via app development. But the money ran out, and in the end the only way they changed the world was by making it into one where their former CEO owned a boat. Around that time, her boyfriend declared they were breaking up, because he was "tired of dealing with her." What he wasn't tired of, though, was living in the city apartment which, through a miracle of a poorly worded listing and months of ramen dinners, she had managed to buy several years earlier. It was while he was explaining how San Francisco's renter-friendly laws were going to keep him there indefinitely that she had made the decision.

"I'm selling it," she had said, barely thinking the words before they were out of her mouth. "The open house is on Sunday. We need to clean the bathroom."

And, thanks to a motivated realtor and a local real estate market that was hovering somewhere between superheated and ludicrous, that was it. Bidding started on Tuesday, and by Friday Claudia was explaining to Oliver that she was sorry, but he was going to have to take up the issue of his continued tenancy with the new owners. It was the most impulsive thing she had ever done, right up until the next one.

She had not set out with the idea she was going to own a marketplace. All she had in mind when she arrived in San Elmo Bay was a month's vacation in the seaside town she had visited with her family as a child. It had been perfect, so completely removed from everything that had seemed vitally important back in the city that she could barely remember why she had cared about all that stuff in the first place.

Pure chance had led her to rent the cottage where she was currently living, and after a week of walking by the empty market building with its "For Sale" sign she had gotten around to asking the rental agent what it was. That was when she had learned about the grand designs of the former owner, to turn the old warehouse into a market hall, with local farmers and craftspeople renting out spaces inside to sell their wares to the visitors who would come from across the world and put San Elmo back on the road to prosperity, and the divorce that had cut off the money that was funding those dreams. She also learned that the sale price was almost exactly what she had cleared from the sale of her apartment, if by "almost exactly" you meant "with the addition of a substantial bank loan." Claudia had decided it must be a sign.

Everyone she knew thought she was crazy, and they were probably right. But for once in her life she was doing something she loved, something that was all hers, and no idiot with a bunch of counterfeit handcrafts was going to ruin it for her.

Which, she reminded herself, was why she had gotten that lease agreement written up in the first place. Lori might be upset that her scheme had been discovered, but there shouldn't be anything she was able to do about it.

And there was nothing anyone was going to do about anything tonight, so Claudia probably should stop worrying and have dinner.

A particularly strong gust of wind rattled the windows as Claudia hauled herself off the couch and wandered over to the refrigerator. It was only slightly larger than the one she had had in her college dorm, and about as usefully stocked. People might think the owner of a marketplace like hers would have a larder packed with the finest in local and artisanal foods, from which she would effortlessly whip up a meal that was at the same time simple and sophisticated, but those people had not seen Claudia stare blankly at a kohlrabi for upward of twenty minutes.

The one part that was true was that she never lacked for ingredients. There was an unspoken agreement among the food vendors at the market that anything that was in danger of being thrown out was first offered to the other tenants, and though Claudia was careful not to be at the front of the line, there was always plenty to go around. She had things to eat; what she didn't have was the energy to figure out how to combine two ears of corn, a cured pork jowl, assorted cheeses, and half a jar of kimchi into a meal.

There were always the empanadas from Carmen, but Claudia suspected they were some of her experimental attempts, and she was in no mood for surprise kale.

So it was with only a moderate amount of shame that she reached into the back of the freezer and pulled out a pizza. Desperate times called for desperate measures.

CHAPTER TWO

By next morning the wind had died down and the day was foggy but calm. The geese were awake and on guard, waiting at the edge of their territory for Claudia to pass. She gave them a wider berth than usual, acutely aware of the beady eyes tracking her progress. Rationally, she knew there was no need for her to be afraid of animals that were a fraction of her size, but on the other hand, she didn't like the looks of those beaks.

There was no sign of the dog, which had probably been someone's pet taking itself for a walk. One of the things Claudia found herself having to adjust to was the different relationships people in the country had with their animals, and this was probably one of those times.

Her view of the parking lot was blocked by the curve of the hill, so she didn't see Lori's car until she was more than halfway there. Claudia's heart sank. She had known she hadn't seen the last of her problem tenant, but she would have liked a little more of a grace period before diving back into the conflict. She hoped Lori had just decided to show up early to pack up her shop before anyone else arrived, and wasn't standing by with a lawyer, ready to turn Claudia's precious market into a dollar store outlet.

Her first surprise on entering the marketplace was that the lights weren't on. The windows did a good enough job of illuminating the shops, but not the interior corridor, and very little light filtered in through the three skylights that were in dire need of cleaning. It was enough to see by, but only just.

Claudia flipped the light switch and looked around. Her first impression was that the place was empty, and maybe Lori had just left her car in the lot for some reason. But something wasn't right. The display at the front of the Pak Family Pickles shop was in disarray, and the giant jar of kosher dills that had been the centerpiece was gone. She found it on the floor in the produce stall, lying on its side next to a bin of tomatoes.

Beyond that, everything was fine until she got to the cheese shop. It was in the far corner of the market, with the largest space, including room for two small tables.

That was where she found Lori, curled around the base of a table, unmoving.

"Lori? Are you okay?" Claudia wasn't expecting an answer, but she had to hope. In a daze, she put her hand on the other woman's shoulder. It was cold, stiff, and unyielding, and in that it told Claudia everything she needed to know. But still she pulled, unwilling to turn away until she was absolutely sure there was nothing she could do.

Then the body finally moved and she saw Lori's face, and she was sure.

Claudia stumbled toward the door, fumbling for her phone and trying not to vomit. She might have screamed, or maybe everything felt like screaming. By the time the ambulance arrived, she had gotten her breathing back under control, though her heart was pounding so loud that she thought the paramedics must have heard it from the road.

She told them what had happened, and they left her to wait at one of the picnic tables at the edge of the parking lot. There wasn't going to be much they could do, but that was for them to decide. Claudia had seen a dead body before, but only because her great-aunt had insisted on an open casket, and while the mortician's heavy-handed makeup job had been disturbing in its own way, it had nothing on this. It had been Lori, but not, her swollen face and bulging eyes making a grotesque caricature that Claudia would never, ever forget.

She didn't know how long she had been sitting there when the other vehicles pulled up, first a fire truck, then all three of San Elmo's police cars, then a van with a picture of a cow in a tutu painted on its side.

"Claudia! What's going on?"

Julie Muller parked the van in the only available space and leaned out the window.

"Did something happen to the market?"

It took a moment, but eventually Claudia was able to find her voice.

"No," she warbled. "The market's fine. It's Lori, she's . . . Lori got hurt."

"Oh no," Julie's expression was appropriately concerned, but the tension had left her voice. She and Lori hadn't exactly been close, and it wasn't surprising that she wouldn't take an injury to the other woman as seriously as something like damage to her shop. She would be horrified when she learned the truth, of course, but Claudia wasn't sure how much she was supposed to be saying at this point. Julie, and everyone else, would find out soon enough.

Julie was the second generation of the family that owned the Dancing Cow Cheese Company. She was a well-built woman in late middle age, slightly overweight thanks to three children and a lifetime of proximity to dairy products. Her father, Elias Muller, had immigrated from Switzerland in the sixties, taken one look at what passed for cheese in this country and declared it unfit for feeding to pigs, so he had decided to start his own creamery and show his new countrymen how it was done. (It was a well-known story, because he liked to tell it loudly at every opportunity, which was why his grandchildren refused to go into the grocery store with him anymore.)

They had been the first vendor to sign on to the market, and Claudia was sure that Elias's seal of approval had helped to bring in the others. She didn't know what he was going to say when he heard their space had been the site of a violent death, but she didn't think it was going to be good.

"Ms. Simcoe? Do you have a minute?" A policeman had emerged from the building and approached Claudia. "We'd like to ask some questions about how you found her."

Claudia allowed herself to be led away, feeling Julie's alarmed stare following her.

Going back into the market was like entering a dream, the kind where you're in a familiar place but it's somehow wrong, like your house suddenly has several rooms you never knew were there. Claudia had spent nearly every waking minute of her past two years in the marketplace building, but it felt alien now. The paramedics had left their equipment scattered around the central hall, blocking the entrances to the market stalls. The pickle jar was still on the floor, and from the fog in her mind a voice she recognized as her own reminded her that she needed to mention that to someone.

There was a crowd of people at the end of the hall, paramedics, policemen, and a few firefighters who might have been doing something important, but at the moment it looked a lot like hanging around and watching. She had seen most of them around town at some point, but the only face she could put a name to was the chief of police, who was approaching her now.

"Miss Simcoe? You found the body?" Chief Bill Lennox was a short, stocky man with a face like a disappointed frog. He was the youngest son of a longtime local family, and he had a reputation of being unpleasant and overbearing, particularly to people he considered outsiders in his town. The only other times Claudia had seen him, greeting guests and making speeches at the department's various charity fundraisers, he had always seemed like he was at least trying to be genial, but there was none of that now.

"I understand you moved the body," he said, his voice booming out into the hall.

"Only to see her face," Claudia explained. "She was curled up there with her back to me, and I couldn't tell what was wrong. I didn't move her very far."

"You shouldn't have moved her at all," he scolded. It was the last thing Claudia had expected, but at least his antagonism had the effect of temporarily knocking her out of the shock that had consumed her since she found the body.

"I didn't know she was dead. I had to be sure there was nothing I could do to help."

"Well, you've certainly helped her killer."

Claudia nearly gasped. It had been in the back of her mind that Lori's death didn't seem natural—with her swollen face and the strange positioning of the body—but she was no expert, and the desire to believe in an explanation other than violence was a powerful argument. But here was the police chief, baldly stating she had been murdered, like it was a secondary problem to Claudia's own irresponsibility.

It seemed like she wasn't the only person there who was surprised. The paramedics exchanged sharp glances, and one of the other police officers started to say something, then stopped himself and gave Claudia a worried look. She wondered how often his boss went off script like this.

Lennox may have realized he said something he wasn't supposed to, because he responded by glaring at all of them, before turning the force of his disapproval back to Claudia.

"I need you to tell me exactly how she was lying when you found her, before you and these yahoos ruined everything." The yahoos in question were the paramedics, who looked more annoyed than contrite.

The police chief was clearly trying to sound authoritative, but the way he kept fiddling with the zippers on his jacket undermined the impression. Claudia had heard a rumor once that he had gotten the job despite having no police experience, because someone on the town council had owed Lennox's uncle a favor, and she wondered if right now he was realizing how badly prepared he was for a homicide investigation, and was taking it out on anyone in range.

He took a step toward the corner, and Claudia realized with a sickening feeling that she was going to have to look at Lori's body again. Her knees started to wobble, but before she could fall too far there was a reassuring hand on her elbow.

"Are you sure you're up for this?" It was the cop who had brought her in, who Claudia had barely registered before. She noticed him now, first in gratitude, then to take in the fact that he was a very attractive man, then to rebuke herself for even having that thought at the site of a friend's violent death. (Well, more of an acquaintance, really, but still.)

"Thank you," she said, fighting to keep her voice from rising flirtatiously. "But it doesn't look like I have much of a choice, do I?"

He smiled reassuringly and gave her a tiny shrug. Taking that as a no, Claudia let him lead her back toward the cheese shop, where the people still working around the body stepped aside to give Claudia the better look she so badly didn't want.

Given the current state of the scene, she didn't think Lennox had much basis to be mad at her for the small amount of disturbance she had caused. Lori's body had been pulled fully away from the table and rolled over next to a set of electric paddles for what had to have been the most optimistic resuscitation ever attempted. The body must have been stiff when they tried, even now it was only slightly uncurled from the position Claudia had found it in.

Lennox was standing next to the table, looking at Claudia expectantly.

"Well?" he said. "We don't have all day."

Claudia stepped forward and gathered herself, trying to focus on the scene without really seeing Lori's face.

"She—the body was curled up over there," she said, indicating the table. "Kind of wrapped around the base. I didn't know why she would be there, so I went over and shook her shoulder, and she didn't move. That's when I pulled her back, just far enough to see her face, and then I went outside and called 911. I didn't move her very much, just maybe a couple of inches."

"And you didn't try to help her at all?"

Claudia wasn't sure what she was being accused of here—moving the body was a problem, but so was not moving it more? On the other hand, this was not the time for her to be indulging her authority issues, so she only let a little bit of defiance creep into her answer.

"I didn't think there was anything I could do," she said. "She didn't—she didn't look like I could help her."

Through her effort not to look at Lori's face, Claudia was starting to notice other things she hadn't seen before, like the wire encircling Lori's neck, ending in two thin wooden handles (somehow familiar, but she couldn't think where she would have seen something like that before), or the dried blood that had run down from the wound it had left.

"Is that it?" Lennox asked. He stared down at Claudia, as if he could glare more information out of her. But there was nothing to give.

"That's all I can tell you about finding the body." She stepped back, relieved to have an excuse to look away. "But there is one other thing. I don't know if you noticed, but there's a jar of pickles on the floor in the produce market. And I know for certain that when I locked up last night it was on the display shelf, where it belongs."

If she was hoping for gratitude, she didn't get it. Lennox just narrowed his eyes and flared his nostrils at her some more.

"Oh yeah? How is it you're so sure of that little detail?"

Traumatized or not, Claudia had had enough of this. She stood up taller and looked him straight in the eyes.

"Because," she said. "It's a very large jar of pickles."

It would have been nice if she had been able to exit on that line, but it wasn't to be. She had to give them all of her contact information, then repeat her story of finding the body two or three more times, then listen to several reminders from the chief that they were going to want to talk to her again later, and she had better make herself available. Finally, when she had assured him enough that she wasn't going to go anywhere but home, she was allowed to leave, followed to the door by the attractive officer.

"Are you going to be okay?" he asked.

"Sure," Claudia said, suddenly preoccupied by the discovery that eyes could be exactly the same shade of blue as the pattern on her grandmother's Delft china. She had never liked those plates, but she was suddenly warming to them. "I, um, I just need some time to recover. Thanks."

"No problem. And take it easy, you've had a rough morning."

That was putting it mildly. And when Claudia got outside, she realized it wasn't over yet. The rest of the vendors had arrived and their cars and trucks were clustered outside of the parking lot. Except for the Pak Family Pickles van, which Mrs. Pak had a habit of treating as an off-road vehicle, and had taken around the blocked-off entrance and parked in her usual space. There was a lot of confused conversation going on, all of which stopped when Claudia appeared.

A chorus of "what happened"s greeted her as she got closer. Claudia looked around for her new cop friend, but he had already gone back into the marketplace. She was on her own.

"I'm sorry about this," she said, as they gathered around her. "Something happened to—Lori is dead. Last night, in the marketplace. I found her this morning. It's—it probably wasn't an accident."

Claudia couldn't bring herself to call it murder, even though the police chief had implied as much, and the wire around Lori's neck seemed to close the question. But to actually say the word out loud gave it more reality than she was able to deal with right now. She would have rather not said anything at all, but her tenants had a right to know. For most of them, their shops made up a major part of their livelihoods, and Claudia didn't know when they would be able to open them again.

There was a moment of quiet while everyone processed her announcement. Robbie, who ran the market's butcher shop, was the first to put it all together.

"Somebody killed Lori? In our market? How? I mean, why? I mean, what's going to happen?"

He looked around nervously after he said it, like he was embarrassed to have had the presumption to ask the first questions. Robbie was one of the younger shopkeepers, in his early forties, tall and lean, with big ideas and an abiding love for the things that could be done with pork. He had called his shop Cure, in honor of the cured meats like salami and prosciutto that were his passion, but the name was causing some confusion among both music fans and people who thought it was a pharmacy.

"I don't know," Claudia said, which was an honest answer to most of his questions. "I'm sure the police are going to want to talk to all of us at some point. If there's anything you know, like if you've seen anybody hanging around, or heard Lori talking about being afraid of someone, you should definitely let them know."

She didn't have a lot of hope for that suggestion, and the blank looks she got in return weren't much of a surprise.

"How will we know if it is suspicious?" The question came from Iryna who, along with her wife Carmen, ran The Corner Pocket, the best combination pierogi and empanada stand in western Sonoma

County. Her car would be full of coolers packed the with pastries they had gotten up at five to make in their rented commercial kitchen space, ready to be heated up in the small oven and cooktop in their shop. They did some business in local farmer's markets as well, and Robbie was trying to set them up with a website so they could take mail orders, but the marketplace was the lifeblood of their business. Claudia felt a flash of anger at Lori for having her death there.

It was a stupid thing to think, and she pushed the feeling back down.

"I don't know," she said again. She had a feeling she was about to be saying that a lot. "Anything you can think of, I guess. But I'm sure there's some obvious reason behind this, and the police will have it cleared up soon."

She wasn't sure of that at all, but the others did her the favor of looking like they believed her. Besides Robbie and Iryna, the crowd consisted of Julie, who had left her cow-bedecked van to join the crowd, a couple of the teenaged employees of the produce stall, and Helen Pak, who was not going to be happy when she found out what had happened to her giant pickle jar, which had adorned the shelf at the front of their shop since it had opened.

It was Helen's attempts to replicate her grandmother's kimchi recipe that had formed the foundation of her business, and her determination that had driven it to grow, past the reluctance, and occasional outright hostility, that had greeted their products. (Since opening the shop, they had added some more Western-style pickles to the line, but if Helen was behind the counter, you were not getting out of there without at least trying a bite of something spicy and unfamiliar.) She wasn't going to take kindly to an extended closure, if by "take kindly" you meant, "not try to break in and reopen it herself."

For the moment, though, she seemed subdued, looking from Claudia to the marketplace building and back again.

"You think they'll solve it right away?" she asked.

"Sure they will," said Claudia, who wasn't sure. "I've heard most murders are done by someone close to the victim, so the police probably won't have very far to look. I'll stay in touch with them, and I'll let you all know as soon as I get an idea of when we're going to be able to reopen the marketplace. There can't be much they can do in there, so with any luck it should be before the weekend."

Fortunately for Claudia, nobody present was taking notes. In the pantheon of famous last words, those should have been up there with "it doesn't look that deep" and "hold my beer."

For the moment, her tenants seemed willing to take her at her word. The expressions on the faces around her ranged from Julie's calm concern, through Robbie being uncertain and confused, and up to Helen who, for some reason, was looking deeply distressed. The last one was surprising to Claudia. Of everyone, the pickle business was the least likely to be affected by the delay, since even their shortest-lived products were good for weeks. But there was no question she was agitated, and Claudia didn't know what she could say that would be helpful.

"I don't know what I can say that will be helpful," she told them. "I'll try to get more information from the police, and I'll let you know as soon as I do. In the meantime, if there's anything I can do to help, let me know."

No one seemed to be able to think of anything at the moment. After that, the group started to break up, as people pulled out their cell phones and got to work on alternative plans for their day. Claudia hung around until the last of the cars pulled away, then, with a sad look back at her marketplace with the police officer still standing guard at the door, she turned and headed for home.

CHAPTER THREE

Back in the cottage, Claudia tried to get some work done, but trying to focus on accounting spreadsheets right now was a battle she was never going to win. Finally, she gave up, fished one of the experimental empanadas out of the refrigerator, heated it up in the toaster oven, and took it outside to eat.

A pair of plastic chairs and an unsteady card table made up her patio furniture, set next to the house on a concrete slab that might have seen better days, but even those hadn't been that good. It would have been an unappealing spot, except for two things. One was that it was on the other side of the cottage from the marketplace, where she wouldn't be tempted to try to watch what was going on and be drawn into useless speculation. (She could manage the speculation on her own just fine.) The other, and more generally applicable advantage was the view it did have, out over the bay and to the ocean beyond. Even when it was foggy it could be beautiful, with glimpses of water through the mist, and on a clear day like this one, when the overnight wind had blown the air clear, it was glorious.

The hill on which the cottages and marketplace sat rose up above the bay, and it was connected to the wider world by a road that ran up from the two-lane highway that cut through the town. Following it took you past a scattering of houses mostly of the vacation-rental variety, a plaza with a laundromat, bar, and small grocery store, and a shockingly rickety pink building selling salt water taffy, then across the highway and down into San Elmo proper. Claudia could see it from where she was sitting, a patchwork of roofs clustered around the marina, punctuated by the neon seagull on the sign for The Lighthouse, the area's one fine(ish) dining establishment. (Their chowder was actually quite good, but Claudia had learned to stay away from the more creative dishes. The sardine pad thai still haunted her.)

The town itself was laid out in a loose grid across the flat land that hugged the edge of the bay, with a small commercial district running for about three blocks near the water, transitioning to modest residences that got progressively nicer and less likely to be occupied year-round as you traveled uphill. San Elmo Bay had had a few scattered heydays, leaving it with a comfortable jumble of architectural styles—a row of Victorian houses here, an art-deco theater turned bookstore there, a monstrosity of sixties church architecture that everyone wished wasn't over there—all conspiring against the local civic boosters who longed for a cohesive postcard image.

Claudia had always loved it, ever since she had come as a child with her parents, getting a scoop of strawberry ice cream and eating it while walking along the pier. She had still liked it as a sulky teen, when they had rented an A-frame house by the beach for a week every summer and she had discovered that she could climb out a window onto a gable roof and sit looking over the stubby pines to the sea. This had always been a place of retreat for her, and it was probably no surprise it was where she had turned to when she had needed somewhere to go.

It hadn't taken long to realize the difference between vacationing in a place and trying to make a life there, but even that hadn't been so bad. Aside from a handful of old-timers, jealously guarding their status as the only true locals, most of the people in San Elmo were from somewhere else, washed up there when the tides of their own lives had turned one way or the other. It was the sort of place where, if you mentioned that you had left your city job to open a probably ill-advised business venture, you were generally met with an understanding nod and the story of the other person's experiences with selling yarn paintings or training yoga goats. Rather than being greeted with the suspicion she had expected, Claudia found that, for the most part, she was just another of San Elmo's seemingly endless supply of people who had never met a bad idea they didn't like.

Not that all was chaos and performing livestock. It was the middle of the afternoon on a Monday, and from where Claudia was sitting the town was so quiet it could have been modeling for a still life. A handful of boats bobbed in the marina, the remnants of the town's long-gone commercial fishing fleet, now pressed into service for day-trippers looking to set Dungeness crab pots or cast a line for salmon, in their respective seasons. Past them, a thin spit of land curved around to form the sheltered part of the bay, and beyond that there was nothing but the Pacific, slate-green and endless. It was all so peaceful, exactly what had brought Claudia to this spot in the first place. Everything was going to be so much simpler here.

Except it wasn't, of course. She had sunk her whole life into a crazy business she knew nothing about, only to see it endangered by the last thing she had ever expected. Contrary to appearances, Claudia was not a fool. She knew there was plenty of risk involved in this venture, and a very real chance that she would be left to start over from scratch. But what she hadn't considered was that she might take other people down with her. With the exception of the dead woman, every one of the vendors in that market was making do with the thinnest of margins, some probably on loans they shouldn't have gotten. But they had taken a chance on her, and on themselves, and they didn't deserve to have it taken away by whatever sort of lunatic had chosen her marketplace to murder Lori. Who, if you were talking about people who didn't deserve things that happened to them, should probably be at the top of the list.

Claudia had been deliberately avoiding thinking about finding the body, but her brain wouldn't let go of the image for long. She kept coming back to the distended features of Lori's face, and how much pain and terror she must have felt, and hoped that somehow it had been quicker than it seemed like it must have been.

That memory should have been enough to shame Claudia out of worrying about her own problems, but questions kept intruding, like how long the police cars were going to be parked in front of the marketplace and what sort of sign she should put on the door if they were going to make her keep it closed. She was sitting there, contemplating her day and life so far, eating her second empanada and wondering if maybe that much nutmeg didn't really work with the beets, when she had a feeling like she was being watched.

Telling herself she was being paranoid, Claudia tried to subtly take a look around, as if it was perfectly natural for her to randomly stretch her arms while turning her body ninety degrees in each direction. She was about to chide herself for being silly when she straightened back up and looked into the face of her visitor.

It was a dog, the same one she had seen the previous evening. Up close, she could tell it was barely out of the puppy stage, with long, gangly legs and ears that were too big for its head, and its ribs showed clearly through a patchy black and brown coat.

Claudia tensed up, not exactly afraid, but definitely wary. She had always been taught to be cautious around strange animals, especially ones that had large jaws full of strong, white teeth. But the dog just looked back at her with a vacant cheerfulness, like it was waiting for her to do something and it didn't matter much what it was.

This state of affairs lasted for a couple of minutes, while Claudia thought about what to do. There was no collar, but the dog might have an owner, and she should really let someone know it had been found, just in case. In the meantime, the least she could do was give it something to eat, and Claudia knew just the thing.

"Here you go," she said, tossing it the partially eaten empanada. "I hope you like nutmeg."

Based on how quickly the pastry vanished, she guessed that her new friend wasn't a very picky eater. Claudia had gone inside to look up the number for the nearest shelter when she heard the crunch of tires on the gravel driveway, followed by the sound of two car doors slamming. Through the window, she saw the dog stand up and trot off. Claudia watched it go for a moment, conflicted as to whether she should try to catch up to it, and what she would do if she did, but the decision was made for her by a heavy hand knocking on the front door of her cottage.

Before she had made it across the room they were knocking again, so hard that it seemed to shake the entirety of the little building.

"I'm coming!" Claudia said. "Hold your—oh. Hi."

She had been ready to give her visitors a piece of her mind, but that was before she saw the chief of police and his attractive new hire. They didn't look happy to see her, and, piercing blue eyes aside, the feeling was mutual.

"Do you have a moment, Miss Simcoe?" Chief Lennox said. "We'd like to ask you a few questions."

They sat in her living room, because there were no other options. Lennox took the one good chair, and Claudia offered the other officer the barstool, leaving her with the sofa. She perched there, a good six inches below the two men, feeling in every way at a disadvantage.

Still, this was her house, and a hostess had certain duties. She turned to the younger cop and smiled.

"I'm sorry," she said. "With everything that was going on this morning, I don't think I ever caught your name."

It clearly wasn't what he was expecting, but it only took a moment of stammering for him to recover.

"Oh, um, it's Derek. Derek Chambers. Officer Derek Chambers." The floor under the stool wasn't entirely level, and the little wave he offered as a greeting caused him to wobble precariously, which made Claudia feel better about her seat on the couch.

"Nice to meet you," Claudia said, and, as he removed his jacket to expose wonderfully muscular forearms, she found herself feeling better about life in general.

"This isn't a social call, Miss Simcoe," Lennox said, and this time she had to admit his irritation was probably warranted. "We're talking about a murder here."

It did occur to Claudia to wonder why he was there at all. The San Elmo Bay Police Department was tiny, and mostly maintained by the town because the county sheriff, who provided law enforcement for the majority of the small towns along the coast, had at one point refused to offer extra support for the crab festival, and the resulting bad feelings had led to the reestablishment of a local force. But they mostly specialized in traffic stops and beach parking lot break-ins, and there was no way they were equipped for a murder investigation. A person who was aware of his own limitations would certainly have realized this, and not be trying to carry it on his own, and the fact that Lennox was not that person only served to support her suspicions from that morning about his ratio of confidence to ability.

"We have a few more questions for you," Lennox went on, sounding suspiciously like he had picked up his interview style from prime-time dramas. "How well did you know the victim?"

"Not very, I guess. I saw her almost every day the market was open, but we didn't really talk. I know she moved here from somewhere back East, and she wasn't a fan of our weather, but that's about it."

"Did she have any reason to be angry with you? Or with someone else at the market?" Lennox asked.

It wasn't a question Claudia had been anticipating, and she wasn't sure she was ready to answer it honestly, so she did her best to avoid it.

"Angry with me? Why? She didn't do anything to me. What's this about?"

"Show her."

"We found these in the victim's purse." Derek reached into the bag he had been carrying and took out a zip-top bag containing two glass vials. He didn't hand them to her, but he held them up so that Claudia could read the labels.

"Stink bombs?" Claudia said once she deciphered the sideways writing. "Why would Lori be carrying around stink bombs?"

"That's what we were hoping you could tell us," Lennox said.

"You think she was planning to set them off in the marketplace? But why—oh." Since finding the body, Claudia had been too distracted to think about her confrontation with the dead woman, and how that might look to other people, but it was clear she was going to have to now. Even if she hadn't just connected the dots midsentence, she had no way of knowing if someone else knew, and to be caught concealing something like that would be about as incriminating a thing as she could do. So she went on.

"Well, yes, I guess she might have thought she had a reason to be angry," she admitted. "Yesterday I learned that the goods she was selling weren't what she said they were, and I told her I was canceling her lease. She was obviously upset, but I certainly didn't get any sense that she was planning any sort of retaliation."

"But when you saw her coming back to the marketplace last night, you went over to investigate, didn't you? And then you got in a little cat fight when you realized what she was up to, and lost your temper?" Lennox said, his voice heavy with implication.

"Of course not," Claudia replied, trying not to let her anger show. "The last time I saw her, she was driving out of the parking lot, one hundred percent alive. I didn't go back to the marketplace until I went to open it this morning."

"Can you prove that?"

"No, I can't. But last night was cold and windy, and you can't even see the entrance to the market from here. There's no way to know that someone was there without walking all the way over. Which I didn't do."

As far as Lennox was concerned, this was obviously an unsatisfactory answer. Clearly, the way this was supposed to go was that he would present his brilliant theories, and she would crumble and admit to her guilt. His fantasy thwarted, the police chief's expression turned stormy, and he might have made an impolitic comment if Officer Derek hadn't stepped in.

"How did you know she was selling counterfeit merchandise?" he asked. "Do you do background checks on all of the sellers?"

The question knocked the tension levels down a notch, for which Claudia was grateful. She took a second to collect herself, then answered in as pleasant a way as she could manage.

"No, I didn't think there was a need. Most of them, it's pretty obvious where their products come from, and honestly, it never occurred to me someone would want to cheat. It's not exactly a big money operation, you know? I didn't suspect anything until the printout from an online catalogue with all of her products showed up on my desk."

Lennox looked over at the card table in the corner that held her laptop and the stacks of paper that were too important to be filed on the floor.

"On that desk? Do people often come into your house to leave you things?"

"I have an office in the marketplace. I keep it open most of the day, since I'm in and out all the time. If people have something for me they leave it there. It's slightly more organized than the one here." That was true, with an emphasis on "slightly." "I found the pages there yesterday afternoon, in an unmarked manila envelope. There was no other information included, but once I saw them, it was pretty clear what it was about."

"I see," Lennox said, making furious notes. "And who do you think might have left it there?"

"I have no idea," Claudia said, and she meant it. She had wondered the same thing herself; grateful for the heads-up but worried about what kind of bad feelings might be going around under her nose. It had seemed like the most obvious candidates would be among the other vendors in the marketplace, but she was hardly going to say that to the police chief.

"So what you're saying is that anyone could have left it for you?" Derek said. "Anybody who knew where your office was, that is."

"Sure," Claudia said, grateful for the prompt. "And honestly, finding out wouldn't be hard. People stop by all the time asking for me—other vendors, tour organizers, whatever—and whoever is around will just point them to it."

"Well, that's convenient," Lennox said, his voice heavy with implication. Claudia chose to misunderstand him.

"It's certainly helpful," she agreed with a straight face. "But I'm afraid it isn't going to shed much light on who killed Lori."

"Let me be the judge of that, Miss Simcoe." It occurred to Claudia that Lennox may have spent too much of his life thinking he was destined for greater things, when he really wasn't.

He went on.

"So how did you feel when you saw the evidence that she was cheating you? If it was in the afternoon, why did you wait until the end of the day to confront her?"

"Because I didn't want to make a big deal out of it. I knew I'd have to cancel her lease, but it didn't make much difference if she had her store open for a few more hours. As far as how I felt, I was mostly annoyed, at her and at myself for not having done a better job of vetting her."

"Just annoyed, huh? At the woman who was threatening to ruin your business? I find that difficult to believe."

There were probably a lot of things Lennox found difficult, but Claudia wasn't going to get into that right now.

"She wasn't going to destroy the business," she said, emphasizing how calm she was. "Who was going to care if one stall out of six in a small-town marketplace was selling things that weren't what they were supposed to be? I had to tell her to leave once I knew about it, and I guess it's a lesson to me to do better diligence next time, but there can't be more than half a dozen people on the planet who would even give it a second thought."

"Well, what about the stink bombs? I guess you're going to tell me that didn't bother you either?"

"Since I didn't know about them until just now, no, they weren't the first thing on my mind. But even if she had used them, those things last for what, a couple of hours? It'd be inconvenient, but nobody's going to kill someone over a prank like that."

"That's a matter of opinion."

"Yes, well, it's mine."

That came out snappier than Claudia had intended and she cringed, cursing her temper and its way of making bad situations worse. She didn't believe that this man she had never met was driven by some sort of personal animosity against her, so she had to assume he was aware on some level that he was in well over his head, and had fastened on the first person he saw as a handy suspect. And now he was trying to bully her into confessing, because hey, why not? Get this done early enough and they could probably get his picture in tomorrow's papers.

Claudia knew she was making a lot of assumptions, and maybe they weren't all fair, but she had been having a rough day.

"Was there anything else?" she said.

At the very least, the chief didn't have the evidence he needed to arrest her, but he wasn't about to leave without letting Claudia know who was in charge here.

"No, I think that's all," he said, standing up and giving her tiny home a final, smug, once-over. "By the way, since it's an active crime scene, I'm afraid I'm going to have to close the marketplace indefinitely. Police procedure."

Claudia was pretty sure it wasn't, but that argument was going to have to wait for another venue.

"How long is indefinitely?" she asked.

"I don't think I could say. Might be as long as it takes to catch this killer. Can't be too careful, after all."

CHAPTER FOUR

"So that's where I am. Dead vendor, business shut down, probably not going to be able to sleep for a week. Other than that everything's fine. How about you?"

"Claudia, I'm so sorry." Her friend Betty sat across from her at the big wooden table, radiating concern. "Why didn't you call me sooner?"

Betty was one of the first people Claudia had met after she had made the decision to move to San Elmo permanently. She and her husband ran a guest ranch a few miles from the town, on the property where his family had raised cattle for eighty years, until economics necessitated a new business plan. Between the animals, the guests, and their three children—twin four-year-old boys and a nine-year-old girl—she must have had more than enough to do, but somehow she always seemed to be able to make time for a chat and a glass of wine.

She was pouring one now, which Claudia accepted with gratitude.

"I didn't want to drag you into it. The last thing you need is for your guests to find out you're associating with a suspected murderer." In fact, Claudia hadn't called at all. It was Betty, ringing her phone off the hook (the poor cell phone reception in San Elmo had driven Claudia to get an actual wall phone, the first of her adult life) as soon as the gossip mill had reached her with the news about the murder. Claudia had been instructed to show up as soon as the guests had been fed and the younger children put to bed, no excuses accepted.

Which was why Claudia was currently settled in the ranch's huge kitchen, a room decorated by Betty to look as simple and rustic as it was definitely not. The apron-front stone sink drew the eye away from the professional-sized dishwasher, and the pattern of the backsplash had been specifically chosen so that, from a distance, it was hard to see how many electrical outlets were in it. The centerpiece of the room was the double oven and six-burner stove, on which Betty produced all of the meals for the ranch's guests. Her cooking had gone a long way to building their reputation as a legitimate destination on the North Coast, despite the distance along narrow backroads from the better-known tourist locations of Napa and Sonoma.

Based on the number of cars in the parking lot, they only seemed to have a handful of guests at the moment, but Claudia's concern about upsetting them was genuine. Betty, on the other hand, just rolled her eyes.

"Please. If they ever looked up from their phones for long enough to notice, we'd just call it authentic local color. They'd eat it up."

She finished serving up the dish of pasta, blistered cherry tomatoes, and basil, topped with a scoop of fresh ricotta and set it in front of Claudia, who thanked her friend and wondered, not for the first time, why she didn't hate her. Betty was a city girl by birth, a self-described "culinary school dropout" who had taken to country life like a duck to a pond full of other ducks that all immediately fell in love with her.

It probably helped that she was beautiful. Not just the ordinary prettiness of a small-market weather girl, but strikingly gorgeous, with a face and figure that made people ask if she was a model, even when they weren't hitting on her. (If pressed, she would admit she had done some catalogue work in college.) Time and children had softened her curves, but she could still stop traffic if she wasn't careful.

Her husband Roy was the quintessential Westerner, tall and taciturn, dressed in a uniform of tight-fitting jeans and worn cowboy boots. He couldn't have been more different from his wife; where Betty was mile-a-minute chatty, Roy spoke so rarely and so slowly that Claudia speculated it must have taken him a week to get through proposing. But they seemed happy, and she hoped they stayed that way. She needed more happy people in her life.

"You should talk to a lawyer." Betty poured a glass of wine for herself and sat down across from Claudia.

"Right. Know any that take payment in week-old pierogis? They've been in the freezer."

"I'm serious, Claudia. You could be in real trouble."

"I know, I'm sorry. I just don't know what I can do, besides hope that Lennox finds someone better to suspect, and soon." She stared down into her bowl, trying not to think about the improbability of that.

"This is delicious pasta, by the way," Claudia said, trying to change the subject.

Betty dismissed her creation with a wave of her hand.

"It's all about the ingredients, really. The ricotta is Julie's, of course. Speaking of which, what's going to happen to your vendors? I don't know what I'm going to do without them. We're starting to get people requesting the pickle and charcuterie platter when they book."

It was nice of Betty to say, and Claudia hoped at least partly honest. The ranch had been one of the first commercial customers for most of the businesses in the marketplace, and their reliance on local producers had even made it into the write-up they had just gotten in a San Francisco paper.

"I don't know," Claudia said. "I hope the closure isn't going to go on too long, and they'll be able to find some other places to sell in the meantime. I was planning to call around to the local farmer's markets once I get my head together, see if they take some of our vendors on for now."

"That sounds like a good idea." Betty ran her finger around the rim of her glass and stared into it, distracted by another thought.

"You know, I talked with her at one point about getting some napkins from her for the dining room, but to be honest, I wasn't that impressed with her work. Which I guess wasn't really her work at all. Anyway, now I'm glad I didn't."

"You have a better eye than I do. God, I wish I had just turned her away. Maybe none of this would have ever happened."

"You can't think that way," Betty said. "Nobody could have predicted this. To have killed her like that, somebody must have really not liked her."

"Ya think?"

"No, I'm serious. Strangling someone, that's not something you do if you just want to rob them, right? It must have been personal."

She paused and took an awkward sip of her wine.

"What did you say she was killed with, some sort of string? Do you think he brought it with him?"

There was a strain in Betty's voice that Claudia had trouble placing. Not that it should be surprising that anybody would be upset by the violent death of someone they knew, however slightly, but for some reason Betty seemed to be trying to make her completely reasonable question sound unreasonably casual.

On the other hand, perhaps recent events were getting to Claudia, and she should stop overthinking everything and just answer the question.

"I didn't look closely, but I thought it looked more like wire, with wooden dowels on the ends. I thought it looked familiar but I couldn't—oh."

"What?"

"I just realized what it was. It's one of the cheese wires from Dancing Cow." Claudia sighed. "So I guess it can't be used as a clue to lead back to the killer. They must have just grabbed it off the counter."

"I'm sure there will be plenty more clues," Betty assured her. "Aren't most criminals supposed to be pretty stupid? They probably left all sorts of evidence lying around."

"I hope so. Or at least a witness or two. Somebody must have seen who was at the marketplace last night, right? Maybe our friend Mr. Rodgers can make himself useful for once."

Until very recently, one of the biggest problems Claudia had was a surly neighbor by the name of Nathan Rodgers. He lived in the house on the hill directly above the marketplace, a situation that bothered him to no end. He seemed to be gone a lot, but whenever he was in the area he found something to complain about, whether it was the cars that occasionally parked on the road, the picnickers who braved the wind and blackberry brambles to sit on the hillside below his property, animals who were attracted to the garbage, or the security lights Claudia had had installed as part of the effort to keep animals out of the garbage. The complaints came in the form of letters—to her, the paper, or the city council—and he seemed completely uninterested in engaging in any sort of dialogue. More than that, in all the time she had been living as his closest neighbor, she had never met the man, or even seen his face. In the early days she had concocted elaborate theories for his invisibility, but eventually Claudia decided that he was simply the kind of jerk who preferred to harass from a distance, so as not to inconvenience himself with listening to other people. She could only imagine what she would be hearing from him once he learned that her business had brought a murder into his neighborhood.

Claudia finished her meal and carried the bowl over to the sink. "Thanks again for letting me come over and eat your food and tell you my woes. I don't think I realized how much I needed a break. This has all been kind of overwhelming for me."

"Of course, you know you can call me up any time. But you aren't going back to that cottage tonight?"

"That was the plan. I'm afraid I'm a little short on alternate homes at the moment."

"You can stay here. There's no way I'm letting you go back to that place less than twenty-four hours after someone got killed right there," Betty said.

"Okay, but how long are you supposed to wait for murderers to clear out? Is it like a bug bomb? I appreciate the offer, but I can't inconvenience you like that. You've done enough for me already."

"Claudia, we literally run a guest ranch. It's right there in the name." Just then her husband entered, carrying a green bucket. "Roy, Claudia should stay here tonight, right? Someone just got killed in the marketplace."

"Sure," Roy said, as he emptied a bowl of kitchen scraps into the bucket. "Plenty of room."

For Roy, that practically counted as a soliloquy. Appropriately impressed, Claudia began to bend.

"But I didn't bring anything. I don't even have a toothbrush."

Betty opened a cupboard next to the door, revealing neat stacks of brand-new toiletries.

"Here at Tyler Ranch, all needs are provided for. And I can loan you a T-shirt and sweats to sleep in, as long as you don't mind that they have some stuff written on the butt. I went through sort of a phase back in the day," she said, as she assembled a collection of the necessities.

"Besides," she went on. "You can help Olive with her project. Her school put together a robotics team for the summer and they're having a competition at the end of the month. I think she's been having some trouble with it, and neither Roy nor I can make heads or tails of that thing."

Olive was Betty's oldest, a third-grader with a serious demeanor who, the first time she met Claudia, had asked if she thought faster-than-light travel would ever be possible. Claudia had never been very comfortable around children, but Olive she liked.

Claudia doubted there was actually any problem with the robot, but she recognized the kindness of Betty making it seem like she would do them a favor by staying. At that point, there was nothing she could say but yes.

"I'll be happy to help if I can. It's been a long time since I did any hardware work, though," she said. "So Olive is liking the new science program at her school?"

"She loves it," Betty said. "I don't understand half of the things she comes home talking about, but at least it's keeping her from taking apart the toaster again."

"Okay," Claudia said. "I'll see what I can do. And thanks. I don't know what I'd do without you."

"You'd eat a lot more frozen pizzas, for one thing."

As Claudia expected, the robot was fine, but Olive was gracious about letting her help, and they spent a pleasant evening refining the control mechanism for the flipping arm.

"Were you on a robot team in your school?" Olive asked, as she worked her fingers through a tiny gap to get at a screw.

"I wish. We didn't have anything this cool when I was a kid. The closest I ever came was one science fair where my project was a marble maze that ended with the marble turning on a light switch."

"What was the science part of that?"

"I'm not sure. Gravity? Light switches? Anyway, this is better."

They were sitting on the floor of the family living room, one of the parts of the house that was off-limits to the guests. The building was, appropriately, ranch-style, arranged in a stunted L-shape around a courtyard. This section had been built in the twenties as a modest, two-bedroom dwelling for the farm's founders and their seven children. The following generations had added to it dramatically, possibly due to some genetic memory of their ancestors' cramped conditions. Most of the guest accommodations were in the newer parts, but for Claudia's money, this room, with its brown-and-orange carpet, oak paneling, and well-worn leather furniture was the most comfortable space in the house.

At the moment, that carpet was littered with pieces of the robot, which Claudia hoped they were going to find all of before someone stepped on one and she never got asked back.

"Could you have built a robot if you wanted to?" Olive asked, bringing her back to the moment.

"Probably not," Claudia said, feeling like the Ancient Mariner. "All that stuff was really expensive and not nearly so good as it is now. That little computer you've got," she pointed to the controller that was resting in an empty mint tin. "That probably has more computing power than anything my school had the whole time I was there."

Olive looked like she found that hard to believe.

"Did you even have the Internet?"

"Sort of. We had a dial-up modem, which sounded like putting an electric violin down the garbage disposal and you couldn't use it all the time because it tied up your phone line. Plus, it was so slow, I kept a magazine by the computer so I'd have something to read while it loaded."

That got a giggle out of Olive. She was a gangly, somewhat awkward child, who clearly took after her father. Claudia hoped that wasn't going to be a trial for her later on, growing up in the shadow of her beautiful mother. Not that Betty would even think it, but for all its modern trappings, San Elmo was still a small town.

For now, at least, Olive was more interested in the past than the future.

"What did you do when you got online? Could you post pictures and stuff?" she asked.

"No, mostly I just went to bulletin boards and talked to other people who were interested in computers. There were some games, too, where you would go on once a day and type in your move, and then wait for the clock to turn over so you could move again."

"That sounds cool."

Claudia laughed. "We thought so. Most people thought it was dumb."

"Yeah, well, people are dumb."

"Hear, hear," Claudia raised her Allen wrench in salute. The kid, she thought, was going to be all right.

CHAPTER FIVE

The next morning, over Betty's objections (but after her delicious breakfast of blueberry pancakes with homemade lemon curd), Claudia returned her borrowed pajamas and headed for home. She had spent a lot of the previous night lying awake, trying to distract herself from dwelling on what Lori had gone through by focusing on what she could do next. She suspected that the police didn't have the right to keep the marketplace closed indefinitely, and that her best step toward getting it open would be to find a lawyer to help her make that point. But she had also gotten a very clear impression that Chief Lennox considered her a decent candidate for the role of murderer, and even aside from Betty's urging, she was aware that the smart thing to do in that situation was to get another, different kind of lawyer.

Unfortunately, Claudia had been telling the truth when she said she didn't have the money for one form of legal representation, let alone two. That was the choice she had been stewing over at four in the morning, even though she already knew the answer. When it came to picking between her personal freedom and her business, there was really only ever one thing Claudia was going to do. As soon as she got back to the cottage, she hunted through her email until she found the contact information of the property lawyer who had drawn up her lease agreements, took a brief, hopeless look at her bank balance, and gave him a call.

Forty minutes later, she wasn't as much poorer as she had feared, but also not as optimistic as she had hoped. The lawyer, who seemed to find this a more interesting problem than he usually saw, did confirm that the police weren't justified in keeping her property off-limits indefinitely but, unfortunately, getting a court to officially agree would likely take months, even in the best-case scenario. Claudia thanked him for his time and expertise and set up an appointment for the next opening he had available, in a week and a half. She hung up the phone and wondered where she was going to be then.

There were plenty of other things Claudia could be doing, from following up on her ideas for alternate locations for her vendors to making all of her social media accounts private before the news of the murder spread too far. But without the immediate urgency of the legal questions, she found it hard to commit herself to a task. The things she had been trying to put between herself and the memories of Lori's stiff body and distorted face weren't strong enough anymore, and ultimately she gave up and faced the horror head-on.

It was, she thought, a particularly horrible way to kill someone. Not that Claudia had spent a lot of time ranking murder methods, but there was something both personal and cold about the idea of taking a wire, wrapping it around a neck, and pulling until life was gone. It wasn't the action of a thoughtless moment, but too risky to have been planned. Whoever it was had done it with strength and determination, not to hurt or incapacitate, but to kill.

Claudia tried to imagine how Lori could have inspired that sort of feeling, but she found she couldn't conjure up that clear of an impression of the dead woman. Not just what would have made someone kill her, but anything at all. Lori had been a tenant in her market for over six months, and most of the impressions Claudia had of her were based on her outfits.

It wasn't like she was deeply involved in the lives of her other tenants, but she at least had a sense of who they were as people. Even Orlan Martinez, who mostly managed the vegetable market from a distance, because it was a small part of his larger business, was less of a cipher. She only saw him once every couple of months, but there were pictures of his farm and dogs posted around his stall, and whenever they spoke on the phone about the market, the conversation seemed to drift to some sort of related issue, like the trouble with getting reliable work out of the high school students he hired in the summer, or the sudden uptick in sales of specialty cabbages. (Claudia still didn't have an explanation for that one.)

She thought about the conversations she had had with Lori, trying to come up with something, some personal topic they had discussed, but came up blank. It hadn't seemed strange at the time, but going back over them now, Claudia realized that every time their personal lives had come up, Lori had changed the subject or otherwise nonanswered. She didn't think of herself as particularly nosy, but if she spent enough time around a person, she generally came away with at least some idea of who they were and where they were coming from, literally or figuratively.

But for Lori she had nothing. No sense of where she had been living before she moved to San Elmo Bay, or why she had come, or what she might have done before she arrived. She might as well have stepped right out of the sea foam; an Aphrodite in natural fibers.

Claudia knew that Lori had lived in a duplex in town, because that was the address on her rent checks, but her social life was as much of a blank as her antecedents. On the other hand, Claudia hadn't had much time for extracurriculars lately either, so she wouldn't have been in the best position to find out. She thought about asking some of the other tenants if they had seen Lori out and about—maybe Julie had run into her at one of her many community groups, or Robbie had spotted her at the bar where he occasionally played drums in a friend's band. Then, as she was planning her list of questions, she wondered what she was doing.

Claudia knew that it was a very bad, very dumb idea to try to investigate this, or any murder. No matter how curious she was, or how worried about her business or her freedom, murder investigations, like brain surgery or stand-up comedy, were no place for the unprepared.

She was not a police officer, she didn't have the training or the resources, or frankly the legal right to go poking her nose into the whys and wherefores of Lori's untimely end.

But, oddly enough, she did have some relevant experience. Not with murder—that was entirely new to her—but through an unusual series of events, she had briefly developed a hobby as an amateur private investigator.

Claudia had been in her twenties when her grandfather showed up at Thanksgiving talking about his brilliant new investment strategy. It was in a company that had been recommended to him by other people at his church, and featured enticements like "no risk" and "guaranteed returns." When Claudia tried to press him about the questions that raised, he had rather snippily pointed out that other members of the congregation had already done very well off the deal, and she should really stick to, in his words "your Internet thing." The rest of the family had smiled and nodded and humored him, because her grandfather was a loud man, and very sure of himself, and on the surface everything looked all right.

So Claudia had taken some time and looked deeper. There were members of her family who believed to this day that she had uncovered the fraud through some sort of top-secret hacking methods, but the truth was she had mostly just put in the time in front of her computer, trekking through a bewildering array of addresses, post office boxes, and personal and business names, real and fictional. What she ended up with was a pretty complete portrait of a team of serial con artists, with arrests and judgements across multiple jurisdictions and a habit of targeting Presbyterians.

She had ended up getting a little obsessed with the project, to the point of driving to one of the addresses her research had turned up, where she took a series of pictures of the scheme's chief player with his luxury cars, boat, and, brand-new backhoe, all of which turned out to have been purchased with investors' money. That part had been determined by the postal inspectors, of all people, because of the group's practice of sending solicitations through the mail. They were the ones who finally sent the investigation staggering slowly through the courts, though fortunately by then the weight of Claudia's evidence had been enough to keep her grandfather from losing more than a nominal amount of his savings.

Not that she had gotten much gratitude for her effort. Reactions from her family members had ranged from grudging thanks to suspicions about her motives, and had centered around a sense that young people should really mind their own business. It wasn't what she hoped for, but ultimately Claudia hadn't minded that much. The hunt had become puzzle for its own sake, and she had discovered she had something of a talent for it. She had even briefly toyed with the idea of changing careers and becoming a private investigator, but at the time the plan had seemed excessively impractical.

These days, impracticalities were the least of her worries. Under normal circumstances, Claudia would never have considered applying her self-taught investigative techniques to the problem of Lori's murder, but what she had seen of Lennox's approach had not filled her with confidence, and if he was really serious about keeping the marketplace closed until he caught the killer, her business could be in real trouble. The way she saw it, she didn't actually have to come up with a complete solution; based on her previous experience, if she was able to assemble a sufficient suite of information, the relevant authorities would be able to take it from there.

That was assuming, of course, that the relevant authorities hadn't already arrested her because they couldn't come up with anything better. And the fact that was even a possibility made it all the more vital that Claudia try her best to figure out what had actually happened.

It was a bad idea, but it was the only one she had.

Anyway, the first thing she was going to do wasn't hazardous at all. Half the town was probably googling Lori's name right now, and one more wouldn't make much difference. It took a while to sort through to find the correct Lori Roth (and, incidentally, Claudia was relieved that the news of the murder didn't seem to have been picked up beyond the local papers), and when she did, the results were disappointing. Lori's social media presence was minimal, and what she had was set to private, with a profile picture that clearly hadn't been updated in over a decade. What Claudia was able to find wasn't much more enlightening: a resume that ended eight years back, detailing a previous career in corporate communications; some streaming music playlists that were heavy on pop-oriented R&B; and a mention in a review of San Elmo on a travel site that the writer had bought one of Lori's bags and been disappointed by the quality. (That one had taken some digging, and Claudia wasn't sure it had been time well spent.)

Frustrated, Claudia leaned back from her computer and looked out the window. She was sure there was more information out there about Lori, but without more of a toehold, she didn't think much of her chances of finding it in the vastness of the Internet. As she considered where that might be found, she let her gaze drift over the view, until it settled on the empty cottage across the way.

Since it wasn't currently habitable, Claudia had been using the building as storage, and she had made it available to the vendors to keep their nonperishable goods too. Most of them only had a few things; Robbie's least favorite butcher knives, three cases of pickle jars that were overflow from the time Helen had found them on sale, some apple crates of unknown origin. But Lori had claimed an entire corner for herself, for what she said were boxes of extra dyeing and printing supplies. That was obviously a lie, so the next step of Claudia's investigation was going to be to find out the truth.

The second cottage had the same layout as Claudia's home, but in skeletal form. The main room had been stripped back to the bare plaster and concrete, with stubs of the plumbing and electrical connections protruding optimistically from the wall where the kitchen might someday be. The bedroom had retained some carpet, and the bathroom its fixtures, and the less said about both, the better.

The electricity had been turned off, for the sake of safety and economy, so Claudia rolled up the paper blinds to let some light in and got to work. She had brought a pair of latex gloves from the box on the shelf in her bedroom, left there for some long-forgotten reason, and put them on, feeling a little silly as she did it. But, while she had good reasons for her fingerprints to be found on pretty much everything in the marketplace, it was going to be harder to explain if they showed up inside boxes of the victim's personal goods. If there was ever a time to develop some paranoid tendencies, Claudia decided, this was it.

With her hands suitably attired, Claudia dove in. The first two boxes were packed tight with Lori's signature "handmade" goods, complete with packing slips detailing how many of each item were there and how much had been paid for them. Initially, Claudia thought it had been some sort of joke at her expense, for Lori to keep the evidence that she was cheating her right under her nose, but after a while it occurred to her that maybe it was just necessity. The wholesaler Lori was ordering from appeared to require purchases in bulk, and since she couldn't have more than one of each identical item for sale at the same time, she would have needed somewhere to store it all.

After five boxes, Claudia figured she had pretty much gotten all she was going to out of this expedition, but there was one more, a box that didn't match the rest, wedged in the corner, that caught her attention.

It was taller than the merchandise boxes, and had begun its life as the packaging for a paper shredder, though based on the dents in the cardboard and multiple layers of tape, it had gone through some other roles since then. It wasn't sealed, so Claudia just had to carefully lift the flaps to see what was inside.

At first, the box seemed to be filled with nothing but office supplies. Some empty three-ring binders, a cup filled with pens, a couple of staplers, an empty tape dispenser; nothing you wouldn't expect to find in the last-day box of someone cleaning out their desk at a job where nobody kept a close eye on the supply cabinet.

The sweat was starting to pool in her gloves, but curiosity kept Claudia digging. Lori was exactly the sort of person to have kept her passwords written down on a sticky note on her desk, and it was just barely possible that such a thing might have gotten jumbled into a box like this.

Unfortunately, no such thing appeared, and she was about to give it up as a dead end when she came across an old-fashioned paper datebook.

Flipping it open Claudia hoped there might be some appointments listed, or the names of contacts who might lead her to someone with a better reason to kill Lori than some counterfeit tie-dye and a couple of stink bombs. But apparently it wasn't going to be that easy.

The first eight pages of the book were blank, and starting on the ninth, they were filled with a list of women's names, scribbled across the lines for appointments with incomprehensible notes, like "Kara Young 5k cousin cancer Philly," and "Rebecca Cobb 10–15? Palmyra." The notes filled a page and a half, getting sketchier toward the end, to the point that the last few entries lacked last names, followed by more question marks than words.

Claudia flipped through the rest of the pages but there was no more writing. Instead, she found a three-by-five photo tucked into the back cover. It must have been at least fifteen years old, from a time when people still took photos and had them developed instead of leaving them to be forgotten on old hard drives. A much younger Lori was smiling at the camera, her arm around another woman who was hugging her back and sticking out her tongue. Both were dressed in early-2000s pink and green, with plaid for Lori and florals for the other, and the non-Lori woman was holding an ice cream cone in her free hand. On the back of the photo someone had written, in purple ink, "Lori + Dana BFF Forever."

It was an image completely unlike the Lori that Claudia had known. Claudia wondered when she had changed, and why. And, more to the point, why this one photo was kept in a book otherwise devoted to the inscrutable notes.

It was past noon by the time she had the storage room put back to rights, and the effects of Betty's breakfast were wearing off. Claudia had locked up and was heading back to her cottage, thinking about lunch, when she noticed her front door was open.

It wasn't the first time it had happened; the latch was old and cheap, and when Claudia was in a hurry she sometimes forgot to go through the ritual of pulling the door tightly closed and then pushing to check it. On a normal day she would have just been annoyed with herself, but the last few days hadn't been normal.

The question was, what was she going to do about it? Standing outside and frowning at the door wasn't a long-term solution, and going for help seemed like an overreaction. Claudia settled on waiting for a while longer and, when nothing continued to happen, approached the door. She pushed it open the rest of the way with her fingertips, standing back as if she expected someone to come bursting out at her. No one did, so she looked inside.

She didn't have to look far. The source of the intrusion was right in front of her, curled up in front of her couch (okay, loveseat) with its ears perked up and tongue hanging out.

Claudia sighed, both in irritation and relief.

"I guess you liked the empanada?" she said.

The dog laid its head down and whimpered in agreement.

CHAPTER SIX

In small towns, like small houses, you rarely had to look for too long to find someone. The local vet (also the florist) had been out on a call, but he was on his way back to the office when Claudia reached him, and insisted it was no trouble to stop by and check on her visitor on his way. He said he would be there in about half an hour, so in the meantime Claudia called the police station to tell them she had some boxes of Lori's stuff, because the last thing she wanted was to give Lennox another reason to suspect her of being uncooperative.

Then she had to figure out what to do with her uninvited guest. First, after some debate, she shut the door. On the one hand, she had the impression it was a bad idea to close oneself up in a confined space with an unfamiliar dog, but on the other hand, she didn't want the vet to make a special trip out to see her only to be told that the patient had wandered off. Tipping the scales was the fact that the dog could hardly have been less threatening if it was a stuffed animal, still curled up on the floor, watching her over the tail wrapped around its nose.

"I think your name is Teddy," Claudia said, and it was.

The vet arrived not long after the appointed time, dirty and smelling of goat. Martin Stephens was a short, round man with a receding hairline and glasses that were consistently either balanced on the end of his nose or pushed up on top of his head, and he drove a truck decorated with dueling magnetic signs advertising his veterinary and florist businesses. The florist part had been his daughter's, until she had met a rodeo clown and decided she preferred a life among the bulls and barrels to buds and bouquets. Her father, who had cosigned the loan for the shop, had reportedly shrugged, said it couldn't be so hard, and occasionally showed up to make wedding deliveries with upward of six cats riding shotgun.

To Claudia's relief, today Martin had no animal or floral encumbrances. He scanned the dog for a chip, checked its teeth, limbs, and eyes, and pronounced "it" to be a "she."

"I'd like to see a few more pounds on her, but that's nothing a few good meals won't fix. Aside from being underfed, I'd say she's in decent health, though we'll need to do some tests to make sure she's not carrying anything. No chip, and she hasn't been fixed, but I'd say she hasn't had a litter yet. Seems to have a nice temperament for a stray, if that's what she is."

He patted the dog on her head and stood up.

"My guess is someone got a puppy, and once they realized she wasn't a toy, they decided to 'set her free.' Damn shame people like that don't get left on the side of the road with nothing more than they were born with, if you know what I mean. Still, she seems to have come out of it okay. If you like, I can take her over to the shelter with me. I've got to go there later anyway."

Claudia thought about that. She had visited the county shelter once, when she had gone with Betty to pick up some chickens that had been dropped off there after their role as Easter basket props had been completed. It wasn't a bad place, as well-maintained as any rural service where the demands outstripped the funding, but it had been crowded and gray and the constant barking of the dogs had been deafening. She looked down at the soft brown eyes of her visitor and rationalized away.

"That's okay, she can stay with me for now. I'll take some pictures and post them around in case anyone is looking. With everything that's been going around here lately, I could use the company."

The vet laughed.

"I'm not sure you've gotten yourself any sort of vicious guard dog, but I do think you've probably found a friend. I'll keep an eye out for anyone looking for a missing shepherd, but I have a feeling we're not going to get many takers."

He started for the door, but haltingly, trying to find a way to ask the questions that were clearly on his mind.

"So, that lady who died here yesterday, well, not here, but over at the market, anyway, you knew her?"

Claudia was probably within her rights to be offended, but the way she saw it, veterinary house calls were a nice perk, and if she was about to become a dog owner, this was probably not the last time she was going to require his services. So she answered without rancor.

"I saw her a lot, but I didn't know her well. Like someone you work with. But I did find her body."

That was clearly getting closer to what the vet was interested in. He moved closer, probably unaware of how eager he looked.

"That's terrible," he said. "It must have been a huge shock."

"It was," Claudia agreed. "I've never seen a dead body before. I mean, not like that."

"She was strangled, wasn't she? That's some nasty stuff. There was a guy a few years ago who got it in his head he was going to strangle one of the Mullers' llamas—you know, the ones they got to keep the coyotes away from the goats? I guess he thought the long neck would make it easier, or something. Anyway, the damn fool got himself trampled nearly to death, and serves him right, I think. They called me in to check on the llama, but it was fine. Might have sprained a foot kicking him, but that was it."

"I guess it's too bad Lori didn't have hooves." It occurred to Claudia that the vet might be a source of some useful general information. His patients might not be human, but he was still a doctor.

"But she must have fought, right? How long does it take to strangle a person?" she asked.

The vet gave this question some serious thought. "How long? I'd say probably at least thirty seconds, maybe a minute until she was unconscious, and longer than that to death. It depends on whether they're obstructing the carotid artery or actually going all the way to crushing the windpipe. And I bet you're right about the fighting. The first thing the police should be doing is checking her fingernails for DNA. That should get them straight to the killer."

It was the most comforting conversation about violent death Claudia had ever had. She hadn't even thought of there being DNA evidence, but of course, that should clear her in no time. Or, at least, as close to no time as the police lab could achieve. She wondered if they ever did rush orders for important cases.

Martin left her with a couple of sample-sized bags of kibble and an appointment to bring Teddy to his office for her first real checkup and shots, and another one for the operation to make sure Claudia didn't rapidly progress from having no dogs, to one dog, to many dogs.

As he left, the vet paused in the door and looked across the field.

"Okay, well, best of luck. By the way, let me know if you want me to have a look at those geese."

As interesting as it was to suddenly find herself a dog owner, it wasn't the main thing going on in Claudia's life at the moment. She would have liked to take some time to do a deeper dive into Lori's digital footprint, but after some consideration, she decided to leave that for later. She had the feeling that that was going to turn out to be an involved research project, and it was the sort of thing that didn't require daylight. On the other hand, considering how little she had known of Lori's personality and her life, one of the first things Claudia needed to do was find someone who could tell her more. And since the only people she knew who knew Lori were from the marketplace, that seemed like the best place to start.

She had obligations to her tenants to keep them updated on the situation, even if she didn't have anything to update them with. And, if in the course of personally delivering her lack of information, she happened to learn more about Lori and what might have led to her death, well, that was just a side benefit, wasn't it?

Her main issue was what to do with Teddy while she was out. There was nothing terribly precious or fragile in the cottage, but what she had, Claudia would rather not lose, so in the end she settled for making a bed out of old towels in the bathroom, leaving bowls of water and food, and hoping for the best.

There was no question what her first stop was going to be. The Mullers and their cheeses had been the earliest tenants of the marketplace, and Elias would expect to be at the head of the line to get an update on its status. So Claudia pointed her aging subcompact inland, across the first line of hills that separated the windswept coast from the sunnier slopes on the other side.

It was a quirk of the local geography that temperatures were determined by how many ridges separated you from the ocean. Almost every day in the summer the cool, wet air blew in from the Pacific, carrying a layer of fog that poured softly along the coastline, seeking openings in the hills where it could sneak inland. The Muller's farm was situated at the base of one of these clefts, taking advantage of the moisture in a place that wouldn't see rain again until October at the earliest. But thanks to the combined powers of fog and irrigation, the farm was a pocket of green, decorated with a tasteful scattering of cows and goats.

Arriving at the farm, Claudia parked and made her way past the barns to the gleaming new cheesemaking facility. It was a white, rectangular building, set close enough to the milking shed that the pipes could feed the milk straight from the cows and goats into the tanks with as little disturbance as possible. But it wasn't only functional; there were concessions to marketing as well, with generous viewing windows on the front for tour groups to watch the magical process of turning milk into snack food.

According to Betty, a reliable source for information on how much anyone in the area had spent on pretty much anything, the facility represented the biggest risk Elias had taken since opening the creamery. Gambling on the growth of the artisan cheese market, he had mortgaged the entire property in order to build a state-of-the-art home for his precious cheeses, against the advice of Julie, who was more cautious than her impulsive father. So far it seemed to be paying off, with wholesale orders growing steadily and the name of the farm showing up on more of the menus of the sort of places that put the names of farms on their menus.

Compared to the glories of the creamery, the Muller family home sat more modestly to one side, awkward with the additions that had been tacked on for a growing family and looking every bit of its sixty years. A scattering of hens wandered around the front yard, pecking at the rose bushes and eyeing everything with chickeny suspicion.

She found Elias in one of the aging rooms in the creamery, carefully washing and turning the soft cheeses. He saw her and waved through the window in the door, motioning to her to wait for a moment. Claudia watched as he finished the last row, then came out of the scrupulously sterile room, pulling the blue paper cap off his head to reveal a magnificent shock of white hair.

"Claudia," he said, enveloping one of her hands with his and patting it solicitously. "What a terrible thing to have happen. Julie told me everything. Are you all right?" Elias Muller was a mountain of a man with the face of a giant baby and hands like Easter hams. Even trying to speak softly, his voice boomed into the small space like he was shouting across mountaintops.

Claudia tried not cringe under the onslaught.

"Thank you, Elias. It was a shock, definitely, but I'm okay now. I just wanted to come by and check on how you're doing."

"Oh, we're fine, we're fine. Haven't found any dead bodies today, have we?" he said, with a laugh that echoed down the hallway.

Claudia smiled dutifully. Elias's sense of humor ranged from "very inappropriate" to "really, seriously inappropriate," and by his standards this was mild stuff.

"Come to my office," Elias said. "We can talk there."

Despite the fact that a bright, spacious office had been built for him on the other side of the building, Elias's preferred workplace was a tiny converted vestibule just outside the cheesemaking room, where he could keep an eye on the workers and should it be necessary, could come bursting out to deal with any failure to keep up with his standards.

By all accounts, the creamery was a stressful place to work, but the pay was good.

Even now, as he led Claudia inside and closed the door, Elias positioned his chair so he could see out of the window, and kept one eye on the other room the entire time they talked.

"So, the marketplace is closed," he said, matter-of-factly. "Do you know for how long?"

Claudia had to admit she did not.

"The police chief said he could keep it closed for as long as the investigation is active. I don't think that's true, but it's going to take some time for me to fight him," she said.

Elias shook his head.

"Don't fight that man. He's as stubborn as he is stupid. I'll talk to some people, see what they can do." He leaned back in his chair, causing it to creak perilously. "Don't forget, when all the vacationers are gone, this is still a small town. I'm still a newcomer, I've only been here fifty years. But people will talk to me, so I'll talk to them."

"Thank you, I appreciate that." It occurred to Claudia to wonder if there was such a thing as a Swiss mafia. If so, she imagined they left very tidy crime scenes. She started to smile at the idea, but then remembered what she now knew about crime scenes, and it didn't seem so funny.

"Speaking of people, I wonder if there's anyone who knows more about what happened to Lori. In a town like this, you think someone would have seen something."

"Maybe they did," Elias said. "Maybe they saw things and didn't know what they saw. If our policeman was something more than an old hen in a uniform, he might find them and ask."

Claudia tried to unpack that, then gave it up as a bad job and wondered what the police chief had done to get himself so thoroughly on Elias's bad side. Whatever it was, she wasn't going to argue.

"I have to admit, I wish I had asked some more questions when I let Lori rent the space. I don't suppose you had any idea about her sourcing her products from wholesalers?"

Elias did not, and he was appalled that anyone in their community would stoop to such dishonesty.

"But why?" he asked, once he was done decrying the degradation of the morals of modern youth. "Why waste so much time and effort for so little? Surely if a person is willing to be unscrupulous, they could do it elsewhere for more money."

"I don't know," Claudia said. "But for whatever reason she seemed desperate to keep it up for a little while longer."

"Maybe she had plans for something big that was going to make her a lot of money? You might be lucky that she died."

Claudia sighed and hung her head.

"Please don't say that. I can't think of anything she could have done to the marketplace that was worse than her dying."

It was the truth, and it was also something Claudia wanted everyone to be aware of. She didn't think Elias suspected her, but there was no harm in making the point.

"Of course," Elias said. "It certainly is very annoying. But I never did like her. Very rude to everyone, and thought she knew much more than she did. Did you know that she once said to me that what the cows ate didn't matter? Didn't matter! Thought I could buy milk from wherever and it would be the same! I'll tell you, she did not get away with that for very long."

Claudia had no doubt that was true, but she hoped Elias wasn't going to be telling that story to too many people. Not that anyone would honestly believe he could have killed Lori to protect the honor of his cows, but a person might look at his hands and wonder. She was thinking about how to phrase a warning to that effect when something caught his attention in the cheesemaking room.

"No!" Elias bellowed. "Esteban, the baskets must be filled all the way up! All the way!"

He rocketed out of his chair and toward the door, pausing only long enough to throw on his hair net, which ended up tilted at a jaunty angle. As the doors closed behind him, Claudia could hear the unfortunate employee get a vigorous lesson in the proper packing of curds. She wondered if her interview was over, but once his task was accomplished Elias came back, looking pleased with himself and ready to pick up their conversation where they had left off.

"Very important to maintain the standards, you know? I look away for a minute and everything goes to hell. Anyway, yes, the poor woman. Nobody liked her, but not enough to kill, I would have thought."

"What makes you think people didn't like her?" Claudia wondered how much there was going on in the market that she wasn't aware of. Lori hadn't seemed to have a lot of friends, but she wasn't aware of any sort of widespread animosity. On the other hand, Elias did have a tendency to extrapolate.

That seemed to be the case here.

"Well, it was more of a sense I got," he backtracked. "Once I saw her being rude to Mrs. Pak, and she was stupid about everybody's work. Except young Robbie, of course, but he had no interest in her."

Robbie was older than Lori, who Elias had just been holding up as an example of the degenerate youth, but Claudia let all that pass without comment. On his broader point, he was probably right, though.

Robbie would have been nice to Lori, because he was nice to everyone, but more than that seemed deeply unlikely, considering how devoted Robbie was to his very devotion-worthy wife.

For his part, Elias seemed to have lost all interest in the marketplace and the people in it and moved on to more important subjects, retrieving a wedge of cheese from the small refrigerator behind his desk.

"Since you're here, you should try this," he said, slicing off a series of pieces from the pale yellow wedge, marked with delicate, smooth holes. "Our new Emmenthaler-style. I didn't want to, but Julie insisted. She says, if we're going to be Swiss and sell cheese, we need to make a Swiss cheese. So this is what we did. It's good enough, I suppose. The sort of thing you give to children."

Elias was trying to sound dismissive and uninterested in this concession to the market, but there was clear pride in his voice, and he watched Claudia take her first taste with undisguised interest.

"It's excellent," she declared, with perfect honesty. The cheese might not have been the most complex masterwork of the cheesemaker's art, but as a thing to eat, it could hardly have been better. The texture was firm and smooth, and the flavor was like the distilled essence of milk; not creamy so much as fresh and light-tasting, and ever so slightly floral. Claudia supposed you could give it to children, if you liked them enough.

"Really excellent," she repeated. "It's going to be a big hit."

Elias harrumphed something about unsophisticated palates, but Claudia didn't even pretend to be offended.

"Anyway, I can't wait to see it in the marketplace. I hope I get a chance."

"Of course you will. Let me talk to some people, and I will find out what Mr. Lennox thinks he's doing, and we will put a stop to this nonsense."

He sounded so confident, Claudia almost believed it could be that simple. She would have liked to ask who these people Elias planned to talk to were, and what he was going to say, but another crisis was brewing in the cheesemaking room and it was clear her audience was at an end. Claudia took a last piece of cheese for the road, thanked Elias for his time, and headed out, offering a silent prayer for mercy on the poor man who hadn't known not to stick his bare arm up to the armpit in the mozzarella vat.

It didn't matter what the business was, she supposed; there was always going to be someone around to muck it up.

CHAPTER SEVEN

It was getting late, and at this point there was no way Claudia was going to be able to make it to all of the people she wanted to see. Carmen and Iryna would be getting ready for their weekly trip to visit Carmen's sister and test their latest products on her nieces (Claudia suspected this was the origin of the ill-fated "birthday cake pierogi," but she had no proof), and Orlan, of the vegetable market, was based out of Petaluma, a good half-hour's drive away. Of all her tenants, he was the least likely to expect a visit—he ran a large operation and while that didn't mean having the shop closed was no problem, she wasn't worried how they were going to keep it together in the meantime. A phone call would be fine.

That left Robbie and Emmanuelle or the Paks. She would need to talk to both of them, but she only had time for one more stop. Ultimately, Teddy tipped the balance. Claudia didn't know how long you were supposed to leave a dog in a bathroom, but it seemed like a good idea to err on the side of caution, and the Pak's home was closer.

They lived in the newer part of town, built up in the sixties during a brief flash of optimism about a freeway extension that would turn San Elmo into a thriving exurb. The freeway never came, but the houses stayed, a patch of stuccoed suburbia tucked against the dunes. Claudia had been to the Paks' house before, but even if she hadn't, it wouldn't have been hard to find. There weren't a lot of houses in town that had a front yard full of carefully pruned yew topiaries, including a surprisingly realistic squirrel. Then, of course, there was the aroma.

Like everyone else, the Paks were required to make their products for sale in a commercial kitchen, but there was nothing to stop Helen from turning her home into a research and development center (as her neighbors had learned, to their annoyance). Today the scent was the usual mix of fermented funk and eye-watering spice, with an added hint of ocean-y tang.

Claudia rang the doorbell and waited through the responding chorus of barks for the sound of approaching footsteps.

"Caesar, Ducky, no. Down. Oh, hi, Claudia," The door was answered by Brandon, the Paks' twenty-year-old son. He had been involved in the business from day one, splitting his time between working in their booth in the marketplace, maintaining the website for their mail-order business, and commuting to a local college where he was studying business administration and art history. Claudia's impression of him was that he was a good kid who could probably use some more free time, but that was none of her business.

He held the dogs back as best as he could and let Claudia in.

"Sorry," Brandon said. "It's almost their dinner time, and they get excited. No, Delaware, no jumping. Are you here to see Mom?"

"Is this a bad time? I just wanted to give you guys an update on the situation at the marketplace and see how you were doing."

"Thanks. We're okay, I think." Brandon led her through the house, spotless despite the trio of small dogs that milled around at ankle level. "Mom was pretty annoyed this morning, but she's mostly calmed down, and Dad's at a trade show, so we were going to be shorthanded anyway. Do you know when we're going to be able to reopen?"

"I wish I did. I've talked to a lawyer about it, but in the meantime I'm going to look into some other options for temporary solutions. How are your online sales doing?"

"Okay. The burst we got from that gift list thing has died down, but we've settled at a higher volume."

It was almost a year now since a major regional magazine had included a short blurb about the Paks' sweet and spicy pickled cabbage in a roundup of food items to put in a holiday gift basket for people you didn't know very well, and the effect on sales had been close to overwhelming. The Paks had pushed their production capacity to the limit, and several of the other marketplace tenants had pitched in to help with the packing and shipping. The consensus was that it was a great thing that everyone hoped wouldn't happen too often.

Claudia followed Brandon to the kitchen, where his mother was lost in contemplation of a pile of shiny brown leaves that looked familiar in a way Claudia couldn't place. Helen was a compact woman in her early fifties, with short black hair and a predilection for bold patterns. Today she was wearing a pink floral tunic over houndstooth-print leggings, paired with the fluffiest slippers known to man.

"Oh, hello," she said to Claudia. "I thought I heard your voice. Sorry I didn't answer the door, I have my hands full with these kelp."

It finally struck Claudia where she had seen those leaves before: in sandy piles on the beach.

'You can pickle those?" she asked.

"Of course you can," Helen said dismissively. "The question is, will people eat it?"

"That's a good question," said Brandon.

Sometimes Helen's ambitions ran ahead of local tastes, to her son's frustration. But Claudia appreciated it; anyone could pickle a cucumber, but who would have known that pickled blackberries could be so delicious? Still, she was dubious of this one.

"It's the local thing," Helen went on to explain, ignoring her son, who vanished back into the living room. "I get all the vegetables from around here, but I was thinking, what is really local? What's right here? And then I thought: the ocean. So I'm pickling seaweed. It's legal to harvest, I checked the rules. You just go out and gather it."

And that was your answer right there, Claudia thought. If there was anything Helen loved more than fermenting, it was reducing overhead.

What she said was, "That sounds great. I'll look forward to trying it. We should think about doing some sort of display once you're ready to sell them."

That brought her back to a more unpleasant thought.

"Speaking of your products, I'm afraid you may need to replace the giant pickle jar from your front table. When I found—when I was in the marketplace yesterday morning I saw it on the ground. I don't know if the jar was damaged but you probably wouldn't want to keep it around anyway."

Claudia was expecting the news to be upsetting, but she wasn't prepared for Helen's response. She stopped what she was doing and remained frozen, with a piece of kelp in one hand and a vegetable peeler in the other, for several seconds. She started to say something, stopped herself, started again and turned that into a hiccup, then finally took a deep breath and laid the peeler down on the counter.

"Well, that is too bad," she said, carefully measuring out each word. "Those large jars are expensive. But maybe it was time to rethink that display anyway."

She looked around the kitchen, as if noticing for the first time that it was there.

"I have a lot to do right now. Could we pick this up later? Please let me know if there's anything I can do to help while the marketplace is closed."

And with that Claudia found herself being politely but firmly given the bum's rush, ending up on the front step, wondering what could possibly be so upsetting about the loss of a jar of pickles, no matter how large.

Claudia spent the drive home simultaneously trying to process the events of the day and her options for the future. Deeply involved in the question of whether it was worthwhile to try to research what kind of printer had produced the sheets that had tipped her off about Lori, she almost failed to notice the police car in her driveway.

"Hello?" Claudia tried the door to her cottage, but it was still locked, and the only sound was a faint whimpering coming from the direction of the bathroom. She was about to go inside when a voice answered her.

"Oh, hey there." The voice belonged to Officer Derek Chambers (funny how easily she remembered that name), who was coming around the corner from behind the other cottage. "I thought I heard someone."

He was in his normal uniform, but somehow on him it looked both sharper and more louche than any of his fellow officers. His short, light brown hair was slightly mussed, revealing a cowlick over his left ear, and the tan lines around his eyes suggested a love of a particular shape of sunglasses. Claudia realized she was staring and mentally slapped herself. This was no time to be distracted by a muscular pair of forearms or a charming smile.

"We got your message about having some of the victim's things in storage, so I was just coming out to pick them up. I hope that's okay?"

"Of course," Claudia said. "There probably isn't anything interesting in there, but I thought you guys should be the ones to make that call." She didn't feel like she needed to let him know she had already been through them, or what she had and hadn't found. Not that she had done anything wrong, but it was the sort of thing that police probably found annoying.

"Good call," Derek said. "We never know what we're going to find until we look. If you can just point me to it, I'll get them out of your hair."

"Okay, right this way."

He smiled again and Claudia had to scold herself for the warm feeling it gave her. It was too easy to be comfortable around him, and that was not a good idea. His boss was treating her like a murder suspect, and no matter how nice he seemed, there was no reason for her to believe that Derek didn't agree with him, and it was his job to charm her into incriminating herself. (Everyone knew about good cop–bad cop, but for her money, it had nothing on bad cop–hot cop.)

"Do you mind if I go and let my dog out?" she said as she opened the door to the storage cottage. "She's been inside for a while and I think she might need some fresh air. The boxes are all the ones in that corner."

"Sure, no problem. I didn't know you had a dog."

"It's kind of a new development. She seems to have adopted me."

Derek's smile grew wider.

"They do that don't they? I'd love to meet her."

Claudia agreed to arrange the introduction and left him to haul the boxes out on his own, depriving herself of the view of those arms in action for the sake of her bathroom.

Teddy was happy to see her, and Claudia was happy to see that the room was still pretty much intact. (She hadn't liked that bath mat very much anyway.) She let the dog out to do her business, and watched Derek load the boxes into the back of his cruiser. She and Teddy were disputing the ownership of a stick when he came back, peeling off the latex gloves he'd been wearing and stuffing them in his pocket.

"This is your dog?" He reached down at Teddy, who immediately lost interest in the stick and came over for some expert-level ear-scratching.

"Apparently," Claudia said. She picked up the abandoned stick and waggled it, hoping to distract Teddy's attention, but it was clear that Officer Chambers's appeal wasn't limited to humans.

"You know, this really is an amazing place. Even the stray dogs are friendly." He finished the scratching job and leaned on the corner of the house, looking out over the ocean.

"How long have you been here?" Claudia asked. Whatever the officer was up to, Claudia didn't see any benefit in sending him on his way, at least not yet. Maybe she could be charming too. Stranger things had happened.

"Almost a year now," he said. "I'd been working in the city and it was wearing me down. Too much violence, too few good days. I thought I'd get away to the country, find some peace and quiet, maybe learn to surf."

"How's that going for you?"

"The ocean's ice cold and I'm knee-deep in a murder investigation. Other than that, everything's peachy."

In spite of herself, Claudia laughed.

"Well, nothing's perfect," she said.

A light breeze picked up, bringing a whiff of salt air, and in the short silence that followed, Claudia allowed herself a moment to imagine the other ways a conversation like this might go, under different circumstances. But that imagined place wasn't here and now, and reluctantly she pulled herself back to the real world.

"So, Officer Chambers—"

"Please, you've got to call me Derek. No one around here is that formal. Lieutenant Derek, if you must."

"All right, Lieutenant Officer, are you really supposed to be talking to me like this? You're in the middle of a murder investigation, and I get the impression your boss only sees mug shots when he looks at me."

Derek looked mildly embarrassed. "Well, a person can have a conversation, can't they? For what it's worth, I don't think the chief really has it in for you. He's just worried about trying to solve the case, and he doesn't want to let any possibilities get by him."

"That's nice for him, but he isn't exactly making it easier for me. Do you have any idea when I'm going to be able to reopen the market? This is our high season, and I've got a lot of people who depend on their shops being open. Myself included." Since she wasn't going to get any pleasure out of the encounter now, Claudia decided that at least she could try to get something accomplished.

But her new friend was having none of it.

"Hey, look, I just work here," he said, stepping back with his hands raised. "I'd love to help, but I can't tell you anything that's going to interfere with the investigation."

"I don't want to interfere," Claudia argued. "I just want to know if I'm ever going to be able to get back to my business."

"I'm sorry, but that's up to the chief. Thanks for turning over the boxes. If you find anything else that belonged to the victim, please let us know."

"Of course," Claudia said, and watched with regret as he got into his patrol car and drove away. Not that there was any other way that could have gone, she reminded herself.

Teddy came up and bumped her head under Claudia's hand, who responded with some clearly inferior scratching.

"Sorry, girl," she said. "It looks like it's just us for now."

CHAPTER EIGHT

It was getting late, and there was only time to make a few more calls before the end of the business day, so Claudia put off any plans to contact her other tenants in favor of calling around to other local businesses and farmer's markets until she came up with enough options to get them through the next week or so. What was going to get *her* through was still an open question, but she'd come up with something. Maybe dig up her old clarinet and try busking. People would probably pay good money to get her to stop.

That got Claudia thinking about more practical steps she could take. She had only scraped the surface on her previous search into Lori's Internet presence, and it occurred to her now that she had a couple of tools that might be helpful. Possibly not legal, and definitely not ethical, but murder was neither of those, so Claudia felt like she had some moral leeway.

The sun was starting to set, sinking into the fog with a last gasp of pink and orange. Claudia heated up a bowl of the chili that Betty had insisted on sending home with her, opened her computer, and got to work.

As a matter of course, Claudia ran a credit check on every one of her tenants. She wasn't authorized to use the information for anything other than leasing decisions, but at this point, a terms of service violation was the least of her worries. With it, and the help of the Internet, Claudia was now able to build a pretty complete resume of the victim's adult life.

Lori Roth had gotten her first credit card in college, listing her address as an off-campus housing complex which appeared to sport an extensive collection of outdoor couches, at least based on the current street-view photos. That was in Ohio, and the résumé Claudia had found earlier indicated that Lori had majored in communications and graduated without doing anything significant. From there she had moved on to a job and apartment in Virginia, after a break of about six months in Connecticut, during which time she leased a used car and was delinquent on paying her credit card bill three times.

The car lease had been cosigned by a John Roth, with a home address near where the purchase was made. That house was a modest suburban split-level with a minivan parked in the driveway and a basketball abandoned on the lawn. A search of the archives of the local paper brought up an obituary for John Roth, a widower who had succumbed after a short battle with cancer eight years ago, survived by his daughter, Lori Natalia.

So Lori had been basically alone in the world by the time she had moved to San Elmo. That was as good an explanation as any for why she had never talked about her family; by the looks of things, there might not have been anyone to talk about. Claudia wondered briefly what was going to happen to the boxes of merchandise Derek had claimed from her storage, before realizing that was probably the least important question she was facing right now, by several orders of magnitude.

Back to the reconstruction of Lori's life. She spent twelve years living in Virginia, working at various marketing jobs and living in apartment buildings that ranged in appearance from okay to pleasant. From Virginia, Lori had moved to Maryland for four years, though that was after the online resume ended. Whatever she had been doing there, she ended it abruptly seven months ago, breaking her lease in Maryland and moving into the duplex she had been living in in San Elmo, all in the space of about a week.

She had put in her application for the marketplace spot two days later.

And that was pretty much the end of the story, at least as far as her current materials could tell it. Claudia looked back over the timeline she had created, hoping something might stand out, but nothing did. Despite the details she had uncovered, Claudia found it unsatisfying. There were all the bones of a life, but none of the meat. Who were Lori's friends, her lovers? Did she enjoy the various jobs she had worked, or were they just a paycheck? What excited her, what did she regret?

And why, with no apparent history with California, fabric crafts, or false advertising, had she decided to drop everything for a new life that combined all three?

She wasn't going to find that in a credit report, so for the moment Claudia set aside the unknowable and did her best with what she had. The additional information was useful for constructing more precise search terms, with which Claudia was able to unearth a few more tidbits.

There were a couple of restaurant reviews heavy on complaints about waitstaff, a mention in Lori's alumni newsletter that she had run a 5k, her name on the list of attendees at a networking luncheon. None of that held Claudia's attention for long, though she did take a moment to entertain the idea that the killer had been a hitman sent by the Food Service Employees of America on behalf of their members.

Frustrated, Claudia was tempted to give up, but she pushed through and tried the next series of combinations. She was starting to reach with some of them, which was why she was surprised when the name of one of Lori's former employers and "fraud" came up with a cluster of hits.

It was a series of old news stories about a member of a D-list boy band who had found a postfame career running a medium-sized cult. They had been doing a fine business in drug running and some light brainwashing in California, but then they had decided to expand their practice to Northern Virginia, to the office building where Lori's employer was located. There were some confrontations, and it turned out that the International Concordance of Love and Light wasn't afraid to fight dirty.

Things escalated quickly, to the point that the CEO of the company came home one day to find a rattlesnake in his mailbox. (Fortunately, November temperatures in Virginia do not make for lively reptiles, and the man got nothing more than a scare and an interesting conversation with animal control.) Eventually, the FBI were able to put together a case, the cult was disbanded, and the TV movie got only average ratings. Lori's name didn't appear anywhere in the coverage. But, if the dates on her resume were to be believed, there was no question she had been present for the events in question.

With further digging, Claudia was able to determine that the cult leader (Serenity Icono Bartok, nee Jason), had been released from prison and was currently living in Humboldt County, about two hundred miles north of San Elmo. It wasn't exactly next door, but a person could probably make the trip in the afternoon, make a short stop to commit murder, and be back home before sunrise.

It was the baldest sort of speculation, of course. With no evidence that Lori had ever interacted with Bartok, it certainly wouldn't be enough for Claudia to take to the police. She could just imagine Lennox's face as she explained that this person who was in the same general area as Lori over a decade ago was definitely a better suspect than herself. Claudia didn't know Lennox very well, but she felt like his response would be less than productive.

She found some pictures of Bartok/Jason and studied them, hoping to tease out some sense of familiarity, but came up empty. In his boy band days he had been a vacuous looking young man with a toothy grin and a hairstyle that answered the as-yet-unasked question of "What if a sea urchin had frosted tips?" In later photos he had acquired most of a beard and an expression that combined divine inspiration with at least two major concussion symptoms.

His booking photo was the most recent she was able to find, and the most telling. Here she found a man, still young, but stripped of the publicist's artifice and beatific styling, so that only the angry boy remained. The round cheeks of his youth had turned hollow, crowned by dark eyes that sat deep in their sockets, like two burnt holes in a blanket. His dark brown hair, long since having abandoned the indignities of bleaching, hung in lank tendrils that framed an expression of sullen superiority.

She couldn't find any photos that dated since his release, and Claudia wasn't very good with faces, but if Jas-tok had made any appearances in the area, she didn't think she had seen him. Still, she printed out the picture to show around. She wasn't sure how she was going to explain her interest, but it seemed like the least she could do.

Claudia finished the chili and let Teddy earn her keep by prerinsing the bowl. (She was aware that there were people who would be horrified, but Claudia considered being able to do what she wanted without fear of judgement one of the primary benefits of living alone. And, frankly, the dishwasher needed all the help it could get.) While her new roommate was hard at work, Claudia wandered back to the computer and stared at it, wondering what her next step should be.

What she needed was more information, something to give her investigation direction, rather than wandering in the figurative darkness. And she had the feeling that the only person who could provide it was Lori, and she wasn't talking.

Or was she? Thinking over the interactions she had had with Lori, one anecdote floated to the top. It had been a slow Sunday afternoon in the marketplace, and Claudia had been helping Helen out in her shop while she was shorthanded. The conversation had somehow worked its way around to computer security and passwords, with Claudia passionately advocating for the value of length over complexity. Lori had been listening in without saying anything, until she interrupted to point out that Claudia, with her years of background in software development, was completely wrong, and it was a stupid thing to worry about. As proof of her position, she offered the fact that she had been using the same password for years, and no one had ever hacked her.

At the time, Claudia had been too annoyed to explain how stupid that was, and now she was glad she hadn't. Because if no one had hacked one of Lori's accounts before, it was high time it happened now.

One of the first things Claudia had done when she decided to take on the marketplace, was to set up a website. It had started out as a bare-bones affair, with a couple of pictures, hours of operation, contact information, and directions, but leaving it at that was not in her nature, and it had evolved into a comprehensive web portal for all tenants, with individual calendars and updatable pages to list their current offerings. Adoption had been inconsistent, but the important thing was that every tenant had their own account, with their own password.

The good news was that Claudia had handled all of the setup of the website herself, and she had control of the system on her own server. The bad news was that Claudia had handled all of the setup of the website herself, and as a result it was built with a level of security more frequently associated with banks or dark web drug sales. Which didn't mean she couldn't get at Lori's password, it just meant that she was going to have to work for it.

She had set up the system to store the passwords with a salted hash, which meant both that a brute force attack was out of the question and now she was hungry again. Setting aside thoughts of browned potatoes, Claudia got to the more pressing issue of how she was going to crack her own security. She knew there were tools available for that sort of thing, and in the end it only took a few more minutes of hunting and an encrypted text to a college friend who had a history of not asking too many questions, and Claudia was the not-very-proud owner of a precomputed rainbow table, suited for cracking the hashed password of her choice. She tried not to think too much about where her money was going—murderers were worse than hackers, after all—but found herself hard to convince.

Claudia had bought a couple of terabyte drives during a Black Friday sale a few years back, with no specific plans for what to do with them but unable to resist the price, and now she pressed them into hosting the attack. Figuring it all out took some time, and employed parts of her brain that hadn't gotten much of a workout in a while, and she found herself chewing gently on her pinkie finger, an old habit from her programming days that turned up whenever she had a problem to solve.

Eventually, she had the program running in a way she was pretty sure was right, and Claudia was able to drag her eyes off the screen and work out the crick that had developed in her shoulder. It all felt so familiar, she had an impulse to IM Sanjay in the next cubicle and see if he wanted take a break to raid the snack room. But there was no Sanjay, and no cubicles, and, sadly, no snack room, so Claudia had to make do with some ranch-flavored chickpea crisps that a distributor had sent as a promotional sample.

Cracking the password could take anywhere from hours to days, so once she had gotten it running Claudia left the tool to do its work. Teddy was whining, so she went to let her out, and stood in the doorway while the dog did her business.

The fog had rolled in too thick to see the ocean, but Claudia could hear the thump of the waves on the rocks and the eternal insistence of the foghorn. Her little cottage felt like an island in the clouds, where even the lights from Mr. Rodgers' house up the hill were like beacons on a distant ship. She tried to center herself in the peace of it, but her heart was racing and she couldn't stop thinking about the investigation, and what she was going to do next.

It was terrible, but Claudia had to admit part of her was enjoying this. It reminded her of what had drawn her to programming in the first place, the feeling that there was a problem to be solved, that could be solved, if only she had the right information and was able to use it in the right way. Claudia loved the marketplace, and she wouldn't give it up for anything, but until now she hadn't realized that there were things she missed from her old job and life.

Some people had normal hobbies, Claudia reminded herself. Treating a woman's murder as an opportunity for self-actualization was skating pretty close to sociopath territory, even for her. But this was something she had to do, and if she was going to do it, then she should take advantage of every bit of enthusiasm she could manage. She had a feeling she was going to need it.

CHAPTER NINE

Claudia woke up the next morning ready to dive back into the investigation, but feeling a little guilty about not spending her time trying to help her tenants. She salved her conscience by calling Julie to talk about the creamery as a possible alternate stop for the two tour groups that were supposed to visit the marketplace in the next week, and listened with sympathy to her account of Elias's meeting with a member of the city council the previous evening on the subject of the closure. It had been apparently going fairly well until he threw the chair.

"It wasn't a heavy chair," Julie said, apologetically. "But you know Father. He does get carried away sometimes."

Claudia said she understood, and told Julie to thank him for getting carried away on her behalf. Privately, she wasn't sure if he had done more to help her case or hurt it, but at this point there probably wasn't much difference.

Her next call was to Iryna and Carmen, ostensibly to make up for not visiting them the previous day, and offer some feedback on the new empanada flavors. (She was able to say they had been well appreciated, without mentioning how much of the appreciation had been done by Teddy.) They went back and forth for a few minutes, with Iryna chiming in over the speakerphone to advocate for herring and Carmen firmly rejecting the idea, before Claudia got to what she was really interested in.

"I was just wondering, Carmen, I know you talked to Lori some—did she ever mention anything about her life? I've been thinking about what happened and I realized I hardly got to know her at all. I can't imagine why she would have been pulling the trick with the fake stuff, let alone what would lead someone to kill her. Do you think she was afraid of anyone?"

Even over the background noise on the speakerphone, Claudia could hear Iryna sigh.

"No, and I don't understand it," Carmen said. "Any of it. She wasn't the nicest person, or the smartest, but that's no crime. I think she had a good job where she was before, but she was hardly making anything with the new business. I thought, well, she must really love to create, but now I don't know what to think."

"Maybe she thought cheating people would be easier and more profitable than it was." Where Carmen tended to be restrained in her judgement, Iryna was prone to flights of fancy, much to her wife's annoyance.

"I bet she moved here thinking it would be an easy life, living on the beach in the sunshine and fleecing the rubes," she went on. (Iryna's tastes in entertainment ran toward the sort of high-end cable dramas that specialized in tough-guy talk.) "And then she gets here, and it's cold and she's not making money like she thought, so she looks around for another way. I think probably the mob."

"You think the mafia is in San Elmo?" Claudia liked the idea of a simple solution, but it seemed far-fetched.

"Well, maybe she went to Santa Rosa," Iryna allowed, referring to the nearest city of any size. It was not, to Claudia's knowledge, a hotbed of organized crime, but she supposed anything was possible. "And when she tried to cheat them too, they killed her. It's the sort of thing they would do. Who would commit a murder like that, except for a criminal?"

Claudia considered explaining the concept of a tautology, but decided this wasn't the moment.

"That's stupid," Carmen said, putting it more succinctly. "Lori wasn't like that at all, and why would she be? If her money was running out here, she could just go back to her old work and forget all about it."

She made the statement with the finality of someone stating the obvious, and Claudia could imagine the two of them glaring at each other across the ancient speakerphone on their kitchen table.

"If that's not what happened, then what did?" Iryna countered. "You think she killed herself for not being a good enough artist to make little bags and stuff?"

The suggestion was sarcastic, but something in her own words set Iryna off on a new theory. Her voice got louder, and Claudia thought she must be leaning in closer to the phone to make her point.

"Or drugs! She put the drugs in the bags, and then people came and bought them from her with a secret code word. She makes the profits go through the business so no one finds out. Maybe the drugs even come in with the bags when they are shipped from China. It explains everything."

"It's certainly something to think about," Claudia agreed. "The police took all the boxes of hers that I had in my storage, so if there's anything in there I'm sure they'll find it."

"I think it's completely wrong." Carmen's voice sounded like she was speaking from a distance, like she had walked away from the conversation, but couldn't keep herself from joining in. "Lori was no criminal mastermind. I don't know what she was doing, but it wasn't that."

This wasn't a disagreement that was going to be settled soon, or possibly ever, so Claudia made some noises about not wanting to take up too much of their time and apologized again for the disruption to their business. Before saying goodbye, she mentioned the possibility of working with the other farmer's markets she had contacted, and resisted the temptation to bring up the possibility of the cult. Iryna would be delighted, but Carmen might never forgive her.

Claudia's next plan was to call Robbie and Emmanuelle, and she was starting to dial their number when there was the sound of tires on gravel and the now-familiar sight of a police car in her driveway.

Her heart bounced up when she saw Derek in the driver's seat, then took a corresponding dive when Lennox got out on the passenger side. She knew they had seen her watching them arrive, but she waited for the knock. Whatever conversation they were going to have, Claudia suspected she wasn't going to like it, and there was no reason to be in a hurry.

"Good morning, Miss Simcoe," Lennox said in response to her greeting. "I suppose you're wondering what brings us back so soon."

He strode into the cottage as smug as a cat with a dead lizard. Derek trailed in behind him, looking apologetic and saying nothing. Teddy immediately trotted over to demand ear-scratches.

"You're done with the marketplace and I can reopen it today?" Claudia said.

Lennox's smirk was almost audible.

"No, not that. We just have some more questions for you. Well, actually, just one question, and it should be a pretty simple one."

He reached into his pocket and took out a clear zip-top bag containing a blue plastic object, about the size of a large beetle, shaped like a focus group's idea of a pebble. There was a clip on one side and a small, scratched LED screen on the other.

"Is this yours?" Lennox asked.

"It could be," Claudia said, cautiously. In truth, she recognized it immediately. It was a fitness tracker, one of those little devices that were supposed to monitor your steps, your sleep, and your general physical activities, making you a healthier person by shaming you with your laziness. She knew it was hers because it was a less-popular brand, which she had chosen because the software it came with was open-sourced, the better for her to play with, and there was a scratch on the screen from when it had fallen behind one of the deli fridges and gotten stuck there. But she didn't see how it would be to her benefit to share that information, especially since she didn't know how Lennox had come to be holding it.

Naturally, Lennox didn't care for her prevarication.

"What do you mean it could be? Either it's yours or it isn't. Which is it?" Lennox waggled the bag in front of her, like he expected her to try to grab it out of his hand so he could snatch it away. It was bizarre, this constant need he seemed to have to prove his power over her, when there was no question he had plenty. Claudia wondered if he was like this all the time, or only when he was faced with a murder he had no chance of solving.

"I do own a tracker like that, but I can't be sure that's it. There must be thousands like it, and I haven't been using mine for a while. Where did you find it?" she said.

"It was found under Lori Roth's body. Does that help jog your memory?"

He obviously expected the revelation to have some sort of devastating effect, but Claudia declined to oblige. It took some effort, considering that her internal dialogue was composed entirely of screaming, but she was able to meet his triumphant gaze with a blank, mildly curious look.

"I see. But why did that make you think it would belong to me?"

"We were informed that you owned a similar item. Do you deny that's true?" Whatever response he had been expecting—weeping, a full confession—Lennox hadn't gotten it, and it clearly unnerved him. Derek hadn't said a word through the entire exchange; he was taking notes, and while his face remained neutral, the rest of him seemed to be engaged in a full-body cringe.

"Of course I don't deny it, I just told you I own one. And no, to answer your next question, I don't know where it is. I stopped using it a while ago after it kept telling me I'd reached ten thousand steps while I was in the car."

"So you don't have it around," Lennox said. "But I'm guessing you could connect this to your computer and tell us if it's yours or not, right?"

"That is technically possible," Claudia said carefully. "But I think you would need to provide a warrant before I agreed to do it."

"So you admit that it's evidence?" Lennox puffed out his cheeks and began playing with the zippers on his jacket again, a tic Claudia was beginning to recognize as a sign that the chief felt like he was losing control of the situation. She wasn't sure if the right move was to try to reassure him, or press her advantage, so she went with her natural inclination.

"I'm not admitting anything," Claudia replied. "But I believe there's a procedure for this sort of thing."

"Okay, so for now maybe we can say that it might be yours," Derek offered, verbally placing himself between them. "If it was, how do you think it might have ended up where it was found?"

Claudia willed herself to respond calmly.

"How it ended up in the marketplace is easy. With the amount of time I spend there, and how little space I have here, pretty much everything but my underwear has shown up there at some point. I don't particularly remember when I used the tracker for the last time, but it's possible it could have fallen off, or I got annoyed with it and took it off and left it somewhere."

"That's all nice and simple" Lennox said. "But how does it get from there to under the victim's dead body?"

Claudia threw up her hands.

"Maybe it was on the floor and it got caught under her when the killer was dragging her around. Maybe it got kicked into that corner some other time and she just ended up on top of it. Maybe Lori found it when she was getting her stuff and thought 'hey, free fitness tracker.' I don't know how it got there, but it wasn't because of me."

This seemed to be a good time to bring up another thing she had learned recently.

"Look." She held out her bare arms so they could see they were completely unmarked. "Lori probably had three inches and at least twenty pounds on me. How do you think I would have been able to strangle her without her fighting at all?"

"By hitting her in the head with a big jar of pickles." There were probably reasons why Lennox wasn't supposed to tell her that, but over the course of Claudia's diatribe he had been growing increasingly agitated, and as soon as he said it, he stood up a little straighter and his hand moved away from his jacket zipper.

"Somebody hit her with the pickle jar? But that thing weighs a ton," Claudia said.

"And how would you know that?" Lennox pounced immediately, but Claudia was having none of it.

"Because I spent an entire afternoon helping Helen move it around the booth when she was deciding where to put it. Which, in case you were wondering, is why my fingerprints can be found pretty much everywhere on it. And my handprints, and I think my forehead print, from when she wanted to have it on top of the refrigerator."

That image had the effect of putting a momentary stop to the conversation. The three of them remained there in a tableau: Lennox standing in the middle of the room, still holding the bag with the fitness tracker and looking like someone who was having things not go the way he had expected, Derek leaning against the couch, attending to his new job of chief dog-scratcher, and Claudia, with her back to the wall, exasperated and hoping neither of the men could tell how scared she was. (She assumed Teddy could smell it.)

"Well," Lennox said at last. "I guess that answers all the questions we have for now. I don't think I need to tell you not to leave town?"

"You can if you want to," Claudia said, letting her mouth get ahead of her brain again. She would have asked her better nature how to handle the situation more appropriately, but it was just swearing and suggesting further insults, so she was about to double down on the attitude when she saw Derek's expression and decided to soften her approach. "But no, I'm not planning to go anywhere. If you have anything else you want to show me or ask me, you can find me right here."

As conciliatory speeches went, there had been better, but at least it managed to take the temperature in the room down far enough for Lennox to harrumph his way through an exit. Claudia didn't think this was a good time to ask about reopening the marketplace, but at least there was a little smile from Derek on his way out. These days, she'd take what she could get.

Once she was sure they were gone, Claudia collapsed on the couch and considered her situation. She hadn't thought it could get worse, but here she was. Lennox might have only had her on his suspect list out of convenience before, but now she had the sense she had been shoved right to the top. And having earned the spot on such a shaky piece of evidence suggested that he didn't have a lot of other options.

And it wasn't the only problem. Her explanations for how the fitness tracker ended up under the body were perfectly plausible; the issue was that Claudia didn't believe them. As lazy as she was about her personal space, she was fanatical about keeping the marketplace tidy, and there was no way she would have just taken the tracker off and left it lying around where it could get picked up or kicked around the floor. If she had left it anywhere, it would have been in her office, but she couldn't think of an innocent way it could have made its way from there to where it was found.

On the other hand, the office door was rarely locked. If a person was looking for a small object that might have fallen off someone while they were in the process of killing a person, in order to plant it on the body, it would probably be the first place they would check.

Until now, Claudia had been thinking of the murder in terms of Lori, her life and the things she didn't know about her. If pressed, she might have said that she expected there to be some unknown outsider, who would prove to have turned up in town specifically for the purpose of killing her, and then escaped to somewhere he or she could be found and arrested later. The possibility of it being someone she knew had been in the back of her mind, and Claudia wished it had stayed there.

Because if the killer had framed her, that meant it was someone who knew her, probably someone who knew her well. And if that was the case, then what had been a critical, but abstract question suddenly became urgently, terrifyingly, personal.

CHAPTER TEN

Claudia got up and began pacing around the room. It felt even smaller than usual; like a tomb with a sofa. What she needed right now was some fresh air, with a side of distraction. For someone who lived by the ocean, Claudia spent surprisingly little time at the beach, and this seemed like a good chance to correct that. She was looking for her summer sweatshirt when her computer dinged with an incoming email. It was from a local mailing list, written by her unfriendly neighbor from up the hill, Nathan Rodgers, with the subject line, "Irresponsible Business Owners Bringing Crime to Our Neighborhood."

Claudia closed the laptop and picked up the new leash she had bought.

"Come on," she said to Teddy. "Let's get out of here."

There were only a couple of beaches nearby that allowed dogs, and neither was likely to be crowded on a weekday morning, even in the summer. Claudia chose the closer one, having discovered the Teddy would ride comfortably in the front seat of her hatchback, but not wanting to press her luck. She parked in the lot and let Teddy lead the way.

Most of the beaches on this stretch of coast were tucked away in rocky coves, but here, where a freshwater creek flowed into the ocean, there was a rare stretch of flat sand. Like all the beaches in the area, it was a public park, so the amenities were limited to a sandy parking lot and a small building housing some questionable bathrooms, and the decorative features were represented by signs detailing which types of wildlife you were least allowed to interfere with.

A row of dunes, loosely covered with clumps of sturdy grass, separated the parking lot from the beach, where spindly-legged shorebirds picked their way along the water line and gulls argued and eyed everything with suspicion. There were a handful of other people, flying kites or walking along the edge of the surf with their hands in the pockets of their fleece sweaters. It was a typical August morning, with the sun just starting to burn off the fog as noon approached.

The waves rolled in, cold and green, and further up the beach Claudia could see some intrepid surfers paddling out to meet them. They did look a bit like seals in their wetsuits, and she thought she could understand how the local great white sharks sometimes got confused.

There didn't seem to be any sharks around today, at least as far as Claudia could see, but she still called Teddy back when it looked like she was thinking about going for a swim. Oceangoing predators aside, she had not come prepared to take home a wet dog.

If Teddy was disappointed by this limit on her freedom, she didn't show it. Within a few minutes she had found a piece of driftwood, which she very much wanted Claudia to throw for her, but she also did not want to give it up, leading to an existential crisis and a brief tug-of-war. Claudia solved the problem by finding another piece, which immediately became more interesting than the first one, starting a stick-tossing relay.

They headed down the beach that way, Teddy chasing, fetching, dropping, and chasing, and Claudia trying to participate without getting too much dog spit and sand on her hands while she thought about life and its alternatives.

Up until that morning, she had been operating on the assumption that her status as chief suspect was nothing more than bad luck. Somebody had to be the last person to have seen Lori, and given the circumstances, it was likely to be her. That their last encounter had been a fight was unfortunate, but unrelated; these things just happened. But the way the fitness tracker had turned up had put a different complexion on the matter.

What if it had been a setup from the beginning? The printouts left for her intentionally, so that she would have no choice but to confront Lori that evening? Had the whole situation been stage-managed, down to the stink bombs in Lori's purse that were supposed to have made Claudia mad enough to kill? Was there someone else who would have been an obvious suspect if the police didn't already have one in hand?

Or an unobvious one, even. If the killer was worried that the police would come up with a connection between himself (or herself) and Lori if they looked too closely at her life, the best thing he or she could hope for is that they would be looking somewhere else. And whoever that was, they had to know enough about Claudia and the marketplace to set up the situation, and to know where to find a small personal item of hers to complete the picture.

It was an uncomfortable thought, and as the wind off the ocean whipped her hair into her mouth, Claudia tried to think her way out of it.

There were six stalls in the marketplace, and in theory all of the tenants and their employees had equal access to any part of it. In practice, it was a little more complicated, but not much. The rotating cast of young people who staffed the vegetable market rarely interacted with Claudia or the other vendors; they were generally too busy in their various internal dramas to pay much attention to the adults around them. Orlan Martinez, the owner, had several other locations to manage, and on the rare occasions he was in the marketplace he spent most of his time dealing with faulty refrigerators or questions of optimal produce display. She couldn't say for certain, but Claudia's sense was that Lori had ranked in his awareness somewhere below beets.

So who else was there? Could Elias have been so insulted by Lori's abuse of the art of cheesemaking that he took it on himself to defend the honor of his milk? Might Robbie have a secret in his past that Lori was threatening to reveal unless he signed over ownership of his farm to her? Or should Claudia stop making jokes and take the question seriously?

She didn't want to.

If she was right, and the murderer had planted the printouts and fitness tracker to frame her, then they must have planned it in advance. That meant someone who not only coldly set out to kill Lori, but who didn't mind bringing Claudia down as well. That was an uncomfortable thought, almost more than the violence. With some imagination, Claudia could come up with situations that might drive one of these people she liked and respected to feel like killing Lori was their only option, but her? What could she possibly have done to deserve this?

It was a moment of appalling self-obsession, but Claudia decided to allow it. She needed the anger. Without it, all she had left was fear.

So, who might have had reason to hate Lori? There was only one incident she could think of, which hadn't seemed like much at the time. Claudia had gone away for a few days, about a month after Lori had opened her stall. When she had gotten back, she had noticed a distinct coolness in the atmosphere that had nothing to do with the marine layer. Some discrete questioning had turned up the information that something had happened between Helen and Lori one morning before anyone else had gotten there. But Claudia had had no luck learning the source of the conflict, and ultimately decided that since they were both adults, as long as they weren't disrupting the business they could work it out between themselves. And she had assumed they must have, because it didn't come up again.

Or had it? Revenge might be a dish best served cold, but maybe Helen thought it could be improved with a cheese wire and side of pickles.

Or maybe Claudia was grasping at straws, because she was unable to deal with the idea that a person she liked and respected might have killed a woman and tried to frame her for it. Either way, she wasn't getting anywhere walking on this beach, throwing sticks and beating herself up over what she didn't know. What she needed right now was someone who would offer her a sympathetic ear, and some lunch.

"And you're sure it was your fitness tracker? Oh, Claudia, that's not good."

"It's not? And here I was thinking this was the thing that finally turned my week around."

The look Betty gave her made it clear that Claudia's sarcasm was not appreciated. Claudia was undeterred.

"Not sure I should have told you that, though. If the police chief asks, you never met me."

"Claudia, there are so many things you shouldn't have done, I don't know if that one even makes the list."

Betty tossed the brush she had been using back into the plastic bucket and picked up a curry comb. Claudia had found her bringing in one of the horses they used for trail rides, and followed to the barn as Betty had explained that one of the guides thought he was coming up lame, though it was her personal opinion that he (the horse) was faking it to get out of work. But she needed to check him to be sure, which was why he was getting prepped for a ride now.

Claudia picked up a second curry comb and talked while she brushed.

"Anyway, there's nothing I can do about it now. Lennox has the thing, and as far as I can tell, that's all he needed to be sure I'm running a business in local, artisanal murder. Not sure what I can do to change his mind, other than finding the actual killer, but I'm open to suggestions."

"Are you sure you couldn't have left it there on the floor?" Claudia was starting to wonder if telling Betty everything had been a mistake. Not that she didn't trust her friend, but the amount of worrying she was doing was making Claudia nervous.

"I can't be positive, but it doesn't seem like something I'd do. But there must be a good reason for how it got there."

"A reason like someone trying to frame you." Betty finished currying the horse's haunches and worked her way back up to his shoulder. "Have you thought about getting out of town? You must have some friends back in the city who could put you up for a while."

"And have Lennox come after me with a posse? No thanks. Besides, I have a business to run, sort of. What's going to happen to my vendors if I cut and run?

Betty sighed. "You know, I don't think I've ever met anyone so stubborn who wasn't a horse." She handed Claudia the curry comb and pointed to the bucket. "If you really want to be helpful, why don't you put these away and hand me the pick."

"The what?"

"That metal thing that looks like a number seven."

"Okay, got it." Claudia's previous experience with horses had been limited to childhood pony rides and one unfortunate experience on a Grand Canyon tour. (Though, now that she thought back, it might have been a mule.) So it always amazed her how at home Betty was with what were, to Claudia's mind at least, large and intimidating animals that may at any minute stick their nose in your pocket to see if you had any apples.

With Betty, though, they always seemed to know exactly who was in charge, and as she leaned down and patted the horse's front leg, it obliging lifted it up, allowing her to start scraping the hoof with the pick.

"Speaking of bad decisions," she said as she dislodged a rock. "What do you think you're doing with this Derek guy?"

"Trying not to get arrested by him," Claudia said, unconvincingly.

Betty was not convinced.

"That's not what it sounds like to me. Just because a guy is good-looking and nice to your dog is no reason to go and fall for him."

"Can you think of any better ones? Seriously, though, do you know anything about him?"

"Well, I—Oof, back off, knothead," she said, as the horse shifted so it could more comfortably rest its weight on her shoulder. Betty shoved back and he straightened up again, huffing in an irritated way. "I met him last spring when we were dealing with some kids riding four-wheelers in the pastures. He seemed nice enough, but he got kind of annoyed when he found out Roy had caught one of them and locked up his bike. Maybe next time I'll use your name and get better service."

"I don't know about that," Claudia said, as Betty put down the first hoof and moved to the other side. "I kind of suspect he's only being nice to trick me into incriminating myself. But I figure, if he's going to be doing that anyway, at least I should get to enjoy it, right?"

This hoof was cleaner than the last one, and Betty put it down and looked up at Claudia.

"No. I'm pretty sure that's not how it works at all."

"Best idea I've had so far," Claudia countered, then admitted. "Which isn't saying much. I really don't know what I'm going to do if I can't reopen the marketplace soon. This is supposed to be our high season—everyone's counting on the sales from this month to take them through to the holidays."

"Especially with the heat wave coming up," Betty added.

"Heat wave?" With all that was going on, Claudia hadn't been keeping up with the weather reports. Betty was quick to fill her in.

"They say it's going to be a big one," she said. "Starting on Thursday and straight through the weekend. Over eighty at the coast, in the hundreds inland. We've already had about a dozen people call, trying to reserve rooms."

Summer in northern California was a funny thing. For most of the traditional duration, temperatures remained resolutely in the sixties near the coast, with dense fog in the mornings and evenings keeping things consistently cool and preventing the development of any sort of outdoor dining culture. However, two or three times a year a high-pressure system would invade and shock the locals with temperatures that the rest of the country would consider "warm-ish."

When this happened, it was the tradition for everybody to go insane. The heat was the universal conversation topic, and any restaurant that had so much as a couple of tables on the sidewalk advertised their patio seating.

And once the work week was over, everyone who had the time and the tolerance for the traffic headed to the coast.

If what Betty was saying was right, Claudia was about to have the weekend of all weekends dropped in her lap, and she was stuck with a closed marketplace and a deeply unsympathetic police chief, with nothing she could do about either. She knew it was irrational, but she couldn't prevent a burst of anger at Lori for having this be the week she got herself murdered. Just a few more days would have made all the difference.

Obviously, that wasn't what she said.

"I wish I had been paying attention. If I'd known about this sooner, maybe I could have set something up for the vendors. Honestly, I'm starting to wonder if they're going to want to come back even after we get to reopen. Are people really going to want to shop for their organic produce in a building where someone was murdered?"

"I wouldn't worry about that too much. This sounds terrible, but it might even become a selling point," Betty said, setting down the last hoof. "Folks love anything a bit edgy and mysterious, as long as it's not too upsetting. Maybe if the murder is never solved you could spin it as some sort of haunting, or a curse?"

"Right. The fish sauce for the kimchi is made with fermented Cthulhu and every cheese contains a damned soul." Claudia shook her head. "I don't even want to think about where Iryna would take that. No, I'm still holding out hope that the killer turns up soon and it's something clear and simple that has nothing to do with the marketplace, so we can get back to normal and forget any of this ever happened."

Claudia realized she sounded insensitive, and it was also untrue. She wasn't going to be able to forget everything, no matter how much she wanted to.

She was trying to find a way to express this when Roy, Betty's husband, came into the barn. He was carrying his tool box, and after nodding hello he settled in to repair a stall door that was hanging crooked. To Claudia it seemed perfectly normal, but apparently Betty knew better.

"I thought you were working on the drip irrigation in the garden today," she said. "Is it done?"

"Not quite," Roy muttered. "Had to fix this."

"The door is fine. What's going on back at the house?"

Roy paused, looking down at the hammer in his hand for long enough that he almost seemed to be holding a separate conversation with it.

"Well," he said at last. "The boys are down for their nap, and Olive is practicing driving her robot. The guests went to the beach, and the lady in room seven asked if they could have something local for dinner. Not sure what that meant."

He paused to take a breath, and Claudia was frankly stunned. In all the time she had known Betty, she had never heard Roy say more than about four words in a row, generally about farm animals or equipment.

And he wasn't done. While his wife looked at him expectantly, he ran his hand over his thinning hair, looked at the door to the barn and back to the stall he was working on, then spoke with exaggerated casualness.

"Also, the fellow who made his reservation on the website yesterday just checked in. He says he's the ex-husband of that lady who died, and he's asking a lot of questions."

CHAPTER ELEVEN

"I'm not saying I won't let you do it, I'm just saying I don't think you should."

"But why? If he's looking for people to talk to about Lori's death, he's bound to come find me eventually. Don't you think it's smarter if I talk to him now, with you guys around?"

"Makes sense," Roy said. Having delivered his news, he had relaxed noticeably, and seemed to think he had joined the proceedings.

Betty threw up her hands.

"Okay, fine. But I still think you should be staying away from him, not using him as a source. And please, remember he's a guest here. The last thing we need is reviews saying we interrogate our customers."

"Right, so no cattle prod," Claudia said. "Seriously, I promise, I'm not going to ask him hardly any questions at all. I just want to know why he's here, and find out some more about who Lori was. She's the key to everything that's happened, and we barely know anything about her."

Claudia also wanted to figure out how, with all of the information she had been able to gather on Lori's previous life, she had managed to miss a little detail like a marriage. Frankly, she thought she was better than that.

Betty put the horse in one of the stalls and they headed back to the main house. Roy suddenly remembered the urgency of finishing his work on the vegetable garden irrigation and left them before they got inside. Betty watched him go with a look of exasperated affection.

"That man is the biggest busybody I've ever known. He'll act all silent and manly, but give him a bit of gossip and he's like a dog with a bone."

"Maybe he was just being helpful," Claudia said.

"Maybe that's not the sort of help you need," Betty replied.

"No, but thanks anyway." Claudia smiled sweetly at her friend, who started to say something, and then just sighed.

"Let me do the talking, at least," Betty said. "It is my business, after all."

In fact, the question of who would take the lead was answered as soon as they got back to the main house. A man was wandering around the living room that served as the reception area, picking things up, putting them back down, and looking generally annoyed. The moment the women entered, he abandoned his examination of a ceramic shepherdess and pounced.

"Hi, do you work here? There was a man who checked me in, but I can't find him now."

He looked like he was in his early forties, with a full head of blond hair and a tall, thin frame that was starting to get a little paunchy around the middle. There was something of the faded college athlete about him; he had probably been a good-looking guy when he was younger, and from the way he held himself, Claudia suspected he believed he still was. For his trip to the country he had chosen an outfit of khaki pants and a polo shirt that still had the creases in the corners from where it had come out of the package, paired with canvas boat shoes.

"That was my husband," Betty said. "He's gone to do some work in the garden, but I can help you with whatever you need. I'm Betty Taylor, and this is my friend Claudia."

He looked at them like he had been stung.

"Are you Claudia Simcoe? The owner of the marketplace?"

Claudia admitted that she was one and the same.

"What are you doing here? I thought this was a hotel. Do you own this too?"

"No, Betty and Roy are the owners, I just dropped by for a visit." Claudia wasn't sure what she was expecting from a recent ex-widower (widower-ex? husband twice removed?), but it hadn't been him interrogating her.

"Claudia is a friend of mine," Betty repeated, before he could ask anything more. "We were about to have a late lunch. Would you like to join us? We usually have a buffet for the guests, but everyone else took boxed lunches today, so I'm afraid it's a bit of a potluck."

The man muttered that yes, that would be okay, and he hadn't eaten all day, with something about airplanes that Claudia didn't catch. He kept looking at her with a kind of confused wariness as Betty led them into the dining room and left them there to go assemble the food. Every few seconds he would look like he was about to say something, then change his mind and stop. Finally, Claudia decided it was up to her to get the ball rolling.

"I'm very sorry about Lori's death. Roy said you knew her?" she said. As the words came out, she realized they sounded bizarrely abrupt, but she wasn't sure what else she was supposed to say. Playing dumb made no sense, since he had to have assumed that Roy would have passed on his introduction, and what little she knew about social niceties definitely included telling people you were sorry when someone they knew died.

"We were married for about a year and a half, so yeah, I guess you could say we had met." Whatever his motivations were, the guest seemed to realize he was overdoing it on the attitude, and made an effort to dial it back.

"The name's Neil Hahn, by the way. I guess this has been kind of a shock."

"Of course," Claudia said. "I'm sorry, I didn't mean to be cruel."

Neil managed a small laugh. "That's okay. It's what Lori would have wanted."

He didn't get a chance to explain that rather peculiar statement, because at that moment Betty came back into the dining room carrying a platter of sandwiches and a jug of ice water, with a bottle of wine tucked under her arm. As always, Claudia was in awe of her friend's hospitality skills. If there was ever a market for a book on how to properly host the previously-unknown ex-husband of a recently murdered acquaintance, Betty would be the one to write it.

"I just threw these together from some odds and ends," she said, setting out the sandwiches and distributing plates and glasses from the stacks on the sideboard. "I hope you're okay with ham? I can do a vegetarian one if you prefer."

A rare slip, Claudia thought. Betty must be more shaken by the situation than she was letting on.

"Ham is great," Neil assured her. "Thank you. I feel like I haven't eaten in a month."

He did perk up a bit as he ate it, as well he should. Claudia recognized the thinly sliced meat as some of Robbie's dry-cured country ham, which wasn't surprising; she knew Betty put her name on the wait list every time he made a batch. It was excellent—rich, well-marbled meat from his pampered pigs, aged to just the right level of salty savoriness, with just a touch of smoke on the finish, and made even better in Betty's simple sandwich of fresh brown bread, with homemade mustard and just enough lettuce to make you feel like you weren't a complete barbarian for wanting two.

"So what brought you out here?" Claudia asked, before realizing that she was setting a land-speed record for getting her foot into her mouth. "I mean, obviously . . . but you aren't, I just . . ."

She looked to Betty for help, but it was clear her friend was going to let her live with her choices this time. Fortunately, Neil didn't seem to mind.

"It's kind of weird, I know," he admitted. "The thing is, Lori and I, we didn't make a very good married couple, but we stayed friends. Neither of us had much in the way of family, so I kept in touch with her aunt. She told me about what happened, and asked me to come out and see what I could do. She's pretty sick, so she couldn't come herself, and Lori's the only family she has. Had. I can't believe she's really gone."

It was the first time anyone had expressed anything like sorrow for Lori's death, and it made Claudia more aware of her insensitivity.

"Is there anything we can help you with?" Betty asked.

"I don't know, I guess I'm still getting my bearings." He was halfway through the sandwich, and giving the wine bottle interested looks, so their hostess took the hint and passed it around. It was an unlabeled red, "just something from a neighbor," and it reminded Claudia of a story Betty had told her about the owner of a local boutique winery, whose daughter was dying for horseback riding lessons.

Sometimes, she thought as she sipped the frankly fantastic pinot noir, it was both what you knew and who you knew.

The wine seemed to have a beneficial effect on Neil, because he went on in a much more relaxed tone. "I found out where Lori lived, but I haven't been there yet. Not sure what the procedure for that is going to be. Do you think the police are going to let me in?"

"That's probably up to her landlord," Betty pointed out. "Do you know if she left a will, or who the executer of her estate would be?"

"I have no idea," Neil admitted. "She didn't have one when we were married, I know that. We never really got around to a lot of that responsible stuff."

"You should probably get in touch with the aunt, then, and have her contact people for you. They can get in a lot of trouble if they let someone start disbursing the effects without going through the proper channels," Betty said, speaking from experience.

"I get that, but I'm really only here as a favor, and I can't hang around forever. I was hoping I could look through her stuff, let Rhea—that's her aunt—let her know what there is, in case there were some family heirlooms or something. You don't think they'll even let me do that much?"

Despite Betty's experiences, neither of them were that knowledgeable about inheritance law, and they said so. Claudia was about to ask about the funeral plans when Neil surprised her by changing the course of the conversation.

"So, it's been a while since I've seen Lori, and I was just wondering, was there anyone she was hanging around with here? Maybe someone she had a fight with?"

As he asked the question, Neil's whole attitude changed. For most of their conversation he had been leaning forward on the table, hovering over his sandwich and ready to take all comers. But now he leaned back in his chair, effecting the attitude of a man who just happened to be wondering if his murdered ex-wife had any enemies.

Claudia didn't know where this was going, but she suspected it was bad for her.

The first question, at least, she could answer with complete honesty. "I really didn't know her that well," she said. "She showed up a few months ago and said she was looking for somewhere to sell her products. I had an empty spot in the marketplace, and I rented it to her. She was generally pleasant, but we didn't talk much. You might ask around with some of the other vendors, but I didn't get the impression she was very friendly with any of them either."

She thought about not telling him that the closest thing Lori had had to a fight recently had been with her, but if this was the sort of question he was going to be asking, he would find out soon enough.

So she added, "Actually, the last time I saw her, I had to tell her I was canceling her lease. The whole point of the marketplace is that we carry only local, artisan goods, and it turned out all of her stock was mass-produced. I was pretty shocked, I have to say. Had she done anything like that before?"

Betty had wandered away to let them talk while she pretended to be very interested in the current state of the flower vases on the sideboard. She was behind Neil when Claudia started her story, and out of the corner of her eye, Claudia could see her friend desperately signaling for her to stop. But it was too late now, and anyway, she was interested in the answer to her question.

It clearly wasn't one Neil had been expecting.

"You mean she just bought them and said she made them? Why would she do that? Lori was never any sort of craftsperson."

"That's what I gathered. I have no idea why she did it; I was hoping you might."

"No, that's just bizarre. And you said you fired her for it?"

"I didn't fire her, I canceled her lease," Claudia corrected. "It was in the terms that anything she sold had to be produced locally by the leaseholder, within reasonable limits."

"That's dumb, why do you care? If people want to buy it anyway, why not let her sell it?" Claudia was starting to see what Lori and Neil had seen in each other.

"Because that's how I decided to run the marketplace," she retorted. "It's my business, I can make bad decisions if I want to."

At this point Betty interrupted, clearly thinking that things had gone far enough.

"You know, I wonder if anyone at the Hobnob might know more about who Lori was hanging out with," she said, referencing the less menacing of the town's two dive bars. "It's so close to her house, she's bound to have spent some time there."

That was enough to distract Neil, and bring him back to the moment. He thanked Betty abruptly and gave Claudia a dark look before finishing his sandwich in a couple of quick bites.

"Thanks for the lunch," he said at last. "I guess I'd better get going."

There was a brief discussion what time dinner was, and before Neil left he stopped and looked back at Claudia.

"I might need to talk to you more later," he said. "I still have some questions about Lori."

"I'll be around." Claudia felt like she had been saying that a lot lately. But the mention of questions emboldened her to try one of her own.

"I was just wondering, has anyone been in touch with Dana?" she asked.

"Dana?"

"Yeah, I, um, saw a picture with Lori that had her name on it. I thought they might be close. Is she someone who might want to be here, if there's going to be any sort of service?"

"Dana Herschel will not be coming to the funeral," he said stiffly.

CHAPTER TWELVE

Back at her cottage, Claudia went out to walk across the hillside while she thought over the idea she had while Betty was telling her about the weather. She had checked the forecast as soon as she got home, and sure enough, there was a warming trend on the way, with a high of seventy-seven predicted for Saturday in San Elmo Bay. It was likely to be the last warm weekend of the summer, and that was an opportunity she couldn't afford to miss. Which was why Claudia was looking at the parking lot next to the marketplace, calculating costs and risks of holding an impromptu outdoor market there.

First, she needed to get the vendors on board. It was going to be a lot of work with no guarantee of profit, and she would understand if they would rather find another way to take advantage of the tourist influx, or maybe just go to the beach. Then, assuming they were agreeable, she would need tables, chairs, signs, and enough goods to sell to make the venture worthwhile. And then there was the bigger issue of how to handle promotion on such short notice. It was no good having all those people coming by if they didn't know there was something to stop for.

It was insane, even imagining she could put on an outdoor market event in less than three days, but the thought of sitting at home while all of those potential customers poured through the town was too much to bear.

The police themselves were another issue; despite the fact that the only place Lennox had said was off limits was the market itself, she didn't think he was likely to be flexible with his interpretations. But that was a chance she was just going to have to take, and if the police chief was that determined to put her out of business, then he could go ahead and explain why her using her own parking lot for its appropriately-zoned commercial activities was going to keep him from finding out who killed a woman inside the building.

Having made up her mind, Claudia made her way over to the lot. Losing the parking wasn't ideal; if more than a handful of people showed up at a time they would quickly fill up the street-side spaces, but that was a risk she would have to take. A glance up the hill at Mr. Rodgers' house reminded her of someone who was likely to be less sanguine about the possibility. If she had been feeling more charitable toward him, she might have thought about at least putting up some signs reminding people not to block the road up, but since he seemed to have decided to drive her out of business without ever having met her, he didn't get that kind of consideration.

Unlike the geese, who got the same respectful distance Claudia always gave them when she passed their home. As usual, as soon as they heard her coming, they came to the door of their doghouse and watched her until she was out of range. They weren't close enough to the parking lot to be a problem, but she did hope no one would wander off and get a lesson in the dangers of irritable waterfowl syndrome.

Claudia spent about twenty minutes walking around, making notes of her ideas and taking pictures so she would know what the notes meant. She came back to the house with a head full of plans and a crudely-drawn map of the potential layout, with an optimistic amount of space for lines to form. The next step was to actually tell her idea to the people whose names she had penciled into spaces on her map, and see if they laughed in her face or not.

She called the Mullers first, not just out of respect for their status, but because they hosted an open house at their farm twice a year, with music and goat-feeding demos, and crowds that numbered in the hundreds. Claudia wasn't planning anything that elaborate, but she hoped

Julie would be able to share her list of service providers, and maybe put in a good word for her.

Fortunately, Julie was more than enthusiastic about the idea. Claudia hadn't even gotten to the point of asking her for the contact information when she was volunteering to call the vendors herself, with a warning that the portable toilet guys would always try to upsell you on the insurance. Claudia thanked her profusely, and went on to call the rest of her tenants, buoyed by this success.

It took very little time to convince Orlan, who was happy to have a venue to sell the produce he had earmarked for the marketplace, and for a reason to call his employees back in before they decided to take the rest of the summer off. He even offered to send them over early to help set up, which Claudia accepted, despite not knowing exactly what they were going to be setting up, or where, or if they were all going to get arrested for interfering with a crime scene before they even got started. Either way, it couldn't hurt to have some strong young people on hand.

She reached Helen next, who gave a more measured response. Claudia tried to think of a way to bring up Helen's fight with Lori, but the opportunity didn't present itself. Neither Robbie and Emmanuelle or Carmen and Iryna were answering their phones, so Claudia left messages and decided to proceed as though the answers were yes. It wasn't ideal, but time was tight, and if she wanted her idea to have any chance of succeeding, people were going to have to know about it, and that meant Claudia had to lean into one of her least favorite jobs: marketing.

It wasn't the first time Claudia had needed to reach out to the media, so she had a list of the local outlets ready to go, once she remembered what folder she had saved it to. (Marketplace_Other, as it turned out.)

List found, she started making calls, with very little success. Even when she was able to reach someone, she was past the deadline to make it into the event listings in any of the local papers, and the best the public access station could say was that they would try to get it into the crawl on the bottom of the screen, but only if Rocky got in before noon.

Still, she persisted, and when she ran out of names on her list she moved on to searching the web for any other outlets that might be looking for local food-event content.

She kept at it until the hunger pangs from her stomach were too insistent to be ignored, then ate a bowl of cereal while she switched to converting the notes she had made earlier with her ideas about the event into a more coherent plan, and a list of the things that were going to have to be done if this was conceivably going to happen. The phone interrupted her work periodically, first with the remaining tenants returning her calls and pledging their enthusiasm for the project, and then, in a less welcome development, from the host of a true-crime podcast who had somehow found her home number. Claudia was momentarily tempted to take him up on his offer of an interview, and then spend the entire time promoting the market, but her wiser self prevailed, and told him he had the wrong number.

At some point, she dozed off on the sofa, waking with a start when Teddy pushed a wet nose into her drooping hand. She had a moment of panic, because the sensation had entered into her dream as a sea creature reaching out of a jar of pickles to grab her, while Chief Lennox screamed that it was all her fault, and once she recovered from that, she was forced to admit that she wasn't going to get anything more done tonight, and went to bed.

The next morning, Claudia woke with an "Oh God, what have I done?" feeling that she previously had only associated with alcohol-fueled online shopping sprees. But fortunately, if her enthusiasm for the project was flagging, there were already other people ready to pick it up.

She had barely gotten her eyelids propped open when Carmen and Iryna pulled into her driveway in their well-worn Subaru. There was something irresistibly delightful about the couple, and as they unloaded a cooler from the back of the car, Claudia could feel her spirits lifting. She came out to greet them, with Teddy right behind her, ready to give everything a good sniffing.

"I know it's early, but we just couldn't wait," Carmen said as she followed Claudia into the house. "We were talking all night about this market idea of yours, and we thought we should try out some new recipes we've been testing, maybe launch them there. Will we have power for cooking?"

"I'm working on that," Claudia said, amazed, as always, at the pair's energy. "I mean, yes, one way or another, I'll have something for you." She wondered how many extension cords she could run from her cottage to the parking lot without fusing a circuit breaker or enraging the geese. Probably better to rent a generator and some gas grills, she thought.

Carmen and Iryna had been the second tenants to apply for space in the marketplace, though their very modest budget meant that they took the smallest space. But they had made the best of it, naming their shop The Corner Pocket in honor of its position in a corner of the building, the pocket pie description of their offerings, and Iryna's past as a pool shark on the river cruise circuit.

The couple had met at a networking event for female food entrepreneurs, and had chosen San Elmo as a home base for their joint business because it was near Carmen's family, and Iryna wouldn't live where she couldn't see the water. Together, they looked like a mismatched set of salt and pepper shakers, Iryna tall and pale, with broad shoulders and a head of wiry silver hair, and Carmen was dark and so petite that whenever Claudia stood next to her she felt like there was a lot of her that must be surplus to requirements, if you could have an entire person who was that much smaller.

At the moment she seemed to be devoting herself to making Claudia larger, if the number of items she was unpacking from the cooler was anything to go by.

"Try the empanada first and tell me if you can guess what's in it," she said, handing Claudia one of the pastries.

She spoke slightly too fast, and there was a strained quality to Carmen's voice that was unusual. From the way she and Iryna had been glancing at each other since they came in, Claudia suspected that there was something more than new product development that had brought them to visit her. She badly wanted to know what it was, but the couple were clearly unsure how to proceed and pressing them now was only going to make things worse. She hoped that if she let them take it in their own time she might find out more than if she forced the issue.

And besides, this was the part of her job she liked best. Claudia hadn't gotten into the local foods business because she was excited about lease agreements and solid waste pickup schedules. What she loved was the food, and the people who made it, and for that she could make some time.

The empanada was done in Carmen's usual style, a palm-sized pie made of a single round of dough, folded over and crimped in a design that identified the individual fillings. Mindful of the nutmeg mishap, Claudia bit into it gingerly, but she needn't have worried. This empanada was packed with fresh summer corn, sweet and creamy, freshly sliced off the cob. The corn was mixed with slivers of caramelized onions and a touch of a funky flavor it took Claudia a moment to place.

"Fish sauce?" she said at last, and Iryna clapped her hands with glee.

"I told you she would get it! Helen kept telling us not to use too much, because it's strong. But I told her, relax, Carmen knows what she is doing. Now you should try mine. This one first."

Claudia did as she was told, and found a pierogi with a thinner wrapper than she was used to, more like a pot sticker, complete with a circle on the bottom where it had browned on the pan. Inside, there was nothing but soft cheese, lightly sweetened, and streaked with fresh basil.

"Perfect," Claudia declared, because it was. "Is that Julie's ricotta?"

"Of course. Nothing but the best! I also got some honey from a nice man out on Underhill Road. Maybe he would want to use the space Lori had? I can ask him."

Claudia thought that might be a little premature, though she had to admit a honey seller sounded like a nice change of pace. She could even go out to see the bees, she supposed, just to be sure.

"Now this one," Iryna said, turning the plate so the other pierogi was closer to Claudia. "I made it specially for you."

Hoping that was a compliment, Claudia took a bite, and was greeted with a rush of familiarity. The filling was a mix of cheeses—definitely mozzarella, probably some parmesan and maybe jack?—with layers of tomato sauce and a fine dice of some of Robbie's best spicy chorizo standing in for the pepperoni. Claudia couldn't help laughing.

"Okay, you got me," she said. "And yes, it's delicious. I'll take a dozen, for my freezer."

"Pepperoni pizza pierogis!" Iryna crowed. "We're going to call it the 'Claudia Special.'"

"You'll sell a million," Claudia assured her. "But I think you need a catchier name."

"Maybe we'll work on that. After all, you aren't that popular with everyone, are you?" Iryna seemed to think this was hilarious, but Claudia was too much on edge for that sort of joke.

"What do you mean?" she asked, just a shade too fast. She tacked on a laugh in an attempt to soften the effect, but Carmen was unconvinced.

"It's nothing, just that neighbor of yours. That Rodgers man must have nothing better to do, with all the time he spends writing stupid things."

Claudia sighed. "Tell me about it. What's he done now?"

"He sent a letter to the town council saying they should revoke the business license for the marketplace because it is bringing a criminal element into the town."

"But you shouldn't worry about that," Iryna added before Claudia could argue. "Nobody listens to him. All he does is sit up in that big house of his and complain, so why should anyone care?"

Claudia thought that might be a slightly overoptimistic read on the situation, but there didn't seem to be much good in pointing that out. But it did give her an opening to bring the conversation back around to the main thing on her mind.

"Speaking of recent events, there's something I've been wondering about. Do you guys have any idea what the issue was between Lori and Helen? I got the idea that something happened with them last spring, but I never found out the details."

Claudia thought she had chosen a fairly neutral question, but it got more of a reaction than she had bargained for. Iryna froze, wide-eyed, and Carmen looked like she might be physically ill.

"We don't know anything—" Carmen began, but Claudia cut her off.

"Come on," she said. "It can't be that bad, can it? What could possibly have happened all that time ago that you can't even tell me about it?"

The pair looked at each other, locked in a silent conversation. Finally, Iryna seemed to win and she turned to Claudia, looking nervous but hopeful.

"I really don't know what the fight was about," she began, then paused.

"But?" Claudia prompted. "What happened?"

"Well, it was a Friday morning in the spring, and you know there's not a lot of business then, so we didn't open until late. When we did come, they were the only people there, with Lori sitting on that silly stool she had in her booth, looking so smug, you would have thought she had just sold one of her coasters to the Queen. And Helen was in her shop, chopping carrots so hard you could hear it in the parking lot. Whack whack whack whack."

Claudia appreciated Iryna's devotion to quality storytelling, but she could have done without the sound effects.

"I tried to find out what it was about, but Helen wouldn't tell me, and I wasn't about to ask that woman. She was always trouble, even before she died."

Iryna did always have a way with words, though the words themselves might have disagreed. Claudia had other things on her mind.

"I wish I had known," she said. "There was no reason to let her stay in the marketplace if she was causing this many problems."

"That's what I told Helen, that she should tell you. But she wasn't interested, acted like she didn't know what I was talking about."

"It was definitely bad," Carmen offered. "I think Helen didn't want people to think of her as causing trouble, so she tried to act like everything was back to normal. But a couple of times I caught her looking at Lori, and she looked like she could—she was obviously still mad."

Claudia nearly asked what Carmen had almost said, but she thought she could guess.

"Okay, but they had a fight six months ago. That's not great, but it's not something to get too worked up about. What is it that's got you both so bothered now?"

This time they didn't make any attempt at denials, and the wordless conversation between the couple seemed more focused on who was going to do the talking. Ultimately, it was Iryna who took up the story.

"I had my yoga class last night, and when I was there I talked to Arlene Davis, who lives next door to Lori's duplex. She's a travel agent and she has to stay up late sometimes, you know? Because someone has a problem in Europe or something and she has to help them."

Claudia wasn't interested in the theoretical problems of European vacationers.

"And let me guess, she was up late on Sunday night? Did she see something?"

Iryna nodded, looked miserable.

"Arlene, she had a run in with the Chief Lennox a couple of years ago, and she said she was never going to talk to him again if she could help it. But she knew I worked in the marketplace, and we knew Lori, so she thought she would tell me and ask what she should do about it."

"What did she see, Iryna?" Claudia asked, with rising concern.

"She said it was about nine o'clock, nine-thirty, when she was on the phone and she looked out the window. It was dark, so she couldn't see so well, but there was someone hanging around Lori's side of the duplex, looking in the windows. She couldn't tell about the face or anything, but she thought it was a man, with dark hair, and the one thing she did see was that he was definitely wearing bright green high-top shoes. She said you could see them a mile off."

"Oh," said Claudia.

There might be hordes of dark haired young men roaming San Elmo in bright green high-top sneakers, but the person the three of them knew who fit that description was Brandon Pak, and his distinctive, favorite shoes.

CHAPTER THIRTEEN

By the time Carmen and Iryna left, they seemed much happier, and Claudia wished she could say the same for herself. Having passed on what they knew, they felt they had done their duty, and they could stop worrying about their unpleasant information. Now it was up to Claudia to decide what to do with it.

In theory, she should have been pleased. After all, this was the sort of thing she had been after, and it had just been dropped in her lap. Good news, right? Except it didn't feel like it. But facts didn't change because you didn't like them, and if Brendan or Helen had killed a woman and tried to frame Claudia for the murder, then that was something she was going to have to face sooner or later.

While she considered how she was going to do that, Claudia went to check on the process of cracking Lori's password. All it said was "processing," but Claudia stared at it for a few minutes anyway, in case that helped.

Her attempt at psychic software intervention was interrupted by the phone ringing. Claudia hesitated in answering it, momentarily afraid to find out what else the world had in store for her. But it was just Julie, calling to let her know that she had successfully contacted several of the rental companies, and the outdoor market event wouldn't be without tables or portable toilets. Claudia thanked her, then paused before asking her next question.

"By the way, do you know anything about an argument Helen and Lori had last spring?"

"Sorry, no," Julie said, in a way that suggested her mind had already moved on. "They didn't like each other very much, did they? I guess you'd have to ask Helen about that. Oh, and one more thing—don't forget you need to call the papers and see if they can get an announcement in the Saturday edition. It's short notice, but who knows."

Claudia promised she would get right on that. (It didn't seem worthwhile to explain her lack of success in that direction.) Julie's other suggestion, though, she decided to take as a sign.

Going to visit the Paks didn't seem very smart, but Claudia couldn't think of what else to do. The pickle-making family were at or near the center of everything she had been able to come up with about Lori's murder so far, and, like it or not, that center was where she needed to be.

After hanging up the phone, she picked up her jacket before she could talk herself out of it. Teddy immediately jumped to her feet, looking expectantly at the door.

"Sorry, girl," Claudia said. "Not the beach this time."

She started to leave, but the look of hopeful enthusiasm on the dog's face was too much for Claudia. Besides, she reasoned, it was probably a good idea to bring the dog with her, just in case. Not that she expected Teddy to provide any protection, but if something did happen, at least she wouldn't be stuck in the house with no one to feed her. If nothing else, the Paks had always been very kind to their dogs.

"Okay, fine, you can come. But you have to be good."

Whether Teddy agreed to her part of the deal wasn't clear, but she enthusiastically followed Claudia and took her place in the passenger seat. Claudia wondered if she was supposed to get her to wear a seatbelt or something.

She parked in front of the Paks' house and considered her plan of action. Her excuse for the visit would be that she wanted to talk about some details of the outdoor market, maybe having them work together with Robbie to pair some of their sauerkraut with one of his sausages. Then she would work the conversation around to the fight, via an as-yet-undetermined method. (Claudia was sure she would think of something, which mostly served as proof that experience is not as good of a teacher as some people believe.)

Claudia had been hoping to catch Helen alone, but she had no such luck. She arrived to find the entire family in the living room, looking like they had either been in the middle of an argument, or a hard-fought staring contest.

"I hope I'm not interrupting anything," Claudia said as she followed Helen into the room where her husband and son were frozen in an unhappy tableau. Victor Pak was facing his son with a mix of anger and hurt, while Brandon sullenly focused all of his attention on the patch of carpet in front of his chair.

Neither of them looked like they had moved in a while, or were planning to in the immediate future, until the Paks' dogs spotted Teddy.

Claudia had meant to ask if she could put her in the yard, but the three furry specks shot across the room like yipping rockets as soon as they stepped through the door. For the next couple of minutes, everyone was involved in the effort to get them separated from Teddy, who didn't know what was going on here but clearly didn't want to get involved, and by the time order had been restored, the ice was well and truly broken.

Claudia apologized profusely, and tried to take the traumatized Teddy back out to the car where she should have left her in the first place, but Helen stopped her.

"No, they need to learn. The trainer said it's important to get them used to being around other dogs, and they're supposed to listen to us no matter what. I think this is a good opportunity." Her voice was bright and brittle and a little bit hoarse, like she had been doing a lot of talking recently.

She turned to her husband. "You do the exercises with them. Claudia, can you just hold your dog there?"

Claudia agreed, and offered a silent apology to Teddy as Victor followed his wife's orders, trying to get the smaller dogs to form an orderly line. The Paks' living room had been designed in the sunken style of the sixties, and Helen had furnished it to a corresponding midcentury aesthetic, though they had replaced the wall-to-wall-to-stairs-to-fireplace shag carpet with something more contemporary. Victor was assembling his students between the glass-topped coffee table and the curved orange sofa, though the smallest dog seemed more interested in attacking his ankles. It wasn't clear what he was hoping to achieve with this activity, in the unlikely event that he ever succeeded at the first step, but Claudia supposed that everyone should have a hobby.

"So, I know we talked on the phone about the outdoor market thing, but I was thinking that maybe we should, um, talk more." It occurred to Claudia that she should have put some more thought into this approach, but it was too late for that now.

"We have plenty of stock to sell, of course. And the parsnip kimchi is ready, but we can't have it packaged in time." From the way Helen was looking at her, Claudia thought she might not have convinced her that the only reason she was there was the necessity of in-person sales planning. The rest of the family was staring at her in polite confusion, and even the dogs seemed concerned.

"But you could offer tastings," Claudia said, doing her best to sell it. "People can sign up for your mailing list, maybe take pre-orders."

There was general agreement that that was something that might happen, followed by increasingly awkward silence.

"Was there something else?" Helen asked, finally.

"Um, well, yes." If there was a good way to ask a friend if they or their child had killed someone, Claudia couldn't think of it at the moment, so, as with most things in her life, she decided to dive straight in and hope for the best.

"I was just wondering, I know you had a fight with Lori last spring, and I wanted to ask what that was about."

A person could have heard a pin drop in that room, assuming it didn't spontaneously combust before it hit the floor.

"I don't know what you mean," Helen said, packing each word with cold fury. "Why would you even ask that?"

"It's just something I heard about, and I wanted to get your side of the story." It wasn't a very convincing argument, but in the moment Claudia was just proud of herself for not hiding under the table. Not that Helen's family was being very helpful on that point. Victor had frozen in the middle of an attempt to arrange the dogs in a diagonal line, wearing an expression of horror, and Brandon was looking like he might think the table thing wasn't a bad idea. And at the center of all of them was Helen, radiating anger.

"Is this your idea to get yourself out of trouble?" she said, her voice rising. "By finding one of us to blame instead? After everything we've done, this is how you are going to treat us?"

Helen was ready for war, and Claudia was feeling distinctly unarmed. She was never going to be able to singlehandedly take on the woman who had silenced an entire busload of German tourists who had taken exception to her more creative sauerkrauts with a single withering glare, in her own home, in defense of her family.

It was time for the nuclear option.

"Lori's neighbor saw Brandon at her duplex the night she was killed. I thought it might be a good idea to give him a chance to explain."

It was like Claudia had taken that metaphorical falling pin and used it to let all of the air out of Helen. In a moment, her righteous anger was gone, replaced by terror and misery. Then the moment passed, and her expression hardened into blankness.

"We do not need to discuss gossip with you. This conversation is over. If you have any concerns, you should take them up with the police."

Claudia wasn't having any of that.

"Oh, come on. You don't honestly think I'm out to get you, do you? I just want to know what happened, and I'm sorry, but this is definitely something that happened." She looked over at the miserable young man in the chair. "Brandon, help me out here. What were you doing there?"

Brandon, who had returned his attention to the carpet, looked up at the sound of his name. His face was drawn and scared, looking simultaneously childlike and aged by the stress.

"Somebody saw me?" he asked, as his mother tried to shush him.

"Lori's neighbor," Claudia repeated. "She told Iryna, and Iryna told me. No one has talked to the police yet." She left the last word hanging there, hoping he would take it as an invitation to see talking to her as a viable alternative.

"I didn't kill her," Brandon said, to his mother's horror.

"Why are you talking! Don't talk, you don't have to tell her things!"

"I was there," he went on, stubbornly. "Please don't tell anyone. But I didn't kill her."

"Then why did you go to her house? Why that night, of all nights?"

But Brandon just shook his head.

"I was just there."

"Really? Is that what you're going with? Four people know you were outside Lori's house on the night she was murdered, not counting whoever else Iryna has told by now. And the best you can do is to say it was just one of those things, what are you going to do? Are you sure you've thought this through?"

Brandon cringed under the assault, but he held his ground. He appeared to have decided to say just enough to incriminate himself, and leave it at that, which was an interesting strategy. Claudia stared at him, thinking about the things she knew and didn't know. Then, out of the blue, a theory started to form. It didn't do a lot for her personally, but it did fit the facts, and filled in some unanswered questions.

"Brandon," she said. "The day before Lori died, someone left a pile of papers on my desk that proved the products she was selling were fakes. Do you know anything about that?"

Helen gasped, and Victor lost interest in the dogs and looked at her, an irritated Yorkie nipping at his feet. Only Brandon didn't respond at first, continuing to stare at the spot on the floor that was, apparently, the key to his escape.

But it wasn't working, and eventually, Brandon moved his head in a ghost of a nod.

"Why did you do that?" Claudia asked, gently, like she was talking to a bird that might fly away at any moment.

Brandon returned to silence, apparently caught in the throes of some internal conflict. Whatever angels were fighting within him were taking their time about it, but eventually they ruled in Claudia's favor.

"She was a jerk," he said at last. "Like, a total—" He stopped there and looked at his mom. "A really bad jerk. She was nice to you, because you were important. But there was this one time some tourists came in and were making fun of how ugly her stuff was, like she wasn't even there, and she saw me laughing, and after that she had it in for all of us."

"It was mostly a ton of little stuff, like pretending to think we're Chinese or talking really loud about how our booth smelled bad. And then last spring I was wiping down the big pickle jar after a bunch of kids got finger prints all over it, and she made this joke about me and, um, the size of the pickles, and she kept laughing like it was the funniest thing, until I just cracked and told her if she didn't shut up I would take that jar and—" He stopped there, possibly realizing he was taking the self-incrimination too far. "Anyway, Mom found out about it and read her the riot act, but Lori just said some stuff about how she wasn't PC and we had to deal with it."

He stopped to take a breath and Claudia was finally able to gather her outrage to the point where she was capable of speaking.

"Why didn't you tell me? I would have had her out so fast, those bags of hers would have achieved escape velocity."

"We had only been there for eight months," Helen reminded her. "None of us really knew what you were like, and we didn't want to be the ones causing trouble." She gave her son a significant look. "Sometimes the best way to handle a problem person is just to ignore them."

"Yeah, well, not always," he said. Having defied her once now, Brandon seemed to be living a life without fear, at least temporarily. "Anyway, a couple of weeks ago, I was online looking for a birthday present for Mom, and I saw one of Lori's bags. So I looked into it more, and that's when I realized that all of the attitude she had been putting on about being this big artist, it was all bull—it was a lie. I wanted people to know what she was doing, but I didn't know how to bring it up. So I thought if I left the evidence for you, you could take it from there."

And Claudia certainly had. That part of his plan had worked, at least. She had some follow-up questions, but they were going to have to wait.

"And that's what you meant?" Helen was almost shouting. "You tell me she's going to be sorry, and then nothing else, and it was about this? Why didn't you explain?"

"Because I thought you would freak out, and I was right," Brandon said. "It was just, it was really bad timing, okay? When I found out she was dead, the last thing I wanted was for anyone to know what I had done. And if I didn't tell anyone about it, then I could be sure that nobody knew." He looked curiously at Claudia. "But how did you find out?"

"Just a good guess," Claudia said. It didn't seem worth going into her thought process, which had leaned heavily on who among her tenants was most likely to be in the further corners of e-commerce and least likely to approach her directly, with a touch of intuition and a healthy portion of luck. Which was probably a long way of saying the same thing, anyway.

"So, the night after you left the papers for me, you went to Lori's house," she prompted.

"I know it was stupid, but I just wanted to see. So I hung around for a while after everyone else had left, and I knew you were going to talk to her, and I wanted . . . I thought it would be fun . . ." He trailed off, embarrassed at his own vindictiveness.

Claudia, who was no stranger to giving in to the baser emotions, filled in the rest for him.

"You knew she was going to be coming home after having been exposed as a fraud and losing her shop in the marketplace, and you wanted to be on the scene for that," she finished for him. Helen was scandalized, but there was no time for that now.

"So, what did you see?" Claudia asked. "Did she do anything? Was anyone else there?"

"No," Brandon said. "There was nothing interesting at all. She walked around for a bit, talking to herself, then she sat down in front of her computer and started drinking wine. That's when I left, because I was starting to feel kind of dumb."

He looked from one person to another for support.

"She was completely fine when I saw her," he said with rising desperation. "And after I left I came right home. I didn't go back to the marketplace, and I never saw her again, I swear."

Claudia was inclined to believe him. Theoretically, she could imagine a situation where Brandon, furious that his plan hadn't produced the emotional response he was looking for, had lured or followed Lori back to the marketplace and made his revenge complete. But here in this living room, with the alleged rage-killer playing nervously with the fringe on a decorative pillow while his father tried to impose order on the movements of small dogs and his mother looked at him like she couldn't decide between hugging and smacking him, it seemed less credible.

"Okay, so you were there," Claudia said. "And as far as the police are concerned, none of us heard that. But is there anything else you remember that you saw? It might be important."

"No," Brandon said, but the way he drew out the vowel suggested otherwise. Everyone waited, and eventually he went on.

"There was a car parked across the street from her house, and when I was leaving something made me notice it. And it took a second, but I realized the driver's seat was lying all the way down, and there was a reflection in the window like someone had their phone on. I figured it was just somebody sleeping in their car, but it made me nervous because I didn't really want anybody seeing me there. Not that I was doing anything wrong, but I just, I didn't want to . . ." He trailed off as his nervousness returned. "I didn't know anything was going to happen to her. I wouldn't have gone if I'd known she was going to get murdered."

Claudia was a lot less interested in this failure of Brandon's planning abilities than she was in this new entry to the scene of the crime.

"What did the car look like?" she asked. "Make? Model? Local plates or out of state?"

Brandon shook his head.

"It was just a normal car. A sedan, I guess? Nothing fancy. I was mostly trying not to get noticed, so I didn't really look."

"Okay, well, it's probably not important," she said, but failed to entirely believe it.

She probably could stand to be skeptical of a few other things, if you came right down to it. Brandon's story was convincing, but that didn't mean she had to be convinced. He had admitted to fighting with the victim, and threatening her, and anonymously exposing her fraud. Could he have just left out the part where he ultimately solved his problem with a blow to the head and a cheese wire? The idea seemed absurd, but every idea seemed absurd, and that didn't make Lori any less dead.

"So, what are you going to do?" Helen asked, and for a terrifying second Claudia thought she had been doing her thinking out loud. But no, Helen only wanted to know what the police's number one suspect was planning for information that would firmly incriminate someone else.

"Nothing, for the moment. As far as anyone else is concerned, this conversation never happened. But I can't guarantee that Lori's neighbor isn't going to tell the police about what she saw, so you should probably have a plan for what to do if that happens."

Helen nodded, and gave her son a look while her mouth set into a firm line.

"We will. And, Claudia, thank you. You didn't have to come here."

"Don't mention it," Claudia said, more embarrassed than when Helen had been accusing her of framing them. "What's important is that we get this settled so we can go back to normal."

There was general agreement on that point, but no one seemed to want to elaborate and the conversation lapsed. Finally, it was Victor who brought it back around to the other issue of the day.

"So, the pickled seaweed," he said, as the smallest dog tried to climb up his pant leg. "Should we offer it as spicy or mild?"

CHAPTER FOURTEEN

By the time Claudia left the Paks' it was past lunchtime, but they had made good progress on the plans for the outdoor market and Teddy would now sit on command. She could have gone home and done some more work, but since she was out anyway, she decided to make a detour to visit another tenant. So, after a brief stop at San Elmo's tiny grocery store for a replenishment of her wine and dog food stocks, and one of their surprisingly good deli sandwiches, she made her way to Robbie and Emmanuelle's home and pork-curing emporium.

They lived at the end of a minor county road, where a sign hanging on a gnarled driftwood tree announced that you were approaching Happy Toad Farm. The name was widely suspected to be a drug reference, but Emmanuelle insisted it related to having found the namesake amphibian under a bucket when they were first viewing the property. What was not in dispute was that this was an agricultural operation like no one in the area had ever seen.

Claudia hadn't spent a lot of time on pig farms, but she suspected most didn't have their entrances framed by a graceful arch of trained fig trees. She passed through it (alone, having left Teddy in the car with the windows cracked and an improvised water dish, not being sure how well she was going to deal with chickens), to a small patio decorated with stylishly dilapidated furniture. Beyond the patio were two raised-bed vegetable gardens, displaying their rows of tomatoes, squashes, and beans under the bird netting like the jewelry case of a vegetable-loving giant.

It all looked like a picture from a magazine, and for good reason. In just the year and a half Claudia had known them, Emmanuelle and

Robbie's "little coastal homestead" had been the subject of three feature articles and one cookbook photo shoot. (Ironically, vegetarian.) The scene was perfect and precise in every way, but whenever the wind shifted there was an undeniable whiff of pig in the air.

Any new farm in the area was cause for local curiosity, but one so far outside the norm drew special attention. As soon as Robbie and Emmanuelle had arrived in town, Julie had gone on a fact-finding mission, which had turned up the information that Emmanuelle's father was a banker of some variety, rich enough to set up his only daughter in whatever lifestyle she desired. What he thought of her choice to spend it here was as yet undetermined.

Then again, maybe it wasn't that hard to understand. Claudia had rung the bell as she came in through the arch, and it was only a couple of minutes until Robbie came to greet her.

As happened every time she saw him, she found herself surprised by how good-looking he was. Robbie was at least fifteen years older than his twenty-something wife (though he affected the look of someone born a good century back), but no one thought of them as a mismatched couple. Between the wax on the mustache, the long, rectangular beard, and the ever-present suspenders, it was easy to get distracted from the person underneath the affectations. But not that easy. The untamed eyebrows shaded bright blue eyes, and the beard covered, but didn't quite disguise, a strong chin and enviable cheekbones. Robbie was thin and not particularly broad-shouldered, but Claudia had it on authority that there were some women who liked that sort of thing just fine, particularly when paired with the tan and muscles that life on even the fanciest of farms was likely to produce. If Emmanuelle hadn't been interested in the country life to begin with, she might have found herself willing to be convinced.

And she wasn't the only one who was susceptible. Claudia didn't have the data to back it up, but she was confident that there were a lot of women, and no small number of men, who left the marketplace with significantly more cured meats than they had intended on buying, and no reason they were willing to admit to for their sudden urge to shop for pork.

Claudia liked Robbie, but despite recognizing that he was objectively attractive, he left her cold. Which was for the best, obviously. She had enough on her plate without going moony-eyed over a married tenant.

Adding to his appeal, Robbie was also quite charming. He greeted Claudia like her arrival was the best thing that had happened to him all day, and only didn't offer his customary hug because, as he explained, he had just come from fixing the gate on one of the pig pens.

"To what do we owe the honor of this visit?" he asked, and somehow it didn't come across as sarcastic.

"I hope you don't mind my dropping by," Claudia said. "I just wanted to see how you guys were doing, and run some ideas I had for this weekend by you. Is Emmanuelle around?"

"She should be. Let's go and find her." He made the act of looking for someone to greet a surprise guest sound like a delightful treasure hunt, and Claudia wondered if she should be wearing a hat.

Robbie's best guess was that Emmanuelle would be in the kitchen garden, and sure enough, they came around the corner to find her crouching next to another set of raised beds at the back of their renovated Victorian farmhouse, pulling dandelions from around the strawberries. She was a petite, slender woman with long, chestnut-brown hair that she had wound into an artfully messy bun. For her work in the garden, Emmanuelle was dressed in blue and white striped overalls and a yellow tank top, with soft leather gloves and surprisingly practical plastic clogs. Aside from the shoes, she looked like the platonic ideal of the "person with a garden," and it was no wonder that she had made at least one thirty-under-thirty list as the "Aspirational Agriculturalist."

But there were no photographers with her today, and she seemed happy for the interruption to her weeding. Claudia expounded on her plan for the outdoor market, with special emphasis on the one-off specialness of the event. She knew from Emmanuelle's social media presence that there was nothing she loved more than things that were made in small quantities or only available after standing in a long line, preferably both. More to the point, she had built up a fairly significant following of like-minded people, who were exactly the type Claudia would like to have show up for her short-notice event.

"That sounds great, and to be honest I was worried about what we were going to do with the fresh sausages. Maybe we can borrow a grill from someone and cook them up to order," Emmanuelle said. "I'll give the bakery a call and see about getting some buns."

"I was thinking just that," Claudia agreed, working her way around to her main point. She tried to make it sound casual, like a thought she just happened to be having as she was examining this pattypan squash plant. "Also, is there anywhere you can think of to publicize the event? We're going to need a good turnout if we want this to work."

"You should be able to do that, shouldn't you?" Robbie said to his wife. "You can post it to all of your friends."

"My followers," she corrected, like a fussy cult leader. She straightened up and brushed a strand of her hair out of her face, casting an appraising eye around the rows of vegetables and herbs. "Of course I'll share it, but I'm not really sure it's going to do that well. Without a good picture, it's hard to get much engagement, and I can't take any pictures if it hasn't happened yet."

Claudia couldn't argue with that, and she was happy to concede the point about the pictures to Emmanuelle's expert opinion. She had been hoping for a little more optimism, though.

But Emmanuelle went on.

"What we should do is get in touch with some of the San Francisco food and event networks. I can see if that girl I met at Coachella still has her newsletter; maybe she can squeeze something in tomorrow."

"That would be fantastic," Claudia said. "The worst thing that could happen is if we did all this work and nobody showed up."

It wasn't even in the top ten worst possible things, but no one said it. Robbie's next question, though, made it clear where his mind was going.

"What are we going to do about Lori?" he asked.

"What do you mean?" said Claudia.

"Well, people are going to ask questions. Do we say the event is in her memory or something?"

Claudia tried to imagine how the police chief would react to that idea, and thought it would almost be worth it to see his face. But even for her, it was a bridge too far, and she said so.

"I don't think that would be a good idea. None of us really knew her that well, and I don't want to give the impression that we're exploiting her death. Maybe we can set up a little table with a book people can write memories of her in?" And then read that book later, because even if you were being considerate, there was still time to gather information.

"That sounds nice," Emmanuelle agreed. "I wonder if anyone did know her, though? I tried to talk to her once, because I've done some shibori dyeing in the past, and I was wondering how she was getting such strong reds with natural dyes, but she got really weird about it. There were times after that I thought she was avoiding me, but I might have imagined it."

"She was always really nice to me," Robbie added. "But yeah, there was this weird thing that whenever Emmie was around she would kind of clam up and vanish."

"I think I can explain that one," Claudia said. She was surprised that the news of Lori's deception hadn't reached them, but Robbie and Emmanuelle weren't very well connected to the general flow of San Elmo society. She gave them an abbreviated version of the story, leaving out the new information about Brandon's involvement. When she was done, the couple looked at each other, sharing a private conversation that ended with a decision.

Robbie took the lead in explaining.

"That actually answers some questions we'd been having. We didn't know if we should have said anything, but there was a thing that we've been worrying about. Emmie's been doing a lot of promotion for our business, and a couple of weeks ago she got a message from a writer she knows at a pretty major publication, asking about scandals at the marketplace. He said he'd been contacted by someone there who had told him she had a big story for him and asking if he was interested in an exclusive. But she wouldn't give any details, so the writer was looking for more information before he wasted his time."

"I told him I didn't know about anything," Emmanuelle said. "And I asked who he'd been talking with. He didn't have a name, but he was pretty sure it was a woman, which didn't narrow it down much, though honestly, I kind of thought it had to be Lori. I mean, there was no one else at the marketplace I could even imagine trying to do something like that, and when I got to thinking about it I remembered there was one time she borrowed my phone to make a call, and when I got it back my contact list was open."

Robbie nodded thoughtfully. "When Emmie told me about it, I thought it was funny too, but we weren't sure what we could do. We didn't want to make trouble, and there was no evidence it was her, or what she might be up to. To be honest, we figured it was probably just some ploy to build publicity for her shop. But then Lori died, and we didn't know what to think."

Emmanuelle added, "Also, I don't know if it's related, but a couple of months ago I was at the copy place in Sebastopol mailing a package, and Lori was there talking to one of the employees about getting a photo blown up to poster size. Which I didn't think was weird at all; she needed something to make her booth look nicer, and I thought I should ask if she wanted some help with composition, because I've done some of that. But as soon as she saw me she looked at me really funny and wouldn't say anything more. So, you know, I just left, because it was none of my business, but it was odd."

She pinched a spent bud off a dahlia, looking thoughtful.

"Do you think she was trying to do something to hurt the marketplace?" Emmanuelle asked. "I mean, selling fake bags, calling reporters, it makes you wonder."

It would make Chief Lennox wonder too, which was one of the reasons Claudia was not excited about this theory. She hoped that when he got around to talking to Robbie and Emmanuelle, these particular details would have slipped their memories. Not that she could say so, so she did the best she could to redirect.

"But why? That's a lot of money and work to try and sink a random business, run by people you'd never met. What was in it for her?"

Robbie just looked thoughtful, but Emmanuelle sighed in exasperation.

"I don't know; it doesn't make any sense. But she was definitely up to something. And now she's definitely dead."

It wasn't the most elegant of eulogies, but it did sum up the problem.

CHAPTER FIFTEEN

Claudia had made it home and was negotiating with herself for how she was going to divide her time between murder investigating and event planning (she had decided on a sixty–forty split, but it wasn't clear which was going to be which) when Teddy started barking at a car that had pulled into her driveway.

It was an American subcompact with Arizona plates and a rental company bar code on the windshield. After a delay that seemed to involve messing with the parking brake, the driver's side door opened and Neil Hahn emerged, looking annoyed.

Claudia retreated from where she had been watching around the edge of the curtains, and had a few seconds to think about this development before it continued to develop. She had not parted from Lori's ex-husband on the best possible terms, and it was unlikely that this was going to be the start of even a moderately attractive friendship. On the other hand, he was someone who might have useful information, and she didn't think he would be pulling up in her driveway in broad daylight with bad intentions.

He knocked on the door, and it was time to make a decision. In a house where no spot was more than twenty-five feet from the front door, there was no point in pretending she was too far to answer right away. So she went to greet him, with Teddy right at her heels and growling all the way.

"Miss Simcoe? Sorry to bother you, but I was wondering if you could spare a couple minutes. I had a few questions about Lori that I hope you can help me with."

He was dressed in a classically preppy outfit of pink shorts and a patchwork button-down, topped off with an honest-to-god sweater tied around his shoulders. He looked so ludicrously out of place on her cracked front step that Claudia almost laughed in his face. The only thing stopping her, other than basic courtesy, was the fact that he already looked irritated enough as it was. So she suppressed her amusement, invited him in, and offered him a seat at her kitchen table and a cup of coffee, while Teddy took up a position next to her chair and kept a sharp eye on the visitor.

"What was it you wanted to ask me about?" Claudia asked as Neil choked down the first sip of the coffee. (It wasn't the first time Claudia's more-is-more approach to caffeine consumption had failed to win a fan.)

"I was looking into some of Lori's affairs," Neil said, once he had recovered his composure. "And there were a couple of things I was wondering about. You said you canceled Lori's lease because you found out that she had been selling mass-produced products, right?"

Claudia agreed that that was the case.

"So how did you find out about that in the first place? Were you checking up on her or something? Did you want to find a reason to throw her out?"

"No, of course not." Claudia didn't know what had inspired this line of questioning, but she didn't like where it was going. "Someone left the evidence for me anonymously. I'm not in the habit of depriving myself of rent-paying tenants, but once I knew what was going on, I had no choice but to ask her to leave."

"Oh, please. You could have kept her on if you had wanted to. Just raise the rent and take your cut."

"I'm not interested in your input," Claudia snapped. "I don't know what you think you're getting here, but if you're looking for some kind of payout, you're going to have to do better than that."

That seemed to throw him for a loop, and a flash of confusion passed over Neil's face before he came up with a response.

"I'm not trying to get any money out of you," he said, sounding offended at the prospect, and putting an odd emphasis on the last word. "I just want to know what happened. Someone I cared about is dead, and I think I deserve to know what happened."

It was a strange phrasing, and Claudia wondered at the psychology of someone who thought that the great injustice of a murder was that no one had properly explained it to him.

"I'm sorry, but you're not going to find that out here," she said. "I don't have any more idea what happened than you do, and I've told you what I know."

"You didn't mention the police have excellent reasons to believe that you killed Lori."

"I didn't mention it because they don't, and I didn't."

"The police chief seems to think otherwise."

"Chief Lennox couldn't find his own backside with a map and a flashlight. He'd like to think I murdered Lori out of some kind of insane rage over her selling mass-produced totes, because that's the answer that requires him to do the least amount of work, even though it makes no sense at all. You can take his word for it if you want, but in that case I don't know what you're doing here talking to me."

To his credit, Neil didn't come back with a retort. He just sat there, holding the mug of coffee he clearly didn't want to drink, looking across Claudia's kitchen table at her like he wasn't sure if she was right or crazy or both. Finally, he seemed to settle in favor of not getting thrown out of her house, and even took another sip of the coffee as a kind of conciliatory gesture. (He immediately regretted it.)

"Okay, so let's say for the sake of argument that you didn't kill her."

"Thank you so much for that," Claudia said, but he ignored her and kept talking.

"Then who did? And why?"

Those were exactly the questions that Claudia had been trying to answer, but she wasn't about to tell him that. It was kind of a shock, honestly, to hear her own internal monologue made real, and placed in another person's mouth, and it was impossible not to recognize that they were very strange questions for either of them to be asking.

Claudia didn't share any of these thoughts. Instead, she took on the role of her own doubts, a position with which she was intimately familiar.

"I don't know," she repeated. "But I don't see how you can possibly expect to find out. What can you do that the police wouldn't be able to?"

"Do you think the police are going to solve it?" he asked.

"They might," she said, but her lack of conviction was hard to ignore. She thought about Lori stealing the number from Emmanuelle's phone, and trying to line up press coverage for something, and it was on the tip of her tongue to ask him if anything he knew about her could shed some light on that, but something stopped her. She didn't know this man, and she had no reason to trust anything he was saying. For all she knew, this entire visit was a ploy to find out what she knew. And even if it wasn't, it was clear that Neil was already suspicious of her, and revealing that she had been doing some snooping of her own wasn't likely to win him over.

"Anyway," she went on. "As incompetent as they are, the police are the ones with all the information and resources. How would you even know how to start investigating a murder? Besides coming here and yelling at me, that is."

"I wasn't yelling, I just wanted some information. And I'm still not sure I got it."

The time for reconciliation was apparently over. Claudia got the impression that Neil wasn't a man who cared for being told he couldn't do things.

"Look, I'm sorry," she said. "Believe me, I want Lori's murder solved too. She died in my marketplace and I found her body, and it's not something I'm ever going to forget. Her death was terrible and cruel, and whoever did it is obviously very dangerous and probably still in the area, so I have personal reasons to want them found as soon as possible. But I don't know what you think you're going to be able to accomplish going around and asking people questions."

By the time she was finished, Claudia wasn't sure if she was talking to herself or Neil. Fortunately, he didn't catch the ambiguity.

"You think so, do you? The thing is, I've got some more resources than you might know about. And you should be grateful, because if I'm right, I could get you out of all of this trouble."

That caught Claudia off guard. Again, she was tempted to press, and bring up her own information, but caution still held her back.

"Then I wish you the best of luck," she said. "But if you really didn't suspect me, then what are you doing here?"

"I need to know some things. Like who Lori was in contact with while she was at the marketplace, and where she might have been keeping some things. Do you have any access to her goods in the shop?"

Claudia didn't, and she told him so.

"She did have some stuff she was storing here, in the other house. The police have it now. It was mostly things to do with her store, so I let them take it."

"You did what?"

She hadn't been expecting to be thanked, but the outburst took Claudia by surprise.

"I didn't know if anyone was going to show up to claim it, and they're investigating a murder, after all."

"Well that's just great. So now I have to go to the police? Why didn't you just toss it all into the ocean and be done with it?"

"I'm sorry, I really didn't think there was anything there that was that important. And it wasn't mine to hold on to, anyway," Claudia said. She refrained from asking what he thought he was going to do with some boxes of counterfeit handicrafts.

Or maybe the boxes had nothing to do with it. There was still the question of that list she had found, along with the picture of Dana.

Could that be what Neil was after? But why? She wished he would leave, so she could take another look at it.

As if on cue, Neil stood up, leaving his nearly full coffee cup on the table.

"I guess I've taken up enough of your time," he said. "I'm sure you're busy."

It might have been sarcasm, but it was true, and as Claudia went to open the door for him she was already thinking about what she was going to do next. He was almost all the way out when she pulled her attention back from thoughts of marketplace prep and search terms and realized she had another question for him.

"One more thing, if you don't mind," she asked from her doorstep, Teddy crouching suspiciously behind her legs. "When was the last time you talked to Lori?"

Neil stopped and thought for a moment.

"I think it was last year. She was moving, and she had found some stuff she thought was mine and asked if I wanted it. It was just a bunch of junk, so I told her to throw it out. She did say something about 'not being in touch for a while, but then I was going to be hearing a lot about her.' I still don't know what she meant by that."

Claudia agreed that it wasn't much to go on.

"I hope she didn't do anything stupid, trying to get famous," she said, thinking of Lori's attempt to reach Emmanuelle's media contact.

"Me too," Neil said. "But she must have done something, right? She's dead."

After he had gone, Claudia went back into the house and cleaned up the mugs, with a bad taste in her mouth that had nothing to do with the coffee.

Neil claimed to be trying to find his ex-wife's killer out of sentiment for her, but his readiness to blame her for her own murder and the fact that he had trouble remembering the last time he had talked to her didn't fit with that. Unless, of course, he remembered everything just fine, and had only been hesitating for as long as it took him to remember what lie he was telling.

In fact, there had been something off about the whole conversation, from his initial aggression about accusing Claudia to suddenly indicating he had some reason to believe she was innocent, and from probing for information to implying he knew more than he was willing to say. That he had come to talk to her was the least surprising part, Claudia supposed. If he really was trying to solve the murder, the person who found the body was an obvious person to talk to, even if she hadn't told him anything of substance. She thought back over his questions, but there was nothing there that made it clear what line he was pursuing, except that he thought there was something Lori had been storing among her possessions, and he either hadn't found it yet or wanted to know if Claudia had. She didn't think she had given away what little she knew, but it was hard to tell when she wasn't sure what exactly that was.

One undeniable outcome of his visit was that Claudia was suddenly much more interested in that list of names Lori had collected. It hadn't seemed like much when she found it, but it was the only thing among her possessions that Neil could conceivably have been searching for, and that meant it was time to give it a closer look.

She had just poured herself another cup of coffee and was examining the pictures she had taken of the list when she got a call from Julie.

"I had an idea," she said, once greetings had been exchanged. "What if we got some of the local community organizations to set up booths at the marketplace? It would be a good way to bring in a few more bodies, and they've all got mailing lists. I have a meeting with some members of the Beach Society at The Breakers tomorrow morning, and I thought you could come along and make your pitch. We're all a bunch of busybodies, and I don't think anyone is on less than three nonprofit boards, so it would be a good way to take care of a bunch of them at once. The only problem I can see is if some of the people who aren't there end up feeling left out, but you can let me deal with them."

"That sounds great," Claudia said, meaning the suggestion in general, but also the idea of Julie dealing with the hurt feelings of left-out nonprofits. The complex politics of small-town living were still a bit beyond her. "What time should I be there?"

CHAPTER SIXTEEN

It was getting late in the day, but Claudia thought there might still be time to try again to reach a few more of her media contacts, none of whom had returned her calls so far. It was frustrating, but Claudia kept trying, stationed at her kitchen table with her phone and laptop, working her way through every name she could find while the wind rattled the windows.

After two hours of work with nothing to show for it but the possibility of a mention on the local traffic-and-weather radio station, Claudia was ready to give up and leave it to luck and the local grapevine. Her one hope at this point was Emmanuelle's social media presence, whatever that was worth. Which, it occurred to her, was something she could determine, or at least estimate. She knew that Emmanuelle was most active on a particular photo sharing site, where Claudia had created an account years ago that she had left to languish, but it was no trouble to log in and find her tenant.

Emmanuelle certainly did have a good number of followers, and based on the amount of comments her photos got, her engagement wasn't bad either. Starting to feel optimistic, Claudia clicked through to look at the list of profiles of the people who were interested in well-lit pictures of strawberries and pancetta, hoping to see some prominent names. She found a few, but almost immediately lost interest in them, because in the long string of thumbnail images her eye had picked out a familiar one. The picture wasn't recent, but there was no question it was of Lori. Dreams of viral fame forgotten, she followed the link.

Sure enough, the face in most of the photos was Lori's, smiling up at a camera held an arm's length from her face. At first glance, the contents of the page were the furthest thing from shocking; the biggest surprise (and, frankly, embarrassment) for Claudia was that her investigating hadn't turned it up before now.

In her defense, the page hadn't been active for a while; the most recent post was from close to five years ago. That one wasn't much, a close-up of a calla lily with a series of crying emojis and hearts as the caption. The post had merited two likes, with one person posting a crying emoji in response.

Further back, the account took on a cheerier tone. Lori hadn't been a steady user of the site; her pattern was occasional bursts of activity followed by long silences, but when she did post, the photos tended to be in the genre of average restaurant meals photographed in low light, and Lori standing in front of things. Most of the things she was in front of were deeply uninteresting—why anyone would think the fact that one was in line for chicken fingers at the ballpark merited documentation was not clear to Claudia, but to each their own.

What she was more interested in was the other people in the photos. Neil appeared in a few, which supported but didn't exactly confirm the case for him actually having been her husband. But the most frequent appearances were from another familiar face, smiling next to Lori at restaurant patio tables, in front of vacation-spot vistas, making faces while wearing hats. In all of them, Dana Herschel—the girl from the journal photo—clung tightly to her friend, giving the same full-teeth, squinty-eyed smile.

Claudia looked over them carefully, trying to guess what had made Neil so sure that this friendship was over. Dana did appear in fewer of the later pictures, and when she did, Claudia thought her smile seemed thinner and more forced. About six months before the final post she vanished entirely, and in most of the remaining photos Lori was alone.

A quick reverse image search on some of the better pictures of Dana didn't turn up anything, so Claudia copied them and emailed them to herself, along with the page address, for further investigation later. Dana remained a question mark for her, particularly since the time she had learned her full name, but Claudia hadn't had much time to devote to research. She made an attempt now, but even with the pictures, it wasn't possible to pick out the relevant people from the endless search results. With enough time, Claudia was sure she would be able to learn something, but before she could get deeper into it the phone rang.

"Hi, I'm calling for Claudia Simcoe?"

"This is she."

"Good evening , Ms. Simcoe, this is Todd Thompson from the *West County Gazette*. I got your message about an event you're holding this weekend?"

The voice on the other end of the line was a little raspy, like he had just finished a coughing fit, but it was the loveliest sound Claudia had heard all day. The *Gazette* was a large local newspaper, taken by most of the households in the county that still took a paper. A write-up there wouldn't guarantee her event would be a success, but at least it would prevent it from sinking into history completely unnoticed.

"Yes, as a matter of fact, we are," she said. "Is there any chance you'll be able to write something about it? I realize it's very short notice."

"It's a little unusual, but we might be able to manage something," he said, this angel of the newsroom. "Why the last-minute planning?"

"Because of the hot weather," Claudia answered, semitruthfully. Unusually for her, she had actually thought this part out.

"It's like Mavericks," she explained, referring to the big-wave surfing competition held near San Francisco. "When they have the waves it happens, when they don't, it doesn't. Same deal."

"Right, well, as I understand it, you've had some other newsworthy events there? Someone was killed? This is the same marketplace, right?"

Claudia went cold all over. She had done her best to avoid the news vans and unfamiliar cars that had been showing up for the last couple of days, but she was aware of the sensation that the murder had caused among the local media.

"Yes," she said, cautiously. "We had a terrible tragedy at the marketplace the other day. I'm not sure I'm comfortable with making that part of a story about the outdoor event, though. If that's the only thing you're interested in writing about . . ."

"Oh no, I think we can work something out to do separate stories. But I was interested in hearing your account of the death. You're the owner of the marketplace, correct?"

The reporter's game was clear now. If she wanted her event promoted, she was going to have to give him a story. Which she supposed was fair, in a way. Everybody wants something.

While they talked, Claudia had been running a quick search on his name. Todd Thompson had plenty of articles on the *Gazette*'s website, all of them having to do with local food and drink events. If he had ever had a byline on a crime story, she couldn't find it. None of his pieces seemed to have made it in the vicinity of the front page, let alone investigative reporting.

She had a theory, and if she was right then maybe they could both get what they wanted, plus a bit more.

"So, I take it that you were hoping for a personal account of the death? Some details about the victim or the investigation? And if I can offer those to you, you might also write up our event?"

"Something like that, yes." If he was put off by her directness, Todd didn't show it. Claudia decided to press her luck.

"Well, the issue with that is that I don't really want to be giving statements. But what if I told you something you could use for a whole new angle?"

This was the bait; she hoped it looked tasty enough. Claudia's guess was that Todd was an aspiring investigative reporter putting his time in on the fluffier beats, who had heard her name in his voicemail and decided to seize the moment. What she needed now was to offer him an even better opportunity, one that wouldn't just get him a shared byline on a follow-up story, but an exclusive of his own. And at the same time, he might be able to get some information that Claudia hadn't. The idea had its risks, but she was willing to take them.

"I'm listening," the reporter said, possibly unaware that his voice had gone up in pitch. "What kind of information?"

"There's actually a couple of things, though I should warn you that I have no idea if either is going to pan out. And I'm only telling you this on the condition that my name is nowhere in the story. I'm just a source close to the investigation, okay?"

"You've got a lot of conditions for someone who's being investigated for a murder," he said, and Claudia's stomach filled with rocks. Her first instinct was to deny it, but she remembered who she was talking to, and the last thing she wanted was to give him any quotes that could be used against her.

"So is that a no?" she asked, hoping bravado could stand in for the confidence she didn't have. "The event is happening whether or not you write about it, but without my tips you don't have any sort of story."

There was silence on the other end of the line as the reporter weighed his options. Finally, for whatever reason, he decided to play along.

"Okay, fine," he said. "Your name won't be in it. But I can't promise the event listing will be in the paper. Might just make the website."

It was less than ideal, but Claudia had the sense that she had pushed the negotiations about as far as was wise.

"Okay," she said. "I guess we have a deal."

"All right then. So what's this big thing you have for me?"

"Three names. There's a man named Neil Hahn who just arrived in town, claiming to be the victim's ex-husband. He says he's here on the behalf of her great-aunt, who's too sick to travel. Which I have no reason to believe is anything other than totally true."

"I see," Todd said, picking up on her tone. "And is there anything else you can tell me about this completely normal and unsuspicious person?"

"Only that for someone who was supposed to be representing the victim's only living relative, he doesn't seem to be very well informed about his legal rights, or hers. And most of the questions he had seemed to have more to do with Lori's life here and her death than things that might be important to her estate. But I've never had to deal with the death of an ex-spouse, so what do I know?"

"What indeed. Well, thanks, that does sound like someone I'd like to find out some more about. Who's next?"

"Dana Herschel. She was a good friend of Lori's in the past, but now apparently no one can get in touch with her. I have reason to believe that she was someone who was very important to Lori, one way or another."

"So? Lots of us have friends we aren't talking to anymore. I can't get a story out of that. You better have something pretty good behind door number three, or otherwise this deal is off."

"I don't know. How do you feel about a former boy band member turned ex-con cult leader who may have crossed paths with the victim in the past, currently living in Humboldt?"

The silence at the other end of the line lasted for so long that Claudia thought the line might have gone dead. Finally, Todd let out a low whistle.

"Well, that's no goat. Okay, you have my attention. How about a few details?"

Claudia filled him in on what she had learned, being careful to emphasize the fact that she couldn't guarantee Lori and Mr. Serenity Icono Bartok had ever actually encountered each other in person. Todd listened intently, asking occasional questions, until he was sure he had gotten all he could out of her.

"Okay, if that's it then that's it. But I hope you realize that this is some suspicious behavior on your part."

"Suspicious? How so?"

"Well, I just have to wonder if you're feeding this stuff to me on purpose, to keep the attention off something closer to home."

Claudia had to admit it sounded like a valid strategy. Not out loud, of course.

What she said was, "You'll have to keep wondering, then, unless you can find someone else to talk to you. Because I'm talking now, and this is what I've got."

Todd laughed.

"I like you, lady. You've got some balls, don't you?"

"Technically, no."

"Fair enough. I'll get to work on these names of yours and see what I can come up with. You can look for the story on your market event to show up on the website by noon tomorrow at the latest. If it's in the paper it'll be the Saturday edition."

Claudia thanked him, and said if she came up with anything else, she'd let him know. They were both aware she was lying, but it was okay. She felt like they had reached a certain level of understanding and the reporter was, if not quite sympathetic toward her, at least aware it was in his interest to stay on her good side, whatever the facts of the case might turn out to be.

As interactions with the press as a murder suspect went, Claudia thought that could have been worse.

By the time they were done, it was too late to make any more calls, so Claudia settled for emailing a few regional bloggers. She was in the middle of making a list of local tourism sites to contact in the morning when it occurred to her that it was after eight, and that uncomfortable sensation in the area of her stomach was probably hunger. The feeling, once acknowledged, took over her thinking to the point where there was no use trying to do anything more until she had some dinner.

Most days, this would have been the time she started coming up with excuses for why she should just heat up another pizza, but the crisper drawer in her refrigerator was full of almost perfectly good produce, and Rob and Emmanuelle had pressed a half-dozen fresh eggs on her as she was leaving, and under those circumstances, the shame of another frozen dinner was too much to bear.

So Claudia took out what seemed like a reasonable range of ingredients and lined them up on the kitchen counter, along with a hunk of cheese to snack on while she contemplated her options. Two lightly bruised zucchini, half a bag of baby spinach, and three heirloom tomatoes weren't the most inspiring starting point, but a couple of Internet searches and a hunt through an old cookbook later, Claudia settled on a frittata as the dish most likely to use her ingredients and not take upward of an hour.

She sliced up the zucchini and tossed it into a pan where she had heated up some olive oil, and while it was browning, she let her thoughts turn to recent events.

It seemed like so much had happened, but she was no closer to knowing what was going on than when she had received those damning printouts four days ago. (Was it really only that long? Claudia felt like she had been living like this for years.) In that time, Lori had gone from being a mildly irritating tenant, to a fraud, to dead. And Claudia's own journey, which had begun with the desire to keep her marketplace free of counterfeit goods, had gone on to having to face the horror of the death of a person she hadn't exactly liked, but who was still a person who should be alive, through being accused of the murder by an incompetent blowhard who was in way over his head and trying to pull her down with him, and into an introductory course in Murder Investigation for Total Morons, for which she suspected she wasn't getting a passing grade.

Claudia tossed the mountain of spinach into the pan and watched it melt down to a couple of tablespoons while she thought about the situation. What, in fact, did she actually know? Lori was dead, and someone must have killed her. (Claudia had no medical expertise, but she was confident that there was no way for a person to hit her own head with a jar of pickles and while unconscious, strangle herself with a cheese wire.) Whoever it was almost certainly had a reason—while she couldn't completely eliminate the possibility of a random attack by a deranged vagrant and/or serial killer, she wasn't giving it high odds.

So, what reasons did people have for killing? Money, anger, and fear were the ones Claudia could come up with off the top of her head. The financial argument was dubious, based on what she had seen in Lori's credit report, but maybe she had had a source of income that didn't go through any of the official channels. Of course, it didn't have to be money that she had. What about blackmail?

Claudia sliced up the tomatoes and tested the edges of her new theory. It was a stretch, but maybe Lori had been using her stall in the marketplace to get close to someone, to threaten them or gather more information? Or maybe her scheme had already blown up on her somewhere else, and a market stand in a rural backwater had seemed like a good place to hide out until things calmed down.

Okay, so it worked as a theory. So what? That and four bucks got you a cup of coffee. Without any proof, Claudia might as well have been theorizing that Lori had been killed by government agents to protect the secret that all of the nation's cats were really aliens in disguise, for all the good it was going to do her.

As if sensing her distress, Teddy came over and pressed her nose against the back of her leg. Claudia reached down and rubbed her behind the ear as the dog whimpered and turned her head to maximize the scratching.

"You'll protect me from the alien cats, won't you, girl?" Claudia said, and Teddy panted her apparent agreement.

That settled, Claudia got back to the business of making her dinner. She cracked four eggs into a bowl, mixed, and added milk until it looked about right. It was going to be a large dish for one person, but it would make good leftovers, and she couldn't see the point in preparing a single-serving frittata.

The eggs and tomatoes went into the pan with the cooked vegetables, floating and sinking according to their individual inclinations. After some thought, she chopped up the remainder of the cheese and mixed it in too, then stuck the whole thing in the oven and hoped for the best.

When it came out, the top was golden brown, with bits of tomato and zucchini poking through, and taking out a slice confirmed the interior was fluffy and cheesy in the appropriate amounts. Claudia was so pleased with herself that she considered taking pictures and posting them, but decided that might be overdoing it for the achievement of managing to cook herself dinner. So she settled for raising a forkful in the direction of the pan, in an eggy toast.

"I dub thee the fridge-ttata," she said.

CHAPTER SEVENTEEN

The next day dawned without its usual blanket of fog. Instead of the normal soft grayness, the sky was bright blue and naked, and the buildings along the edge of the bay stood out clearly in all their faded, tin-roofed glory. There wasn't even a breath of wind, and the regular tone of the foghorn had fallen silent.

It was unnerving, to say the least.

Claudia had set an early alarm, and only gave herself one snooze cycle before she got up, let Teddy out, and started gathering the mental resources she was going to need to face the day. That required caffeine, so she loaded up the coffee maker and set it on "kill." It was Friday, just over twenty-four hours from the start time for the Hail Mary event Claudia was hoping would save her business, and she did not have one damn thing ready.

Breakfast was a cold piece of leftover frittata, eaten out of hand as she tried to identify her ducks and figure out what kind of row they should be in. She was writing up a schedule for what she was going to have to get done by what time, when she remembered that one of the first items on it should be her meeting with Julie in twenty minutes.

The Breakers Bakery and Coffee Shop was a local institution in San Elmo. Housed in the same Victorian building it had occupied since it outgrew its beachside lean-to in the eighties, it was a rambling space, with uneven, creaking wood floors and well-worn furniture tucked into cozy nooks. The former dining room was dominated by a long oak counter, jammed with raspberry bars, apple turnovers, allegedly healthy granola wads, and the stickiest cinnamon buns to ever challenge dental work.

Upstairs, the space had been converted into a series of small meeting rooms, popular with the apparently endless need of the locals to organize themselves around various causes and interests. Claudia had been meaning to join one of them, or at least make the appearance at Betty's book group she had been promising, but at the end of a long day, the option of staying in her cottage, wearing comfortable pants and not talking to anyone had always won out. But now, as she ordered her latte and felt the eyes of the other patrons on her, she cursed her weakness. At a time when a not-insignificant portion of the population was likely to believe that she had hit a woman over the head and strangled her with a wire, it would have been nice to have a few more people who at least felt obligated to greet her in public.

There was no sign of Julie, so Claudia took her drink and looked around for an empty spot. Even on a weekday morning, the cafe was so popular that it wasn't easy, and it took a few minutes of wandering around before she found an appropriately isolated seat.

At least, that's what it looked like. The spot Claudia had selected was a high-backed chair upholstered in shocking pink, facing the fireplace with its painted concrete logs. She was just settling in, ready to look innocent and return the text she had gotten from the manager of the local waste management agency about the possibility of getting some extra trash bins, when she realized there was another chair about eighteen inches away, previously blocked from her view, and it was occupied.

By Officer Derek Chambers.

"Oh, I'm sorry. I didn't see you there," Claudia said, awkwardly shifting to try to make it look like she had done anything other than walk straight across the room and sit down right in front of him.

Derek didn't seem to put out by her sudden appearance.

"No worries," he said. "There's plenty of space. Want the funnies? I'm done with them. I'm afraid someone's already done the crossword, though." He offered a rumpled section of the paper, and Claudia accepted it with thanks.

"You know, I'm not sure I've laughed at a newspaper strip in twenty years, but they're still my favorite part of the paper. Does Mark Trail still talk in all caps whenever he sees an owl?" she asked as she tried to smooth the sheets to the point that she could comfortably hold them.

"I think it's bears this week," Derek said. He was out of uniform, dressed in blue jeans and a polo shirt, with a tan line on his upper arm illustrating the difference in sleeve length from his uniform. The pile of paper on the seat next to him and his nearly empty mug suggested that he had been here a while, and Claudia wondered if this was usually how he spent his days off.

"Is this how you usually spend your days off?" she asked.

"One of the ways," he said. "It's nice to find a place to come and sit for a while, and their apple turnovers are amazing. What about you? What do you do with your free time?"

"Free time? I'm sorry, I'm not familiar with the concept. This is the longest I've gone without putting in a full day at the marketplace since it opened. Nothing like being forced to take an unpaid vacation to really catch up on your R&R." It had started out as a joke, but as the words came out of her mouth, Claudia could hear the bitterness in them. She cringed, but there was no way of calling them back.

"Sorry, I guess that was out of line. I don't really know what the protocol is here," she said, forcing herself to smile and relax a bit. She was confident that police officers weren't generally supposed to mingle with suspects, and vice versa, but San Elmo was a small town, and things would have to be different. There just weren't that many people to talk to.

"No worries. To be honest, I'm kind of at a loss when it comes to socializing these days," he admitted. "Back in Raleigh, the chances I was going to run into anyone I'd met on the job were pretty slim, but here it seems like I can't avoid it."

"Well," Claudia said, raising her paper cup in a mock toast. "Here's to being unavoidable."

Derek laughed and returned the gesture. "I'll drink to that. Have you always lived in small towns?"

"No, this is all new to me, too. I grew up near San Francisco. Plenty of experience with panhandlers and streets closed for random protests, none with meeting people everywhere who know all about you and want to chat." Claudia frowned. "Did you say Raleigh? For some reason I thought you were from the Northeast."

"I am, originally. Got tired of the snow and started looking for other options. Then I got tired of the paperwork of a big-city job and thought I would look for something a little more slow-paced. Got that part wrong, but I can't say I regret the decision." He looked out the window at the blue sky. "Though I've gotta say, this is the first time since I've been here that it's really felt like how I imagined California would be. When I moved here, I didn't even pack a jacket in my suitcase. Had to wait for the movers to arrive before I could feel my fingers again."

"Rookie mistake," Claudia said. "But at least you can go inland to warm up."

"And we can all be grateful this weekend that we don't have to."

Derek seemed to sense that this discussion of the weather had run its course and, looking around for inspiration to keep the conversation going, had settled on an amateur painting of a fishing boat that was hanging over the fireplace.

"Um, so, do you like going out on the water?"

"I do, but I get seasick," Claudia admitted. "But I've been meaning to go out fishing for crabs once Dungeness season starts. According to Betty, you just sit there for a while until it's time to pull the pots up. I think I could manage that."

"The dull-diest catch," Derek quipped. It wasn't very funny, but Claudia gave him points for effort. It was difficult carrying on a conversation with someone when you couldn't talk about the one thing you had in common, which was also the main topic occupying both people's time and attention. Still, Julie hadn't showed up yet, and the corners of Derek's eyes crinkled up when he smiled, so Claudia decided to give it another try.

"Teddy was really taken with you," she said, hoping she didn't sound quite so much like a Victorian matron as she thought. "Do you have any pets?"

"I would, but my landlady isn't so into the idea. I'm thinking maybe I can get a fish and she won't notice, but I'm not sure I want to take the chance. I'm pretty sure whenever I'm not there, she sneaks in and turns down my thermostat."

The conversation turned to terrible landlords they had had, and Claudia had almost forgotten what she was there for when Julie appeared next to her chair.

"There you are," the cheesemaker said. "I was starting to wonder if you had abandoned us." She turned to Derek and smiled. "Do you mind if I steal her for a second? I've got a few people waiting to talk to her."

Appropriately chastised, Claudia followed her friend to the back of the room, where the other committee members were waiting.

"I'm sorry, I guess I just lost track of the time," she said.

"I can't imagine why," Julie said, with raised eyebrows and a smile. "Did you find out anything interesting about what happened to Lori?"

"That wasn't what we were talking about," Claudia insisted, suddenly confused about how much Julie might know or have guessed. Had she figured out that Claudia was trying to solve the murder? Had everyone? She suddenly felt very exposed, so she tried to cover by redirecting. "And I wouldn't expect him to. He's very professional."

"I'm sure." Julie left it at that and started the round of introductions.

The informal meeting went well, and Claudia left with promises for appearances from the Firefighter's Aid Society, the Rotarians, who could bring their own booth, and a corgi rescue organization who didn't have any corgis yet, except the founder's not-quite-housebroken pet, but they were hopeful. They all agreed it was short notice, and said they were going to have to talk to their other board members (or, in one case, Mr. Wuffles), but the general attitude was one of optimism and Claudia left feeling slightly more like her event wasn't going to be a total disaster, at least from the attendance standpoint. That only left her about eighty other things to worry about, or more if you counted natural disasters and zombie invasions.

Claudia left The Breakers feeling proud of herself for having spent so much time working on the market, instead of the murder, and she decided to reward herself with some time spent looking at Lori's list.

She had initially thought it was just an impenetrable collection of names and numbers, and a closer examination did little to alter that impression. If there was a code, it wasn't an obvious one, and why would Lori be writing coded messages to herself? It seemed more likely she was gathering information about something or someone, and this was all she had managed to get before she died. In which case, it was up to Claudia to take it from there.

She started with searches on the names, which was largely an exercise in futility. Most were too common, with too little other identifying information, to narrow the choices down from the thousands, and even the best weren't that great. There were fifteen Kara Youngs in Philadelphia alone, though she thought she could exclude the two-year-old and the 19th-century trombone player—and no Rebecca Cobbs at all in the nearest Palmyra (New Jersey). The only other information she had about them was that Lori had written their names down, so Claudia decided to search for any connections there.

She hadn't had a lot of hope for the new approach, but in fact it turned out to be almost immediately fruitful. One of her Kara Youngs had attended college with Lori, and while being a graduating class of twenty thousand meant there was no guarantee they had known each other, she was able to find them both on the professional networking site where Lori's resumé was posted, linked by only three degrees of separation.

That Kara was a real estate agent now, and the webpage for her office listed an email address and a phone number. She dialed the number before she could talk herself out of it, and a woman picked up on the third ring, which was exactly two rings after Claudia realized she still hadn't worked out exactly what she was going to say.

"This is Kara Young, how can I help you?" The voice on the other end of the line was clipped and professional, with just a touch of boredom.

"Um, hi. This is Claudia Simcoe. I'm a friend of—I knew Lori Roth. I think you might have known her? I was just calling because I thought I should let you know that she died."

If she was going for garbled and incomprehensible, Claudia would have given herself full marks, but as an investigative strategy it left something to be desired.

The woman on the other end of the line clearly felt the same way.

"I'm sorry," she said. "I don't think I know that name. Are you sure you don't have the wrong number?"

"I don't know," Claudia admitted. "Possibly." Nothing else was working and she had a feeling the call was very close to being over, so she decided to risk it all and go with honesty.

"I'm sorry, I just have this list here that Lori made, and I'm trying to figure out what it means, and it has your name and '5k cousin cancer' in it. Does that mean anything to—"

Claudia was suddenly aware that she was talking to a dead line. Whatever that note had meant to Lori, to Kara Young it meant time to hang up.

Claudia spent a while staring at the phone, but it didn't have any more to offer her. She had no business being surprised, and she certainly wasn't mad. She would have hung up on herself a lot sooner. The call had been a shot in the dark, and like most it had probably missed, and now Claudia found herself left with just as many questions and less chance of them getting answered.

She was about to turn her attention to the major sales event she was planning to hold in less than twenty-four hours, when there was a soft chime from her laptop. Claudia had so many alerts set for so many things that it didn't immediately register which one this was, but she wandered over to check it anyway.

There was nothing immediately different on the screen and it took her a moment to figure out what she was looking at. Then she realized: the status bar for the hacking attempt on the password was gone, replaced with a dialog box that said, somewhat anticlimactically, "Progress Complete."

Claudia clicked through with shaking hands, hardly believing that this particular idea had worked. And there, in front of her was the prize, the secret password of Lori's that she had spent all of this time pursuing: Passw0rd123!

"You have got to be kidding me," Claudia said.

She stared at it for a while longer, wondering if she should laugh or scream. Had she honestly just spent all that time and effort for something she could have gotten with five minutes and a list of the world's laziest passwords? It wasn't the only time Claudia had outsmarted herself, but it was definitely going to make the top ten.

Regardless, she had it now, and it was time to test her theory that it would get her into Lori's other accounts. She went to the webmail portal for Lori's email and was about to type the password into the box when she stopped herself. It was only because of her own love of security that Claudia had set the requirements for passwords for the marketplace system to require at least twelve characters, including letters, numbers, and at least one symbol. Knowing what she knew now, she thought that the odds that Lori would complicate things that much on her own were slim to none. She wasn't going to have too many tries at this, so she tried to put herself in Lori's place. What would a person who didn't care about their information security at all do?

Claudia typed:

password

Password Incorrect

password123!

Password Incorrect

Most sites had a limited number of fails they would allow, and three was a common choice. One more attempt and the account might lock, and all of her efforts would be wasted. Claudia went back and looked at the password Lori had used for the marketplace site.

There were two things that stood out to her. First, the requirements Claudia had instituted didn't include the need for capital letters. And second, if she already had the numbers at the end of the word, there would be no reason to change the o to a zero. So, going by the theory that Lori wasn't going to make any changes that weren't absolutely required, Claudia made her final guess.

Passw0rd

The screen went blank, and then the interface for the email inbox loaded.

CHAPTER EIGHTEEN

The number of unread messages that filled the screen were enough to tell her that no one had accessed the account since Lori's death. Most of them were from mailing lists; sale announcements, listserv updates, general advertisements, and requests for money from her alumni association. There were a few information requests about her products that had come in through the marketplace portal, and one thing that looked like an invoice from her overseas supplier, but it seemed that no one, on finding out that Lori was dead, had emailed to ask if it was true.

Digging deeper into the inbox wasn't much more enlightening. There was nothing in the days leading up to Lori's murder to suggest she was being threatened, or felt worried about anyone around her. Giving up the present day for the time being, Claudia went back to the beginning, to see what Lori's communications could tell her about the woman.

Lori seemed to have acquired the email account about ten years ago, and in the early days she had used it mostly for signing up for retail loyalty programs. The personal messages started about six months in, and were generally on the subject of five to seven people trying to decide on where and when to meet for dinner. Neil Hahn and Dana Herschel appeared in several of them, so Claudia branched off from her chronological search to check all of the messages to and from their respective addresses.

If she still had any doubts that Neil and Lori had been romantically involved, the series of increasingly explicit messages would have dispelled them, and that was before she got to the one with the attached video. (Which Claudia didn't open, but the thumbnail image was enough to make her open all of the following messages with her eyes slightly out of focus.) Later on, the messages got less intimate, but remained friendly enough to support Neil's claim that their breakup had been amicable. The most recent email was just a list of website links, with the subject line "here are the links I was talking about." Claudia hesitated to follow them, given what she had just seen, and compromised by downloading the message to save for later, then moved on to the emails from Lori's former friend.

The only reason she had to be particularly interested in Dana Herschel was she had found her picture in the same notebook that had held the mysterious list and, along with the list, it was one of the only things she could imagine Neil had been looking for. There were certainly plenty of messages from her, particularly in the early days of the account; chatty missives heavy with gossip about shared acquaintances. Dana seemed to be in the habit of recommending bright lipsticks and embellished jeans for Lori to buy, and asking for opinions on recipes she found on the Internet. Lori's responses were briefer, and more negative than not, to the point that Claudia started to wonder why anyone would try to have a conversation with her.

It went on that way for a while, and then about five years back the emails grew less frequent and the tone changed. Most of the remaining exchanges were initiated by Lori, and the responses were brief and disinterested. Dana also vanished from the group get-together threads, and the prompts from others to try and reach her went largely unanswered. Eventually, the communications dwindled to nothing, except for one lone message, sent by Lori several months after her last attempt went ignored.

I tried to help you and I'm sorry you're not listening to me. If you're going to be an idiot there's nothing I can do, but don't say I didn't warn you. whatever happens to you now is your own fault.

There was no response.

Hoping for enlightenment, Claudia searched the rest of the folders for any other emails that included Dana's name. She only came up with one that post-dated Lori's ultimatum, in the sent mail file, to someone named Sandra Herschel-Wilson.

I'm so sorry for what happened. Dana was my best friend, even after what went on between us I will always love her. She didn't deserve any of this and I would give anything to go back and change it.

It was the rawest and most heartfelt thing she had ever seen from Lori, and so out of sync with everything else Claudia knew about her that for a moment she wondered if it was some kind of a joke. But that seemed unlikely, and when she cross-checked the dates on the photo-sharing site she found, as she expected, the email lined up fairly closely to the picture of the lily.

So Dana was dead. And before she died, she had gotten involved with something her best friend was sure would doom her, but she refused to listen to warnings. Claudia would very much like to learn some more about what that had been, but she had exhausted her normal information-gathering routes. This was going to take some more thought.

The cell phone she had been ignoring while she was doing her research buzzed, knocking her out of her reverie. It was Julie, asking if she had drawn up a plan of the layout in the parking lot for where they were going to set up the booths tomorrow, because she was running into some difficulties arranging her community groups to minimize conflicts. Claudia lied and said it was almost ready, then set about making the lie into the truth. She could think just as well while she got some work done.

"The booths with hot food are going to have to go along this side, so that puts the charity tables over here, and the performers can set up over there. Except, no, that doesn't leave enough space from the exit."

Claudia was talking out loud to herself, wandering around the parking lot with a tape measure in one hand and a copy of the fire department regulations in the other. Every few minutes she would stop and redraw the map, only to realize some problem with it, stop, cross it out, and start over. Teddy was trailing along behind her, not sure what this new game was about, but enjoying it nonetheless.

The work hadn't gotten her much closer to thinking of a new way to find out what had happened to Dana. Asking Neil was the obvious option, but that presented the minor problem of having to explain to him how she knew as much as she did. "I was just hacking into your dead ex-wife's email, I hope you don't mind," didn't seem like a very promising way to begin a conversation, but so far she hadn't been able to come up with a useable lie.

Claudia stopped what she was doing to respond to a text from Emmanuelle, asking for an opinion on what hashtag they should use for photos of the event. Claudia said she would leave it up to her expertise to choose one, and promised to start using it as soon as she did.

She had drawn out the placement of two more booths when she was interrupted again. This time the text was from Betty, saying that she had to get dinner ready at the guest ranch but she was free to help after that, and should she bring anything to eat? Claudia thought about telling her not to worry, that she had everything under control, but Betty wasn't going to believe that for a second, and she didn't have time for a tedious dance of oh-no-you-shouldn'ts. So she wrote back that help and dinner were welcome, and when, three minutes later, Julie and Helen sent near-simultaneous texts offering their own assistance, Claudia gave up, declared it an open house, and sent Betty another message asking how many she was willing to cater.

It was midafternoon, and in the open parking lot the air was uncomfortably hot and still. Claudia looked longingly at the locked-up marketplace and wished she could go inside, if only for a couple of minutes. For the last two years it had been her second home, and looking at it now, she felt like she could see straight through the redwood-shingled walls and tightly closed blinds, to the polished concrete floors and closed shops.

It would be dark in there, and cooler. The power was still running to the refrigerators, but Claudia didn't want to think about what the cleanup was going to be like, particularly at the produce market. If things went on much longer this way, she was going to need a flamethrower just to get past the fruit flies.

Claudia ended her survey of the building at the door, still decorated with two bands of police tape. One had come loose and drifted in the air like a bit of abandoned spiderweb. Nobody from the police department had been inside since they took Lori's body away, which strengthened Claudia's suspicion that the closure had been more out of spite than necessity.

She spent a few entertaining, if pointless, minutes imagining the devastating put-downs she would have for Lennox once she had solved the murder and he was forced to come to her and apologize, begging her not to make him lose his job. (Somehow, in this fantasy, she had acquired that power.)

With some difficulty, she pulled herself away from the question of whether she should be vengeful or magnanimous, back to the more immediate issue of what she was going to use to block the door from the curious eyes of what she hoped was going to be a throng of customers. She had just worked out that the bookshelf in her living room would fit there, and would be a good place to display pickles, when her phone buzzed again.

Assuming it was another person inviting themselves over, she was already composing a "the more the merrier" reply in her head, but the number wasn't in her contacts, and the message wasn't an offer of help.

I've got a bottle of wine that needs drinking and you need a break. Meet me at Clover Beach at 6? Derek

Claudia stared at the screen for a lot longer than she had any business doing. She was a busy woman, with way too much on her plate to even consider going on a date, no matter how charming the man or how well-shaped his forearms. Still, she hesitated. She had been single for too long, and dates over these last few years had been infrequent and unsatisfying.

But that was just a trend that was going to have to continue, Claudia thought as she put the phone back in her pocket. Because she had a mystery to solve and a business to save, and she wasn't going to do either by sitting on a beach on a beautiful evening, sipping wine with a handsome man who might be trying to get her to make an incriminating statement.

She was putting the finishing touches on her layout plan when a glint of light caught her eye. It had come from the direction of Mr. Rodgers' house, and at first she thought it had just been the reflection of the sun off a window. But then she saw it again, and it came from an object on the otherwise-empty porch, a long tube ending in a lens that was pointed right at her.

Claudia wouldn't have expected her neighbor had a lot of things left he could do to surprise her, but she hadn't thought of a telescope.

She wanted to laugh it off, but the discovery unnerved Claudia more than she liked to admit. Her unseen neighbor had always been more of an annoyance than anything else, just another headache that had come with the marketplace, like health inspectors and the geese. But the thought of an unknown pair of eyes on the other end of that telescope, getting a close look at her when she wasn't aware, was not comforting, to put it mildly.

The planning wasn't exactly done, but Claudia decided she could just as well finish drawing her diagram back at the cottage, with the doors locked and the blinds closed. She was aware that there was a possibility that she was overreacting, that Rodgers was simply an astronomy enthusiast who had bumped into the telescope on his way back into the house, but she wasn't finding herself very convincing on that point.

Nathan Rodgers. Could he be the killer? It was a crazy thought, and Claudia wondered why she hadn't come up with it sooner. But why would he kill Lori? He had no reason to be mad at her. Except, what if he didn't know it was her? For all their confrontations, he and Claudia had never met, and today was the first time she had even noticed the telescope. What if he had seen a woman going into the marketplace late at night and decided it was Claudia, up to something that was going to annoy him. Could he have decided that this was the right time to air his grievances and gone to confront her? And could Lori, still annoyed at having her lease revoked and already planning a revenge of her own, seen an opportunity in antagonizing him while pretending to be Claudia, and inadvertently drove him to such a rage that he hit her with the pickle jar, and strangled her with the cheese wire?

Or maybe she never got a chance to say anything to him at all. Maybe he had been planning murder all along, and it was only Lori's ill-timed brainwave with the stink bombs that had kept Claudia from being killed in her own bed. Either way, it would have been a rude shock for him to discover he had missed his target so completely, though with the closure of the marketplace maybe he felt like he had achieved his goal regardless.

It was all the baldest sort of speculation, but suddenly Claudia's cottage felt less cozy and more exposed. By holding the outdoor market event she had made it clear she wasn't going to give up on the business without a fight. What if that meant it was a fight she was going to get?

For the first time in her life, Claudia wished she owned a weapon more effective than her set of department-store kitchen knives. But she didn't, and it was probably a bad idea anyway, so she decided to arm herself with information instead. She didn't have the time to do a deep dive, so she started with a simple search of Nathan Rodgers' name with San Elmo, and when that didn't turn up anything, expanded it to all of Sonoma County. That returned too many results, none of them immediately useful. She thought she could be fairly confident that none of the obituaries were relevant, though she looked through them carefully, in case one of the men was survived by a namesake son. Otherwise, she had a notable former brewery owner, a high school track champion from ten years ago, a person who had applied to register a business name for something called "Love vs. Crepes," an optometrist in Healdsburg, and the assistant winemaker at a Russian River winery.

That was the most interesting one to Claudia, not because she was in the market for a nice pinot (though that was also, and always, true), but because that particular Nathan Rodgers had been arrested five years ago when he got into a fight with a fellow patron of a local bar, resulting in a broken nose for the other guy and forty hours of community service for him. That seemed like something she should know about, so Claudia dedicated a few more minutes of searching and came up with his arrest report.

The booking photo showed a white man in his mid-forties, looking like he had had better nights. His thinning gray hair was sticking out in all directions, and he appeared to have a black eye under development. She studied his face, trying to remember if she had seen him anywhere around, but there was nothing familiar.

Property records would narrow it down, but they weren't searchable online for her area, and as much as Claudia would like to know who she was up against, she didn't have time to go look through the county archives right now.

She wanted to do more searching, but the phone rang and Claudia spent the next fifteen minutes dealing with the question of how she was going to get the tables from the rental shop to the marketplace, and whether they were willing to stay open long enough for her to figure it out. Then there was another call from the corgi lady, and then the portable toilet company wanted to know what the percent grade was on the parking lot, and Claudia was forced to concede that figuring out whether or not her neighbor was trying to kill her would have to wait.

CHAPTER NINETEEN

"Where should I put this?"

It was three hours later and Claudia had finally gotten her plans into something resembling order, just in time for all of her helpers to show up and start disrupting them. Betty, the first arrival, didn't bother to knock, which showed that, for all her paranoia, Claudia had failed to lock the front door. But she was too happy to see her friend to be annoyed with herself, and she greeted Betty and her cooler full of food with more than usual warmth.

"Thanks so much," she said. "Hang on, I'll see if I can make some room in the fridge."

It didn't take much time to move the bag of wilted greens, leftover pierogis, and various condiments, and even with the argument as to whether ketchup belonged in the refrigerator, they had Betty's perishables put away before Helen showed up with Brandon trailing reluctantly behind her. No mention was made of his indiscretion, but it was clear from the way his mother was keeping a close eye on him that, if he might be forgiven, it was definitely not forgotten.

Next to arrive was Julie in the van, followed closely behind by Elias in the farm's oversized pickup truck. Claudia went to meet them, hopeful that their arrival might have solved one of her chief remaining problems.

"It's good to see you," she said, mostly meaning the people, but also the vehicle. "Thanks for offering to help."

"Of course," Julie said. "Anything we can do. Do you want me to make some signs? I brought pens and some leftover poster board from Beryl's science fair project."

"That would be great," Claudia said. "But actually, what I really need is someone to run over to the rental place and pick up the tables and things. We did it on such short notice, they were able to get us the stuff, but their truck wasn't available."

"I can go, but I cannot lift more than fifty pounds. That's according to my doctor who's a little gir—" Elias caught his daughter's eye and corrected himself. "A little too much concerned with my back. Maybe the boy can come with me? He doesn't want to stay here and make signs anyway."

Brandon looked pained, but his mother nodded vigorously.

"That's a good idea. Brandon, you go along and do whatever Mr. Muller tells you."

Claudia watched with amusement and some amount of pity for the young man. She wasn't exactly pleased with some of his decisions herself, but three hours in a truck cab with Elias (and his opinions) was punishment enough for anyone.

And, from the way he kept checking his phone, she suspected that there was somewhere else he would very much rather be. (Claudia briefly thought of the invitation she had gotten to be elsewhere tonight, but pushed it out of her mind. She had made her choices.)

Elias left with his reluctant assistant, and no sooner had they pulled out of the driveway than Carmen and Iryna showed up to take their place. With six people and a dog, the cottage was approaching capacity, but the women found a way to squeeze themselves in, dispensing suggestions and accepting Betty's mascarpone-stuffed cherry peppers with enthusiasm. Claudia put them to work folding the brochures she had ordered in bulk when she opened the marketplace, and stored behind the couch ever since, because it turned out ten thousand was slightly more fliers than she was ever going to need.

Helen settled in to help Julie with the signs, and while Betty took over Claudia's layout plans and made corrections, Claudia thought she might have a minute to gather her thoughts and strategize how she wanted to approach the next twenty-four hours, both in terms of the marketplace and the murder investigation. But no sooner had she picked up her other notepad (Betty had taken possession of the first one) than her cell and wall phones rang simultaneously and she was plunged back into a world of people who wanted her decisions on things.

One of the calls was Emmanuelle, updating her on the progress of her social media campaign, which sounded like it was going well, and wondering if it would be possible to set up a spot with a display of marketplace goods that people could use as photo backdrops. Claudia didn't know what the appeal would be of having a picture of yourself in front of a lot of pickles, but Emmanuelle was insistent, and she figured it couldn't hurt. The other was the dispatcher for the delivery company that the produce market used, confirming drop off times and unsubtly angling for gossip on the murder. Then a reporter for one of the papers she had been trying to reach finally returned her call, and she was back into sales mode.

It was tiring, bouncing from one demand on her attention to another, but there was something comforting about being able to do something. Sitting there, in her cramped, crowded house, trying to carry on professional phone conversations over the sound of arguments about whether every word on the poster should be different colors, or just the nouns, she felt calmer and safer than she had for a while.

She took a deep breath and repeated her patter about the outdoor market being a special, weather-dependent event, and mentally dared the reporter to bring up the murder. She didn't honestly believe it wasn't going to come up in the coverage, but she hoped at least she would be able to temporarily redirect the conversation.

While Claudia was on the phone, Helen had a brainstorm about making individual packs of kimchi and sauerkraut for picnickers to add to their sausages, and hurried off to see if she could find the plastic cups she thought she had stored at her rented prep kitchen. That reminded

Carmen that she might not have enough raisins for the beef empanadas and, unable to get in touch with her regular supplier, she took off for the grocery store.

Even with the reduced numbers, they were able to get a lot done, and Helen was back before Betty had to leave to put the twins to bed and Julie remembered that she was supposed to drop in to the Friends of the Library meeting she was currently skipping, to see if they would bring along the book table.

For the next hour or so it went on like this, with whoever wasn't off running various errands being put to work on whatever needed doing. By the time Julie got back with news that the table had been secured, and Betty returned with a plate of fresh cookies, they had pretty well gotten most of the details settled, and assuming about fifty improbable things went exactly as planned, the First Possibly-Annual San Elmo Outdoor Artisan Marketplace would go off without a hitch.

The sound of another car pulling up didn't draw much attention. By this point there had been so much coming and going that Claudia only registered it with a vague thought that she hoped whoever it was wouldn't be too annoyed that they'd eaten all the cookies. She didn't even bother getting up to respond to the knock, just covered the phone mouthpiece, shouted, "It's open!" and went back to answering the question from the representative from the tourist bureau who she had manage to pull away from his dinner. It wasn't until she had noticed that the room had gone suddenly quiet that she looked up to find the chief of police glowering back at her, with a concerned looking Derek trailing behind.

"Can I help you?" Claudia said, after ending her call. She wasn't surprised that he had showed up, but she had been hoping for a little more time to get things moving to the point where he would have trouble disrupting them.

"That depends." Lennox clearly hadn't been expecting a crowd, and it was throwing him off his game. He looked around a couple of times, licked his lips, and went on.

"Where were you between five and six-thirty this evening?" he said to Claudia.

"Right here," she replied. "Why?"

"You let me ask the questions. Can anybody verify that?"

Claudia looked around at the assembled group who were watching the scene, goggle-eyed.

"Pretty much everyone. We're setting up for an event, and people have been helping me all evening."

Lennox, faced with a collection of eminently respectable women staring back at him, was dismayed but undaunted.

"Yeah, well, anyone who isn't a personal friend of yours?"

Claudia was flattered that he thought she was so popular that half a dozen people might perjure themselves for her, but even for that she had an answer.

"Yes, as a matter of fact. For most of that time I've been on the phone, the land line, talking to a variety of people who don't care about me at all. I can give you their contact info, and I'm sure you can get the records of the calls from the phone company. Now, would you please tell me what this is about?"

"Neil Hahn was found in Half Moon Cove. He was stabbed with a butcher knife less than an hour ago."

"Is it bad?" Iryna asked.

"Yes, ma'am," Derek said. "He's dead."

Even with the entrance of the police, there had been a certain busy energy in the room, but the effect of the news was like flipping a switch. Everyone was suddenly still, and for Claudia the silence made the horror of the moment that much more vivid. Neil had been alive and well and bothering her in this very room barely more than twenty-four hours ago, and now he was gone, just like Lori. The shock of facing two murders in a row was so severe that Claudia could barely manage to be relieved that she had an unassailable alibi this time.

The rest of the gathering seemed to be working through the issue in their own ways. Unsurprisingly, it was Iryna who recovered her voice first.

"Could it have been an accident?" she asked. "What do you mean, stabbed?"

"I mean that a large knife had been plunged into his body multiple times and left several feet from the body. If you can tell me how that's an accident, I'd like to hear it."

To her amazement, Claudia realized that Lennox was actually shaken. She had become so accustomed to thinking of him as a sort of avatar of obnoxious officialdom that it seemed unbelievable that something like a horrible, violent death might actually be upsetting to him. She wondered what made this body so much worse for him than Lori's. Was it the blood? The outdoor setting? The fact that the sleepy small town where he was supposed to be keeping the peace had experienced two murders in the course of the week, and he had no more ability to solve them than he did to pilot a bumper car to the moon?

Julie had other questions. "Who found him there? Not many people go to Half Moon Cove; there's no light and the trail down those cliffs is beyond dangerous. So how can you be so sure of the time he died?"

"Because he left the Hobnob alive at five, and someone walking by spotted him from above at six-thirty. They spotted some other things, too." He gave a look to Claudia that might have been meant to be menacing, but devolved into confusion. He seemed to be flagging, but then remembered something and rallied.

Lennox turned to Helen, accusingly. "Where's your son?"

The question sent a jolt down Claudia's spine, and out of the corner of her eye she saw Iryna and Carmen exchange a worried glance. She hoped this didn't mean Iryna's friend had gotten over her dislike of Lennox enough to pass on her information, but she couldn't think why else he would suddenly be interested in the boy.

Helen must have been thinking the same thing, because she froze, visibly wilting under the force of the chief's glare.

Ultimately, it was Julie who came to the rescue.

"He's in a truck with my father, somewhere between here and Santa Rosa," she said. "They left over two hours ago to pick up the tables. It's a good ninety minutes each way, and they had to load everything when they got there. I'm sure the folks at the rental place will be happy to confirm when they arrived and left, unless you want to accuse them of being in on it too."

It was obvious that this encounter was not going the way Lennox had expected it to. What Claudia was curious about was, why? There was no secret who his favorite suspect in Lori's death was, and it was possible he knew about Brandon's late-night visit to Lori's house, but even given that, he had been awfully confident when he arrived, and was awfully surprised now.

"Why did you think Brandon or I would have anything to do with killing Mr. Hahn?" Claudia asked. "I've only met him twice, and I don't think Brandon ever heard of him."

"We had received information that certain individuals had been seen in the area," Lennox said stiffly. "It's possible our informants were mistaken."

"Seen in the area? How is that possible? Why would anyone think I was there?" As Claudia said it, a chill of fear gripped her stomach. She turned to Derek.

"Wait a minute. Did you—Did you, um, send me a text earlier today?"

The officer looked back at her with blank confusion.

"A text? No, of course not. Why?"

Reluctantly, Claudia picked up her phone.

"Because I got one, allegedly from you, suggesting that I meet you at Clover Beach tonight. That's only about a mile down the coast from Half Moon Cove." Cringing, she held up her phone as proof. Lennox reached for it, but she retained her grip.

"That's evidence," he protested.

"Then get a warrant," Claudia said. "I'll send you the relevant information, but I'm keeping the phone."

Under other circumstances he might have thrown his weight around some more, but the chief was so discombobulated by the turn of events that he didn't even argue.

Unlike his boss, Derek had been more focused on the content of the message.

"That's not my number," he said. "I don't even know what area code that is. Is it from around here?"

Claudia glanced at the screen.

"No, looks like somewhere near Bakersfield. But nobody has a local phone number these days." A thought struck her, and she got to work excavating her computer from where it was doing vital work holding up a pile of dirty plates.

"Actually, I wonder . . ."

What she was wondering would have to wait to be revealed, because at that moment the truck pulled up with Elias and Brandon and a load of rented furniture. Helen took off like a rocket to meet them, with Lennox right on her heels, and the others followed, Julie to prevent Elias from throwing anything important, and Carmen and Iryna because they weren't about to miss out on the next act. Only Claudia and Betty were left in the house, one focused on her computer screen while the other unpacked another batch of miniature tarts from her seemingly endless supply of plastic containers.

"That's what I thought." Claudia said.

"What?" Betty stopped looking for something on which to serve her baked goods that was more appropriate than a frisbee and came to look over her shoulder.

"Solar panel salesmen? IRS scams? What's going on?" Betty asked, reading down the page Claudia had brought up.

"It's spoofed," Claudia explained. "You pay one of these services and they'll disguise your call or text with a different number. They're mostly used by telemarketers and scammers to trick people into answering. The spoofing services reuse the same numbers all the time. Some people go online to make notes about the calls they get, on sites like this."

"So that's it? There's nothing you can do to find out who sent that text?"

"Nothing I can do," Claudia said, as she made a copy of the page and attached it to an email, along with a screenshot of the text on her phone, then sent both to the printer. "But there's something that can be done."

She found Lennox arguing with Helen about the evidentiary value of the extra canning supplies in her car, while Brandon stood quietly by.

"Brandon," she said, ignoring the others for now. "Did you get a text today? One that asked you to be somewhere tonight? From a number you didn't recognize, but it said it was from someone you knew?"

Brandon's eyes bugged out and for a moment she thought he might be about to accuse her of witchcraft.

"Yea—Yes, how did you know?"

She ignored the question and held out her hand.

"Can I see it? It's important."

Wordlessly, he took out his phone and unlocked it, even as his mother started to protest.

"No you hold onto it," Claudia instructed as he went to hand the phone to her. "I just want to see."

The number wasn't the same as the one she had, but the message was similar.

"Hadley's Point? That's about twenty minutes north of here, right? Pretty remote spot to be going out to at that time of night."

Brandon didn't say anything, but he was blushing so vigorously that Claudia was worried he might pass out. In the interests of kindness, she didn't read the message out loud or comment any further on its contents, though she did have some questions about the sort of people who would name their daughter Kaiylleigh. Instead, she made a note of the number and led the way back into the house, where she put it into the search box on the same website and came up with a similar list of complaints.

"So that's what happened," she said after she finished explaining the existence of phone number spoofing for the second time. "Someone used one of these services to make fake numbers, and sent both of us texts that were supposed to get us out in the area where Mr. Hahn was killed, so one or both of us could be framed for his murder."

It was hard for Claudia to believe that she was talking so casually about a man's death, but this was no time for emotional crises. Lori having died on her doorstep might have been a coincidence, but there was no mistaking the malice in the current situation. Unfortunately, if anyone was going to fail to see that, it was Chief Lennox.

"How do I know you didn't send those yourself?" he said, grasping at the remaining straws that were holding up his beliefs.

"In what universe would I send myself and Brandon fake texts, to set us both up to have no alibi for a time when we both had perfectly good ones?" Claudia said. "Do you have something against evidence that would actually stand up in court? They don't offer these services for free. Someone must have paid for it, and they probably left some sort of paper trail. Find out who they are and maybe you'll get somewhere."

The rest of the volunteers had crowded back into the house at this point, giving Claudia a significant audience for her rant.

Elias, at least, was entirely on her side.

"This is ridiculous," he said, stepping into the doorway and completely blocking Iryna's view. "You say this man was killed tonight? You're sure of that?"

Lennox had to admit that he was.

"Well, then the boy didn't do it, because he was with me. And I am not someone you sneak away from, you know? And Claudia didn't do it because she was here. So stop bothering these people and take the information she is very nicely giving you and go find the real killer. That's what you want to do, right?"

Lennox couldn't argue with that, and facing the only man in the room who was larger than him, it seemed he didn't want to. After making a minor show of reminding everyone who had the authority around here, he finally accepted the printouts that Claudia was offering him (in lieu of handing over her phone, which she kept in a death grip) and left in a huff. Derek paused for a second on their way out the door, and Claudia almost said something to him, but the words, whatever they were, stuck in her throat.

CHAPTER TWENTY

When the police were gone, the air of tension in the cottage relaxed noticeably. Thoughts of planning for the marketplace were forgotten, as they passed around Betty's tarts and exchanged theories.

"He was probably her partner, laundering the money from the drug operation," Iryna said. "He came to find it, and then the mafia killed him too."

"That makes sense," said Helen. "Where do you think she hid it?"

"We don't have any reason to believe Lori had anything to do with drugs," Claudia said, trying to keep the conversation from getting completely out of control.

"Another thing then. Smuggling, or cheating the banks." Iryna was not to be deterred. "She must have been doing something. Otherwise why would she be murdered? And now him?"

"People do get murdered when they haven't done anything wrong," Betty protested. "Mr. Hahn has been staying with us for the past two days, and nothing he's done has made me think he had anything to do with a criminal conspiracy."

"He did seem to be looking for something Lori might have had," Claudia said, thinking out loud. She regretted it almost immediately.

"Something she had?" Julie asked. "Like what?"

"I don't know," Claudia said, trying very hard not to give away her guess. "But the police have been looking through everything of hers, and if there was something incriminating there, you'd think they would have found it by now."

"I don't like it." Elias had been uncharacteristically quiet for most of the conversation, and Claudia was surprised he broke his silence for such an obvious observation. The rest of the party waited for him to elaborate, which, after some more thought, he did.

"The lady dies, okay, it's sad, but it's a big world and lots of crazy things happen. But now this? A man who knew her comes to town, and he's dead too? And why? What could be here that would be worth killing two people for? We sell cheese and pickles and pork, not diamonds and drugs."

"Not everyone gets killed for money," Carmen said. Like Elias, she had mostly stayed out of the conversation, but now she entered it with a vengeance. "A woman moves to a new town and starts a business where nobody knows her. And she keeps it that way—in all the time she was here, did anyone have any sort of conversation where you learned anything about her? Or ever see her spend any of this huge amount of money she's making with all these drugs or whatever?"

A series of sideways looks and shrugs brought the group to a consensus of no on both questions.

"So, yeah, maybe she decided to move here to run a vast criminal enterprise that no one seems to have heard anything about. Or maybe she had other reasons."

"You think she was running from somebody?" Julie asked.

"She might have been." Carmen looked around like she was daring someone to contradict her. "Why else would she have gone to all that trouble? And cheating on her shop like that, it doesn't make any sense. Even the extra money she was making, how much would that be?"

"Not much," Claudia admitted. "I was wondering that myself. As scams go, it's about as small-scale as you get. She would have been better off setting up on the Internet and saving herself the overhead."

"See? That's what I mean. It makes no sense for her to have been here. And it makes no sense that someone killed her. So maybe together, they make sense?" Carmen said.

Claudia looked around the room and marveled at the group she had somehow gathered around her. Five women and two men, all clustered around her table, helping themselves to the pot of mint tea that Betty had somehow conjured from the kitchen cupboards. (Claudia hadn't been aware that she even owned a tea strainer.) Their attitudes covered the gamut from Deeply Apprehensive (Helen), through Concerned But Embarrassed (Brandon), Just Concerned (Julie, Betty), and all the way up to Much Too Enthusiastic (Elias and Iryna, despite Carmen's best attempts).

If you had asked Claudia what she expected to come of her opening an artisanal marketplace in a seaside town, "assembles a mismatched team to investigate a murder" would not have been her first guess.

"But if she was killed by someone she was running away from, then what happened to the man who died tonight?" Julie asked. "Was he running from the same person?"

"Or he might have known who it was," Claudia pointed out. "He was here yesterday, asking me questions. From the way he was talking, it sounded like he was going around to a lot of people. Maybe he found out something that someone didn't want him to know?"

"And did you ever think that person might think you know the same thing?" Betty asked. "You're staying with us again tonight."

"I can't. There's way too much to do," Claudia protested. "Besides, I can take care of myself."

"Claudia, two people have been murdered and somebody just tried to frame you for one of them. Could you just humor me by making a good decision for once?"

Even with the suspicion that everyone else in the room was going to gang up, kidnap her, and force her to take the offer, Claudia might have still tried to decline. But then she had an idea. It might even have been a good one.

"Okay," she said. "You're right. Let's just get finished up here and I'll follow you over."

By the time they got to the ranch, the police had been and gone, taking the dead man's possessions with them and seriously upsetting the remaining guests. Betty took over the job of soothing them from her husband, who was well out of his depth. Claudia hung back and offered to help clean up the dinner dishes while she waited for an opportunity to make her suggestion.

She had armed herself with a dishcloth and was doing her best to keep up with Celene, Betty's part-time employee who helped out in return for boarding her horse in their stable, when Olive appeared at the kitchen door.

"Mom told me to get the eggs for the French toast tomorrow. Are you gonna be here for breakfast?"

"Probably not," Claudia said, adding a clean plate to the stack in the cupboard. "I have a lot to do, so I'll be getting out early. But isn't it a little late to be getting eggs now?"

"Oh, the chickens don't mind if it's me," Olive said airily. "They don't even notice."

Claudia didn't know enough about chicken psychology to dispute that, so she settled for expressing her regrets that she was going to miss the fruits of their labors.

"That's okay," Olive said. "I'll come over and make it for you some other time. You're busy solving the murders right now."

Claudia froze in place, holding a half-dried coffee mug suspended over the dishtowel in her other hand.

"Who told you I was doing that? I mean, I'm not doing that. That's the police's job."

"But they aren't any good at it," Olive said, picking up a dishtowel of her own and taking a water glass from the rack. "And you need to know, don't you? They might come after you next."

"Um, well, I guess that's a possibility. That's why your mom invited me to stay here tonight. But I don't think you should worry about it too much."

Claudia was acutely aware of Celene behind her. She was giving every appearance of someone who was paying no attention to the conversation, but Claudia noticed she had turned down the flow on the tap of the kitchen sink, so that the sound of it didn't interfere with her ability to hear. Claudia didn't blame her; she would have done the same. But she wasn't about to give her anything interesting to share.

So, to Olive, she said, "Is your mom done in the living room yet? I need to ask her about some stuff before she goes to bed?"

"About the murders?" One thing you could say for Olive, she was persistent.

"One hundred percent not about any murders, here or anywhere else." Which was essentially true. Using the ranch's network monitoring software to give her insight into Neil Hahn's recent browser history was not, strictly speaking, about murders, though that could change quickly if she found anything.

If Olive suspected the prevarication, she was kind enough to let it pass. And Celene, having finished her work, reluctantly gave up the hope of hearing any more, leaving Claudia alone to carry out her plan.

"No." Betty's response was firm, and not unexpected. Claudia had come prepared for this.

"But what harm can it do?" she argued. "No one will ever know. And what am I supposed to do, hide in your spare bedroom forever? I need to get a handle on this mystery, or I'm never going to get my life back. If it makes you feel better, you can tell the police tomorrow that you thought of it, and give them anything that's relevant."

Her friend hesitated. There was no question that what she thought

Claudia should do was to go to bed with a borrowed book and a mug of her excellent homemade cocoa. But Betty had once backpacked across Vietnam with nothing but two changes of clothes and an iguana named Sid, and there was enough left of that woman that she was willing to take the occasional risk.

"Okay, fine. But if you find anything, leave it to me to decide who gets told, and how. I don't want guests to think if they come here someone will be going through their underwear."

Claudia gave her solemn word that no laundry, dirty or otherwise, would be aired, and Betty reluctantly led her to the computer, to do her worst.

The room that served as the Tylers' office had started its life as a storage closet, done some time as the heart of a failed mushroom-growing operation, and reached its current status with the addition of a used school desk and a suite of computer equipment, purchased on Claudia's recommendation.

She had also been the one called in after the unfortunate episode of the guest whose combined interests in downloading pirated movies and watching pornography with the sound turned up to eleven had given them a difficult week and made it clear that simply handing out the password was not a good long-term plan. She had gone with one of the simplest security systems on the market, which monitored every device connected to the network and blocked access to a regularly updated list of malicious and inappropriate websites. When she installed it, she had described it to Betty and Roy as a filter for their Internet, and now she was going to see what had gotten caught in it.

She was still able to sign in as an administrator, which was something she was going to need to talk to Betty about, but for the moment it was convenient. Claudia had mostly chosen the software for the website blocking, but another feature it had was that it recorded every URL visited through the ranch's network. There was no record of the contents of anything that might have been transmitted, but she was hoping it might give her something to go on.

Teddy, who had come along on the evacuation and been given her own dinner with the Tylers' dogs, was curled up in the small amount of floor space that wasn't taken up by the chair or the carefully-stored stacks of old copies of *National Geographic*. (The office doubled as storage for anything deemed sufficiently office-y, which also included several boxes of Christmas decorations and old vegetable seed packets.) The chair was one that had been retired from the dining room set after a guest had had the wine-fueled inspiration to reenact one of the velociraptor scenes from *Jurassic Park*, to damaging effect.

Having gotten herself settled as comfortably as possible, Claudia opened the program and reacquainted herself with the interface. There was nothing she particularly expected to find in Neil's browsing history, but his behavior had convinced her he was up to something, and it was Claudia's experience that the modern person, when confronted with a question, looked for answers on the Internet. She had barely known Neil, and what she had known she hadn't particularly liked. But, like Lori, he had been someone who had come into her life and left it violently, and Claudia had had enough of that sort of thing.

The software didn't identify the users by name, but it did assign unique identifiers to their devices, and since there were only three other rooms occupied at the ranch at the moment, plus the family, it didn't take long for Claudia to narrow it down to the likeliest candidate. Of course, there was always the chance that he was the one who had been looking at horses for sale in San Diego county, or the person who seemed to be fixated on a string of news stories about fraud at a small pharmaceutical company, or even the guest who rotated between four different social networking sites with such vigorous regularity that Claudia suspected some sort of compulsion, but she thought she would go with the one who had searched her own name in several iterations.

He had visited the main website for the marketplace, a couple of places that had posted the press release she had created for the opening, her out-of-date professional networking page, a moribund blog she had maintained when she was in college and under the impression the world was more interested in her opinions about classic television shows than turned out to be the case, and an archived obituary for a different Claudia Simcoe, who had died in Omaha in 1987. Nothing he found was private or particularly interesting, but Claudia was sufficiently creeped out to wonder if Neil's death had really been such a bad thing.

Whatever he had been looking for, he seemed to either have found it, or decided it wasn't findable, because from there the history branched out, to a webmail page, from which he seemed to have sent and received several messages (contents unknown), then to a department store's selection of brown shoes, then customer reviews of restaurants in and around San Elmo. Claudia worked her way diligently through them all, not wanting to miss anything that might be relevant.

About halfway down, the list took an odd turn. First there was a fashion blog that had opened up its comment section for readers to chime in with stories of their worst dates, then a syndicated advice column from five years ago, followed by three different dating sites where he had narrowed the search to an area of about fifty miles around San Elmo. None of it made the slightest bit of sense to Claudia, but there was something familiar about some of the URLs. Then it struck her: they were from the list of links that Lori had sent him. Suddenly much more interested, Claudia dug deeper.

She went back through the pages, reading them in detail to look for something that would tie them together. She found it, of all places, halfway down the page of bad date stories. There, intermingled with the tales of creeps and jerks and dates who spent the entire meal talking about the novel they were going to write and then walked out on the check, there was a comment by a woman with the username BeccaC, who had a different story to tell.

"*dating sucks. i used to use one of those sites and all i ever met was losers and then one time i thought i was with a good guy and he lied and took all my money. i never want to trust anyone like that again it's not worth it"*

It was a sad story of broken faith, but that wasn't what Claudia found interesting. In addition to their usernames, each contributor to the site was identified by their city and state, and while it was possible that it didn't mean anything that both this BeccaC and the Rebecca Cobb on Lori's list were from Palmyra, she wasn't accepting any more coincidences at this time.

Claudia leaned back in the chair and let out a gust of breath. So Lori had made a list of names that she kept hidden along with a picture of a former friend, and she had sent a series of website links that were related to that list to her ex-husband. And after her murder he had referred to those links, before being murdered himself. That had to mean something, but what?

She thought about the theories that had been discussed earlier that night around her dining table, specifically, Carmen's idea that Lori had been running from somebody. Could the names on the list be people Lori was trying to get away from, or other victims trying to make the same escape?

Claudia went back over the other webpages, looking for more points of similarity to the list, but if they were there, she didn't have enough information to recognize them. It occurred to her that the list she had might have been an earlier version that Lori had abandoned when she moved on to a different system—that would explain why it was in such an inaccessible place in her storage.

Whatever the list meant, Claudia was more certain than ever that it was important. What she wasn't sure of was how it was going to get her any closer to finding Lori's killer.

CHAPTER TWENTY-ONE

It was late, and Claudia was starting to get loopy, but inertia kept her in front of the computer. She had no reason to think that anyone else who was staying at the ranch might be involved in the murders, but she didn't know for sure, and going through the rest of the recent browser histories was a thing she could do without getting up from her chair and going to bed.

On some level, Claudia was aware that this was snooping beyond the level that Betty had agreed to, and her guests could reasonably be upset if they found out, but Claudia justified her actions by not really looking when she came across anything that didn't look like it could be of interest to her. Which must have been how she didn't notice that she had wandered out of the file for the guest users, into the family's computers.

Curiosity or not, Claudia absolutely was not going to look through what her friend's family had been up to online. That was none of her business and, frankly, she didn't want to know. At least that was what she was planning to think, until she came across a web search for a word with recent connotations. Not a question, just one word plugged into the search box: "garroting."

There were probably a lot of very good reasons why a completely innocent person might look that up, and then click through to a page full of images so unnerving that Claudia instinctively covered her face with her hands the moment they loaded, but thinking of one was causing her some trouble.

There was no turning back now. It took less than a minute to determine that she was looking at the history for Roy's computer, thanks to the farm-supply-focused browser history and the fact that it was identified in the software as "Roy's computer."

Claudia's first hope was that the search had been made after Lori's murder was discovered, in a moment of gruesome but understandable curiosity, but no luck. The timestamps on both page visits put them clearly over a week back, and even a desperate theory about a calendar error that would have changed the date was easily disproved.

No matter what Claudia tried, there didn't seem to be any getting away from the fact that her best friend's husband had been looking into the finer points of killing a person with a piece of wire a mere four days before Lori was murdered in exactly that way.

For a hot moment she considered deleting the record, but better sense prevailed. She wasn't positive, but that seemed like it might be the sort of thing that could be considered tampering with evidence, if there was any evidence to be tampered with. And, more disturbingly, it would be a clear indication that she had seen what she shouldn't have seen, and that could be dangerous.

Claudia didn't like to think about it, but she had to. Personal bias and loyalty to her friend said there was no way Roy could be the murderer, but, thinking rationally, she knew she had to admit the possibility. He would have easily been able to overpower Lori and Neil, and she knew that his habit was to spend the evenings while the guests were eating dinner out in his shop, where he expected not to be disturbed, which would mean he had no alibi for the time of Neil's death.

And, unfortunately, probably not for Lori's murder either. His wife would be the obvious one to provide that, but Claudia knew what a lot of people didn't, that Betty had a snore that could raise the dead, or at least keep them up for a few hours, and because of it, she and Roy had slept in separate bedrooms for most of their marriage. It didn't seem to have done much damage to their relationship, if the three children were anything to go by, but it meant that he could easily have slipped out in the night to kill a moderately annoying woman who, to the best of Claudia's knowledge, he had never met.

She couldn't begin to fathom what his motive would be to kill two people, but what did she know about him? About anyone? And more to the point, what was she going to do right now?

There was a good chance that Betty had told her husband what Claudia was up to; after all, someone accessing their guests' Internet usage was something any responsible host would want to know about. He had been deeply uninterested when Claudia had tried to explain the monitoring system when she installed it, but she didn't doubt that he had understood the basics, and if he had any concerns about someone seeing his browser history, it shouldn't take him long to get worried now. The best Claudia could hope was that the possibility hadn't occurred to him, and to get herself out of the room and away from that telltale link as soon as possible.

So that's what she did, taking only the time to edit her own history. She kept Teddy close to her and hurried down the hall to her room, while simultaneously trying to look as casual as possible (which turned out to be not very). Fortunately, she didn't meet anyone, and the pleasant, softly carpeted hallways of the ranch house remained as unmenacing as ever.

Betty had invited her to let Teddy stay in the rather luxurious kennels her own dogs used, because the room was small and large dogs didn't necessarily make the best roommates, but there was no way Claudia was going to take her up on it now. Fortunately, Teddy didn't seem to mind the tight quarters, waiting patiently on the bed as Claudia tried to pull a chair in front of the door without making too much noise. The room next door was occupied, and she didn't want to have to face questions in the morning about late-night furniture arrangement.

Curled up on the bed, with the light off to not draw attention, the ridiculousness of her situation was not lost on Claudia. She was in her friends' home, with their paying guests a thin wall away, and the idea of anything happening to her here was absurd. But a lot of absurd things had been happening lately, and here in the dark, with those coldly clinical images of strangulation fresh in her mind's eye, being afraid didn't seem very irrational at all.

Claudia didn't know when she fell asleep, or for how long, but she must have because eventually it was morning and she was woken by the alarm on her phone, with sunlight coming through an unfamiliar window and Teddy breathing gently and fragrantly into her face. She got up and changed quickly into the clean clothes she had brought, at the same time wondering how a person could so consistently forget to pack a hairbrush.

Having done the best she could using her fingers as a comb, Claudia went to leave. She planned to leave Betty a note, explaining that she had to get back to get the market set up, which was true, if not absolutely honest. It was early, but not farm-early, and there was no good reason Claudia couldn't have sought out her hosts to say goodbye. But she wasn't doing good reasons these days. So she was just going to leave now, and apologize later.

At least, that was the plan. Just in case, she was rehearsing in her head what she would say if she saw Betty on the way out, which probably would have gone fine except that the person she ran into was Roy.

"Leaving?" he said. Roy was dressed in his usual work clothes of brown pants in heavy-gage denim and plaid shirt, both bearing a variety of unidentifiable stains. He must have been on his way to the stables, because he was carrying two pieces of a broken harness and a small, bladed tool that was probably somehow involved in harness fixing. Under normal circumstances, she wouldn't have found it at all disturbing, just weird that anyone could be doing work that early in the morning, but right now the very last thing she wanted was to be around Roy when he was holding leather straps and a knife.

"Yeah, um, gotta get back and get the market set up. Lot of work." Claudia hadn't meant to imitate his taciturn style, it just came out that way.

Roy nodded.

"Coming back?"

"I don't know. I don't think so. We'll see." That was something she was going to have to deal with later, Claudia thought. In the meantime, it occurred to her that she wasn't being a very good guest.

"Thanks, by the way. For letting me stay. I really appreciate it."

"Any time. Take care of yourself."

Claudia had almost convinced herself that she was getting wound up over something that was no more than a bizarre coincidence, but the way he looked at her as he spoke, wary and like he was looking for some kind of response, made her deeply uncomfortable. Gripping Teddy's leash a little more tightly, she thanked him again and headed down the hallway, only to glance back as she was rounding the corner and find him watching her.

But why? Why would Roy want to kill Lori? That was the question that kept repeating in Claudia's mind as she pulled out of the ranch's driveway a little too fast. Had he somehow been involved with her scheme to sell the handbags, or some other fraud she didn't know about? Was Lori someone he knew from his past? The mind boggled at the possibility—Roy and Lori weren't the sort of people Claudia could ever imagine meeting each other, let alone develop a history.

She tried to remember what Betty had told her about the early days of her and Roy's relationship. She knew they had met on a blind date set up by Betty's roommate when Betty was working as an event coordinator at a Napa restaurant. According to the account told over an afternoon of slightly too much wine, it had been a brief but intense courtship, culminating three months later when the two of them had headed to the courthouse to make it official. Claudia remembered having trouble reconciling that story with a man who seemed to think that multisyllabic words were an unnecessary indulgence, but at the time she had simply credited it as another example of life's rich tapestry.

Now, of course, every unusual thing took on a sinister air. Had her friend been rushed into marrying a psycho? Were there other unsolved deaths in San Elmo that nobody knew about? Wouldn't a successful psycho already know how to garrote someone, without having to look it up on the Internet?

Back at home, Claudia could easily have spent the rest of the day trying to answer those questions, but she had a lot to do and, as early as it was, the day was already getting away from her. Reluctantly, she decided that anything to do with the murders would have to wait for a more convenient time. She hoped the murderer would agree.

That was the plan, anyway, and she was getting her last minute to-do list in order when the phone rang. At this point, Claudia was expecting so many calls that she didn't even check the caller ID, just grabbed the receiver and mumbled "Hello?" through a mouthful of paperclips.

"Hi," said the uncertain voice on the other end of the line. "This is Kara Young. Are you the person who called me the other day?"

Claudia's heart leapt into her throat and got stuck there.

"Yes, I am," she said, trying not to croak. "I'm sorry if I said something to offend you. I didn't know, well, anything really. I was just trying to find some answers."

"Yeah, I looked up that lady you mentioned, Lori Roth. She got murdered?"

Claudia admitted that was true.

"Do you think it had anything to do with, with that list you said you found?"

"I don't know," Claudia said. "That was what I was trying to find out. Have the police been in touch with you? They're the ones who have it now."

"No, I haven't heard anything. But I, I think I know what it was about."

Claudia held her breath, not wanting the least sound from her to derail the revelation.

"It was a man," Kara went on, her voice thick with bitterness. "The best, worst man I ever met. Left me with a broken heart and a pile of debt."

"Um, wow. I mean, I'm sorry." She cast her mind quickly back over Kara's entry in the book. "Is that what the '5k cousin cancer' thing was about?" The produce truck was supposed to arrive in twenty minutes and Claudia's cell phone was buzzing with a call from Julie, but for the moment her real-life responsibilities were dead to her. She cradled the phone with both hands, as though she could coax the answers out of the receiver, and waited for more.

"Yes, that's how I knew what you were talking about," Kara said. "It was a guy I was dating for a while. He'd borrowed some money from me before, small amounts here and there, but then one day he comes to me with this story about his little cousin who has cancer, and she's going to die if they don't get her this experimental drug. So, like a chump, I totally fell for it. Gave him all the money I could scrape together, held up my family and friends, the whole deal. I even passed around flyers at work. Anyway, long story short, there was no cousin, there was no cancer, and as soon as he cashed the check there was no man."

"What did he look like?"

"Tall, Caucasian, brown hair, and the most amazing green eyes you've ever seen. Seriously, I think those eyes got me for at least two grand on their own. He said his name was Steve Mann, but I'm pretty sure that was an alias. After he left with the money, I tried to track him down, and none of the info he gave me about himself checked out. I guess I could have done more, filed a report with the police or something, but I was just so damn embarrassed, you know? I never thought I could be that stupid. That's why I hung up on you last time. I couldn't deal with the idea that anything about him was coming back into my life."

"When did this happen?"

"About ten years ago now, I guess. It doesn't seem like that long."

"Do you have any photos of him?"

"Not really. We met online, and there was a photo on his profile, but it wasn't very good quality, and when I went back later he had taken it down. Actually, a lot of our relationship was on the phone and the Internet, and when we were together he was always the one offering to take the pictures. It didn't seem like anything at the time, but after it was over I went and looked, and it seemed like any time I was taking a photo he had his back turned, or was just out of the frame. I guess having a bunch of pictures of him with different names floating around would really cramp his style." The bitterness in her voice was blended with anger, though whether it was at herself or the alleged Steve was unclear.

Claudia hated to press her, but she couldn't let it go at that.

"Do you think there's a chance that someone else might have gotten a clear shot of him? The number of pictures people take these days, he must have slipped up at some point."

"I'll ask around, but I'm not sure it'll do much good. Steve tended to avoid hanging out with my friends, and he didn't want me to either, which I totally didn't think was a problem, because I'm an idiot. Actually, we didn't see that much of each other at all, even after we met in person because he had so many work commitments. Honestly, there were so many red flags there, I could have started a semaphore school."

"You're being too hard on yourself. This guy has probably been doing this for years," Claudia said, as another question occurred to her. "How old would you say he was, anyway?"

"Twenty-seven, according to him, but that was probably a lie too.

I even suspected that at the time, just because there were some things he would get wrong. I just figured he was self-conscious, because I was younger. God damn, I was so young."

Claudia agreed that it was an unfortunate condition and tried to work the conversation back around to more relevant information.

"What city were you in then, if you don't mind me asking?"

"Baltimore, but Steve didn't live there. He said he was in D.C., but I never saw his place, so who knows. Why do you want to know all this, anyway?"

Claudia was ready for that one.

"Well, like I said, I found that list after Lori, the woman who was making it, was killed. I don't know how much of the story you've been following, but nobody knows who did it, and now another man was murdered last night. So, you know, I'm feeling kind of nervous, and if there's someone around here who isn't who they say they are, I'd like to find out who it might be."

"Wow, okay. Yeah. Obviously, I didn't have the best impression of Steve, but I can't really imagine him as a murderer. But I can see why you would want to know. I wish I could draw a picture of him for you, or something, but that's not really something I'm good at. Maybe I could use one of those sketch sets like they have for police artists?"

"That would be fantastic," Claudia said. "Anything you can do. I really appreciate you talking to me, by the way. I know it can't be fun, revisiting all of this."

"You're welcome. But it's okay, actually. I've spent so long beating myself up about it, I never actually got to looking at what happened and what I did. I mean, I was dumb, but I'm okay, and it's not the worst thing anyone ever did, right?"

"Right," said Claudia, who could think of a few worse things right off the top of her head. "Absolutely."

CHAPTER TWENTY-TWO

They talked for a little while longer, but there wasn't much more Kara could tell her. The romantic hero formerly known as Steve Mann had been tall, probably over six feet, but not by much (though Kara revealed that, at five-foot-two herself, she wasn't the best judge of heights), no younger than twenty-two and no older than, say forty-five, even with really good plastic surgery. Everything else about him could have been changed with time and cosmetic enhancements, though Kara thought that if she got a look at him she would be able to pick him out, regardless of superficial changes.

Claudia promised to put together a set of pictures of possible candidates and send them to her, ignoring for the moment that that was something she absolutely did not have time for right now. But time was what you made of it, and for now Claudia was making herself some by drawing the curtains, turning off her phone, and taking her computer down onto the floor behind the couch so no one could spot her.

She had no doubt now that this was what Lori's list was about; the details from Kara and the comment from the mysterious BeccaC confirmed that. Unfortunately, with those answers came more questions, and there was one in particular Claudia didn't relish asking, but she was going to need to if she was going to send those pictures.

Brandon was too young, Elias was too old. Victor, Brandon's father, roughly fit the age range, but he was unlikely to pass for Caucasian. Technically, Roy was still in the running, though she would have to find out if he had spent any significant time out of state early in his marriage. Orlan, the vegetable market owner, couldn't be more than five foot six in tall shoes, and none of his regular employees would have been out of grade school for the critical time. That left her with Robbie, and Claudia didn't appreciate the gift.

He was the right age, height, and general attractiveness, probably more so if you shaved off the beard. She knew he and Emmanuelle had only been together for four years, and whenever he was asked about his previous life, he had a tendency to be genially vague about the details. What's more, she realized, as she scrolled through his various web presences, for someone whose wife was so deeply involved in social media, there weren't many good pictures of him.

She put a few of the best she could find, plus a cropped image of Roy from Betty's last Christmas card into an email to Kara, and included a link to a local website that had collected photos from various town events, just in case there was a familiar face there. After all, it didn't have to be anyone associated with the marketplace at all, or even living in San Elmo. But it did have to be someone who had her and Brandon's phone numbers, and knew enough to send them the messages.

That certainly included her two main candidates, but there must have been someone else. What about Neil? Not that he was likely to have participated in his own murder, but could Lori's ex-husband have been a con artist, and killed her when she tried to expose him? He hadn't struck Claudia as a particularly attractive or charismatic man, but a lot can happen in ten years, and beauty is in the eye of the beholder. Still, that left the question open as to who killed him—Claudia thought it was stretching belief to have two separate murderers at work.

But maybe there didn't have to be. What if Lori hadn't been a victim in the scam, but a participant? Maybe she had helped Neil identify the victims and string them along until he got them to empty their bank accounts. And maybe their latest victim had caught on and taken her revenge on both of her tormentors.

That opened up her field quite a bit. Helen, Julie, Emmanuelle—if she was being open-minded about it, Carmen and Iryna could even be suspects. Which pretty much took her back to where she started, suspecting everyone and knowing nothing.

That wasn't completely true, but the theory did leave a lot of unanswered questions, like why Neil had showed up and made a point out of his connection to Lori if the goal was to keep from being exposed. The only reason he would do something like that was if there was some sort of evidence in Lori's possession that was worth the risk to prevent anyone else from finding. The list was a candidate, Claudia supposed, though it seemed too vague to count as hard evidence. But there was no denying that Neil had been eager to get at Lori's things, and agitated when he found out they were gone. Claudia was starting to regret that she hadn't done a better job of searching, but in her defense, there had been a lot of bags in there.

She was stewing over that when the rising noise of voices from outside pulled her back to the present. The outdoor market had been her idea, after all, and she could work on her theories and regrets while she set up tables.

The sun was well up now, and the day was bright and sharp, without a hint of wind. By the time Claudia made it down to the parking lot it was already starting to crowd with people and trucks and a rising sense of chaos that served as a rebuke for her tardiness. She hurried to join them, trying her best to look like someone who had been detained by something important and unavoidable, and hoping no one had seen her close the curtains.

Elias had come back with the truck and the tables he and Brandon had picked up the night before, and was directing them to be set up in exactly the wrong places. She spent the next twenty minutes or so sorting that out, and by the time they had been arranged to most people's satisfaction, the rest of the vendors and the charity groups had shown up and were squabbling passive-aggressively over who needed to be where.

Claudia brandished her plan, found herself ignored and brandished it a little louder. Eventually they got things settled down, with Carmen and Iryna having enough power to heat their offerings and Julie and Elias with enough shade for their cheeses, and the corgis kept well away from all of it. (Victor was helpful in that regard.) Throughout the activity, Claudia kept sneaking glances at all of them, trying and failing to reconcile the friendly, mostly helpful faces around her with the brutal murders of two people.

"What do you think? Too harsh?"

"I'm sorry?"

"The colors. I'm worried the green and the purple together are ugly." Helen was standing back and contemplating her display with a critical eye. "I was going to do red, but Brandon said that would look like Christmas."

"The green is pretty much unavoidable," Claudia agreed, surveying the array of pickles. "I think the purple is fine. We want a festive atmosphere; this isn't a New York cocktail party."

Helen was unconvinced, so Claudia said she'd leave it to her judgement and moved on. She would have liked to slip a question in about whether she had ever had a dalliance with a younger man who may or may not have stolen a lot of money, but it was difficult to introduce the subject. She ran into the same problem a moment later, when Julie came to her with a question about sales tax.

"That should take care of it," Claudia said, once they had settled the matter. "By the way, I'm sorry that you all got dragged into that scene last night, with the police and everything. I hope your father wasn't too upset by it."

"Are you kidding? Pop hasn't had that much fun in ages. I could barely get him to go to bed last night, he was so convinced that it was up to him to keep poor Brandon out of the electric chair. If we hadn't had to be here this morning, he'd be over at the rental place, getting signed affidavits from the employees."

"Well, I'm glad he's enjoying himself." That sounded more sarcastic than Claudia intended, so she quickly backtracked. "I mean, this whole thing has been a horrible mess, and I appreciate you all sticking with me and having such a good attitude."

"Don't think about it," Julie said. "None of us are having it nearly as rough as you. Honestly, I'm amazed you're doing all this. I have to admit, most folks thought you'd pack up and head back to the city."

It wasn't the greatest vote of confidence Claudia had ever gotten, but she could hardly blame them for doubting her. It was no less than she had thought of herself.

"Well, I didn't," Claudia said, unnecessarily. "And I'm not going to." The activity level in the parking lot was picking up, and she didn't have time for many more questions, so she decided to skip the formalities and get right to it.

"By the way, yesterday, when you went to the library, you would go past Half Moon Cove, right? Is there any chance you saw Neil Hahn there, or anyone else?"

Julie looked thoughtful, like she was trying to remember, then shook her head.

"If I did, I didn't pay them any mind. I never met Mr. Hahn, so I wouldn't recognize him, and I wasn't paying much attention to who was out and about anyway. If I'd seen someone walking along with a bloody knife, I would have mentioned it to the police, you know."

"Of course, sorry. It was a dumb question." It was also a question that didn't seem to rattle Julie at all by reminding her that she could be placed in the general area of the second murder. Not that that proved anything. It was possible that a person who was engaged in a campaign of murderous revenge might not be too upset by the occasional inconvenient question.

The market was scheduled to open at eleven, and though it was barely past ten, a scattering of cars were starting to line up in the parking spaces along the road. Claudia hadn't been expecting this, and from the way the rest of the vendors kept sneaking glances at the early arrivals, she guessed neither had anyone else.

Except, it seemed, Emmanuelle.

"Not bad," she said, like a connoisseur surprised by an inexpensive bottle of wine. "My post from yesterday wasn't tracking very well, but I had a nice uptick in faves this morning, so I think we'll do okay. But it's so hard to tell, you know?"

"Oh, definitely," Claudia said. (She didn't know.) "By the way, is Robbie around? I was hoping he could help me with something." She didn't care to specify what that thing was, and fortunately Emmanuelle didn't ask.

"He'll be here soon. He had a batch of bacon in the smoker, and he wanted to get it done in time to debut it today. He's been experimenting with some new curing techniques, and trying a sort of honey infusion."

"That's great. I can't wait to try it. Is that what he was working on last night?" Claudia wasn't sure whether bacon could be an alibi, but it was worth asking.

"I think so. To be honest, I was kind of busy with some new greeting cards I'm designing for this collaboration thing, and I wasn't paying attention. I'm sorry we didn't come over to help with the setup, I'm sure you had a lot to do."

"Don't worry about it, I had plenty of help." And witnesses for her alibi, which Claudia couldn't help noticing was something Emmanuelle and Robbie lacked. She also thought it was interesting that they couldn't vouch for each other. Which might not mean anything, but it might mean a lot.

But there was no time to get into that now, and Claudia was about to move on, when it occurred to her that there was something else she needed to ask Emmanuelle.

"You know, I really appreciate you taking point on all the social media for this event. It's been a big help. There's one thing I'm worried about, though, with Lori's murder, and then Neil Hahn last night, are people talking about that a lot?"

Emmanuelle looked uncomfortable.

"Well, it has come up," she admitted. "Mostly just jokes, but there have been some theories. I guess I should warn you, there might be a few people who think they are going to come here and solve the murders themselves."

"That's crazy," Claudia said with a completely straight face. "Why would anyone do that?"

Emmanuelle shook her head.

"It's the Internet. What are you going to do?"

Claudia was still determined to get a conversation in with Robbie at some point, but he had just arrived with a carload of pork products and was too busy for chatting. She tried to make it over to him several times, but there were a few setbacks with getting the burners set up to cook the pierogis, and not lighting the rented tables on fire seemed like a slightly higher priority than whatever she was going to say to Robbie.

She did get a chance to try some of the bacon, though, when Julie brought her a piece. It was good enough for Claudia to wonder if maybe some crimes could be excused for the sake of truly fine cured meats.

There was one quiet moment, when all the tables had been laid out and before the gates were opened (or, more accurately, the piece of temporary fencing untied from the signposts), which Claudia was using to center herself and ask herself why she actually hadn't left town when the trouble started, because that seemed like a pretty good idea. Naturally, this was when Robbie vanished into one of the portable toilets, where he stayed far longer than Claudia would have thought anyone would find bearable, and in the meantime she was approached by Carmen.

"Have you tried the pear empanadas? Iryna wanted to call them 'em-pear-nadas,' but I put a stop to that," she said with a snort. Carmen's legendarily low tolerance for foolishness was respected and feared by everyone but her wife, who seemed to view it as a personal challenge. There were certain branches of the local grapevine that considered this a sign their relationship was doomed, but Claudia suspected they both thought it was part of the fun.

"I did, and they're great. When did you find the time to make them?" she asked. Carmen and Iryna hadn't left the cottage until after nine, and judging by the setup at their booth, they had been some of the first arrivals that morning.

"Oh, I hardly sleep anymore. Because I'm getting old, I think. My grandfather was the same way. So I figure, as long as I'm up, I might as well get something done, right? Papa used to make magazine racks in his woodshop. Do you know how many magazine racks a person needs? Not that many, I can tell you."

Claudia admitted that she had zero, and had never felt the lack. Carmen wasn't high on her list of suspects, but since she had her, she figured she might as well take the opportunity.

"I'm still getting over what happened last night," she said. "I only met Neil Hahn twice, but I certainly didn't expect him to turn up dead like that. Did you run into him at all while he was in town?"

"No. I hadn't even heard his name before that oaf Lennox showed up and started tossing around accusations. You said he was Lori's husband? The dead man, I mean, not Mr. Police Chief."

"Ex-husband, yes. Which is weird, isn't it? It wasn't totally clear what he was doing here, and now I guess we'll never know."

Carmen shook her head. "What crazy times these are. The whole time we've lived in San Elmo, I don't think there's been a single murder, and now two at once. You don't think of that happening here. A day like this, what could happen?" She gestured toward the distant view, where the bowl of bright blue sky met the sparkling ocean, as though nice weather was a guarantee against violence.

"You were living in a big city before, on the East coast, right? I guess this doesn't seem so scary by comparison," Claudia said, trying another approach. But Carmen wasn't biting.

"It's different here, though. And having it be someone I knew—not the man, but Lori at least. You don't expect that."

"No, you don't." Claudia was trying to think of a way to work the conversation back around to whether Carmen had really never met Neil before, but before she had the chance, a luxury charter bus pulled up alongside the parking lot. The doors opened and a young woman with a clipboard leaned out and looked around.

"Is this where the fine foods event is?" she asked, in what Claudia could only describe as an authoritative yelp.

"Um, yes?" she said. She wasn't aware of any promotional material that had used that wording, and she was definitely sure she hadn't ordered a bus, but it seemed like the only plausible answer.

"Good," said the interloper. "When do the tours start?"

CHAPTER TWENTY-THREE

They were eventually able to convince the tour guide that, regardless of what her clients had been promised, there was no pickle production facility available to be visited, and she finally settled on letting them in for the "market preview hour" Claudia made up on the spot. Everything was pretty much ready, so it wasn't too great of a hardship. And there was no question it was a relief when the first sales started to go through.

The next couple of hours were a blur. Cars pulled up, blocked traffic, parked inappropriately, people got out, packed into the lot, wandered out of the lot and irritated the geese. Sales were made, cheeses were explained, pickling techniques were argued about. The crowds waxed and waned, and varied between random passers-by who got distracted on their way to the beach, and a surprisingly dedicated crowd of food-enthusiasts who mostly seemed to have found out about the market through Emmanuelle's outreach efforts.

Claudia's informal polling efforts were interrupted when she was approached by a man she didn't recognize.

"Claudia Simcoe? Hi, I'm Todd Thompson."

The society reporter for the *West County Gazette* was a barrel-shaped man who looked like a cuddly Viking, but with more earrings. He was probably in his early forties, with curly brown hair and a tightly trimmed beard, dressed in battered cargo shorts and a T-shirt advertising a long-past music festival, and accessorized with an array of woven bracelets and a scrimshaw necklace on a leather cord.

"Nice to meet you in person," Claudia said. "And thanks so much for getting that story in the paper." It had been barely more than a blurb, but so far the market was enough of a success that she was happy to spread the credit around.

"Not a problem. I like to think of myself as the guy with his finger on the pulse, and this crowd you've got here is making me look good. Are you going to be doing more of these?"

"We'll see. Not right away, at least. I don't think this weather is set to last through tonight, anyway," Claudia said, keeping half an eye on the group of people who had descended on the pickle table, led by a man who was loudly holding forth about the products to a deeply unimpressed Helen, plainly unaware of how much trouble he was asking for. She was set to intervene when Betty swooped in, driving off the kimchi-splainer with an exchange Claudia didn't quite catch. As he stalked away, Claudia's friend caught her eye and gave a quick thumbs up, and she smiled back, grateful for the support.

". . . and that's why it was so short. But next time I should get more space."

"What? I'm sorry, I was distracted for a minute there." Claudia had come back into the conversation just in time to catch the last of what he was saying, but not enough to be able to respond without embarrassing herself further.

Todd was unruffled. "I was just saying that my bosses weren't very enthusiastic about writing up this event, but with things going this well, I think they'll change their minds. People who spend money are a newspaper publisher's favorite people."

"Yeah, they're pretty popular with me, too." Claudia had the sense that they were talking around the main point. However pleased he might be now, Todd had only done the original write-up as a quid pro quo for information about the murder, and Claudia didn't think he would have forgotten that for the sake of a crowd of cheese shoppers.

As if on cue, Todd ran a hand over his beard and raised an eyebrow at her.

"So, I have to ask, do you have some sort of direct line to the underworld?" he asked.

"What do you mean?" Claudia wondered for a minute if Iryna had been sharing her theories about mob involvement.

"You gave me three names the other day, and two of them are dead."

"Two of them?"

"Looks that way. The ex-husband, obviously, and that other one, the friend of the victim? I looked her up, and if I've got the right person, then she committed suicide five years ago."

"Suicide? Are you sure?" Claudia tried to look surprised, but given what she had learned from Lori's emails, she had already suspected Dana might have killed herself.

"She left a note. I couldn't find out what it said, but I guess the police didn't find anything suspicious, because there was never a case filed on it. She was cremated, and her family held a small, private memorial service, no obituary."

"You found all that out in two days?"

"I have skills, lady."

"I guess so. What about name number three? I take it that at least our favorite cultist is alive and kicking?"

"You could say that," Todd agreed, suddenly cagey. "Nothing to do with Ms. Roth, that I could find, but he's, well, let's just say he's an interesting guy. I have to thank you for pointing me to him, and that's all I'm going to say right now."

"Any time." Claudia thought about what she knew of Mr. Bartok and how he had dealt with previous opposition to his operation, and added, "Watch out for snakes."

"Will do. So, is there anything else you'd like to mention? Between you and me, it's been a slow news week, and the publisher is looking for us to bump up the coverage on this murder thing. I don't suppose you'd be interested in getting out ahead of that, would you?"

Claudia was about to upbraid him for not even concealing his threats better, but before she got the words out, she realized there was a better option.

"I don't know what you think I'd be in front of," she said, in the coldest tone she could manage on short notice. "But if you want to do some actual reporting, I have someone who might be willing to talk to you. You have a lot of pictures from events around here, right?"

Todd agreed that this was the case.

"Okay then." Claudia fished a piece of paper out of her pocket, making sure it didn't contain anything incriminating before scribbling Kara Young's email address on it.

"Write to this woman and mention my name, and see if she's willing to look through your photo archive for someone she might recognize. I can't guarantee that she will, but if she does, then you've got all the story you could ever want."

"Can you be a little more vague there?" Todd complained. "Want to throw in a reference to a Bible verse, or something about the phase of the moon?"

"Sorry," Claudia said, quickly seeking out something that needed her attention. She had said as much as was safe, and possibly more. "That's what I've got. Looks like there's a bit of a situation with the pierogis; I'd better go. Why don't we catch up later over email? Enjoy the market."

She walked away before his disappointed look could penetrate her defenses, reminding herself that she needed to keep herself safe a lot more than she needed a new friend. Todd Thompson might have thought his information should have bought him more in return, but she hadn't made any deals like that. And besides, the pierogi situation really was getting critical.

From there on, Claudia didn't have a lot of opportunities to investigate. Nobody working at the market had done anything like this before, so the opportunities for problems were extensive, and thoroughly explored. Eventually, though, the stream of crises slowed to a trickle and they were all able to catch their breath. The sun was getting low in the sky and the wind had picked up, carrying a cold edge that promised the fog was on its way. Iryna and Carmen had sold out of all their stock almost an hour ago, and the Paks' booth was adorned with a single, lonely tub of pickled seaweed. A few stragglers stayed on past the official closing, and by the time they were finally ushered out of the parking lot, there was only a narrow window to get the tables taken down and loaded back onto Elias's truck in order to return them to the rental place on time.

Claudia tried to maneuver herself into having a chance to talk to Robbie alone, but even when she did, it was hard to get the conversation to the point where she could naturally bring up Lori or her former friend's tragic end. It wasn't until they were going around doing the final cleanup that she got a chance to corner Robbie near a bad patch of detritus.

"Thanks for staying," she said. "You didn't need to, you guys have done so much."

"Hey, no problem. Keeps the party going, you know?" He smiled like they were friends having a great time, not a landlord and leasee picking up dirty paper plates. Robbie still wasn't her type, but the charm went a long way. Which brought her back to the investigation.

"I just glad there was a party in the first place. The promotion Emmanuelle did for us was a big help, and it was great that we were able to get a mention in the paper. By the way, I was talking to the reporter, and he mentioned someone he thought you knew—a Dana Herschel?"

Her attempt got her nothing but a blank look in return.

"I don't think so. There was a girl named Dana I worked with down in San Diego, but I think her last name was Chen. Maybe she got married?"

"Maybe that's it." Claudia had no business being disappointed with that pathetic gambit, but she was.

"When were you in San Diego?" she said, trying again. "I didn't realize you'd spent much time on the West Coast before. Weren't you living in DC for a while there?"

That got a response.

"Who told you that?" Robbie asked sharply, before catching himself and reverting to his previous, relaxed self. "Actually, yeah. But that was a long time ago. Different life."

He made it sound tossed-off, but with a dark edge to his tone that made it clear the subject was closed. Claudia wasn't interested in pressing her luck, so she moved on to another line of inquiry.

"I tried some of your bacon, by the way, and it was great," she said as she carefully maneuvered a half-eaten cheese sandwich into her trash bag, trying not to think about why it was so damp on the edges. "Emmanuelle said you were working on it all last night."

"Yeah, you really have to watch the smoker when you've got something with so much sugar. A little too much heat and you're halfway to charcoal."

"Right, of course." Claudia wasn't sure how she could check it, but nonburned bacon seemed like a pretty thin alibi.

"Is everything under control here?" From the way she was carrying her bags, it was clear that Julie meant this less as a request for information and more as a prelude to leaving. Claudia answered in the affirmative, because what else could she say?

"Okay then, I think we're going to head out. We're releasing the two-year gouda next week and I need to make sure everything is ready to ship."

"Of course, thanks for everything you've done," Claudia said.

"By the way," Claudia added, as Robbie moved out of earshot. "There was a reporter who was here earlier who was asking some questions about Lori's murder. I didn't tell him anything, of course, but I was just wondering, have you ever heard of someone named Steve Mann?"

Claudia figured she was only going to get one question in before it looked weird, and gambled on the chance that Julie had been one of the mystery man's other victims, and he had used the same name on her.

"Sorry, doesn't ring a bell. Who is he?"

"I'm not sure," Claudia said with absolute honesty. "But it seems like Lori might have gotten tangled up with him in the past. Him and a lady named Dana Herschel."

That was probably less subtle than was ideal, but Julie's mind was on her cheeses, and the question barely seemed to make an impact.

"No idea. I hope that reporter knows what he's talking about, and he's not just throwing people's names around for no reason."

"Me too," Claudia said, feigning a sudden concern for the feelings of a pseudonymous scammer and a dead woman. "He did seem pretty aggressive about his theories. But I can't imagine a reporter for a small regional paper is going to be able to do that much."

"I wouldn't be so sure," Julie warned. "It doesn't take a lot for a person to make trouble these days. I hope he wasn't trying too hard to get information from you?"

"I had to be nice, because he was doing a write-up about the marketplace," Claudia said, by way of deflecting the question. "But I don't think I told him anything he could run with."

"Don't believe that. Those people can spin a story out of two guesses and a hiccup, and the whole world will believe them. The best thing you can do there is lock your doors and pretend to be deaf."

Julie had never said anything like this to her before, and Claudia had no idea where this animosity against the press had come from. But that didn't seem like a question she could ask, so Claudia just promised that she would be more careful when dealing with the dastardly members of the local media, and thanked Julie again for all she had done to make the market day a success. On those cheerful terms they parted, and Claudia tried not to think too much about what would happen if her marquee tenant turned out to have killed two people in a vengeful fury. It would take out the Christmas season, at the very least.

Once the Dancing Cow van pulled away, the rest of the vendors didn't take long to follow. The weather was also done with its contribution, and soon there was just Claudia, cleaning up the last of the detritus of the day in the gathering fog.

She was involved with the problem of whether she could leave the extension cords out overnight, or if she really needed to haul them back to her cottage, when she remembered she had left Iryna's cooler behind the marketplace building to keep it out of the way of crowds who had started opening everything in reach. She went to retrieve it, discovering on the way back that some of the guests had turned the back corner of the building into an impromptu smoking section.

She spent the next couple of minutes bussing cigarette butts and swearing about people in general until she caught a glimpse of movement in the corner of her eye and realized she wasn't alone. Mid-swear, she looked up and found herself face to face with Roy.

"Betty sent me to get you," he said.

CHAPTER TWENTY-FOUR

"Um, I'm not sure. I have a lot to do here still." It hadn't occurred to Claudia that her friend would send her husband, and she was torn between fear and the awkwardness of the situation.

"Want some help? Be dark soon."

It was an innocuous comment, said in Roy's normal, level tone of voice, but it was about then that the paranoia started to overtake Claudia. Why didn't Betty just call? Did she even know Roy had come? Claudia looked around, but the last car had pulled out of the lot several minutes ago, and there was no one left for her to casually inform where she was going.

"I appreciate the offer, but it's all accounting stuff that I've got left," she said, casting around for a topic that Roy wasn't likely to want to help with. "But maybe if I get done before it's too late I'll come over. Can you tell Betty that, and thank her for me?"

If anything was going to happen, that was the moment Claudia thought it would. But Roy seemed to take the rejection the same way he took everything: with a thoughtful blankness, as if he was going to have a reaction as soon as he worked through all the implications.

"Okay," he said.

He left, and Claudia decided that she had had enough of being out in the parking lot on her own. She had brought her car, because even a short distance was too much to carry all she had over the uneven and rocky hillside, without any hands free to defend herself against the geese (who had been seriously annoyed by all the activity, and had spent most of the afternoon glaring goosily at the customers). She felt silly doing the loading and unloading so close together, but she consoled herself with the fact that there was no one around to see her.

At least, that was what she thought. Claudia had just finished bringing in the cash box and pay point hardware, stowing them in her high-security spot behind the couch (if there was one thing she had learned from this experience, it was that she needed to get a safe that was located somewhere other than the marketplace itself), when she noticed someone wandering around the parking lot, among the scattering of chairs and other large items she had left for last.

The last thing she had patience for right now was some jerk messing with her stuff, so Claudia took off across the hillside, barely stopping to lock her front door. She came over the crest of the hill at full speed, and was about to shout at him that the market was closed, until she recognized the uniform and realized who it was.

"Oh, hi," she said to Derek, as she arrived, slightly out of breath. "Sorry, I didn't see you drive up."

"No worries, I wasn't sure if you had the lot opened back up yet so I parked down the street. I was just passing by, thought I'd see how things went." He looked around the remains of the day's activities with a rueful smile. "Looks like I missed all the fun."

"All over but the shouting," Claudia agreed. "And I don't think I have the energy for much more than a whisper at this point. But I think it went well, on the whole."

"That's good." Derek looked awkward and embarrassed, shifting his flashlight from one hand to the other and avoiding Claudia's eyes. "Look, I'm sorry about all of the trouble this is causing you. My boss, he gets an idea in his head, and that's got to be the truth, you know?"

"I didn't kill Lori," Claudia insisted. "I swear, I had nothing to do with it."

"Yeah, I think even the chief is starting to come around on that, after what happened last night. Like I said, once he gets an idea, he tends to stick with it, but he doesn't deal with contradictory information real well. The thing where you had such a good alibi for Mr. Hahn's murder, and the texts, that really threw him for a loop. He was going pretty crazy about it for a while there, but he's settled on a new theory, and I probably shouldn't tell you this, but you aren't his first choice anymore."

"Thanks, I appreciate that." Claudia was surprised, both by the information and who it was coming from. That he wasn't supposed to tell her was the understatement of the day, assuming it was true. She reminded herself that this could still be some sort of setup, and not to lower her guard, and then promptly forgot to take her own advice.

"I don't suppose you can tell me who he's suspecting now?" she asked as she gathered the remaining supplies into one place, for easier loading once she brought her car back. Derek shook his head reproachfully.

"Of course not. I've talked too much already. But I can do one better." He reached into his pocket and pulled out a familiar set of keys. "That lawyer of yours has been bugging the chief, and now that you're off the top of the suspect list, he was okay with letting you back into the marketplace."

"No kidding?" Claudia stared at the keys dangling from his hand like she couldn't believe they were real.

"No kidding at all. We were done with the crime scene a long time ago, unofficially, of course. I think it's starting to occur to the chief that he might be setting himself up for some trouble down the line, and he's hoping you'll let bygones be bygones."

"I'm not making any promises," Claudia said cautiously, still eyeing the precious keys hungrily. "But a person is a lot less likely to complain about a problem they don't have, you know?"

As assurances went, she thought that was pretty vague, but apparently it was enough for Derek, who handed over the keys and removed the crime scene tape from the door with a theatrical flourish.

"Your palace, madam."

Claudia was so happy and relieved she almost giggled.

Entering the darkened marketplace, the first thing that struck her was the smell. Despite the mostly cool weather, five days turned out to be beyond the coping limit of even the most farm-fresh cabbage. The second thing, as soon as she turned on the lights, were the memories of the last time she had been in here. She had spent a lot of time in the last few days thinking about what had led to Lori's murder, and it occurred to her at that moment that one of the reasons might have been to avoid having to think about finding the corpse, and the terrible violence of her death.

Desperate to distract herself, and hoping for a little more information, she turned the conversation back to what Derek had mentioned about Chief Lennox's ideas about the killer.

"So, this new theory of your boss's must be pretty good if he's letting you do all this for me. Is it something you guys learned about Neil Hahn while he was here?"

Fortunately, Derek chose to be more amused than annoyed by her transparent bid for information.

"Nice try, but no. We didn't even know who he was until he turned up dead. Had to get his name from his driver's license, and it was your friends at the ranch who told us how he was related to Ms. Roth."

They were standing near Lori's booth, which Claudia hadn't really seen since the night she had told Lori she needed to close it. Looking at it now, it seemed painfully obvious that the bags and napkins and fabric-covered journals weren't handmade, with their vivid colors and curiously uniform designs. But she had fallen for it, never even asked a question. That was the problem, Claudia thought. She had to learn to be less trusting.

The goods were in minor disarray, like someone had looked through them, but hadn't made much of a job of it. She wondered if the police had even paid that much attention to the boxes from Lori's storage. Her hope, in not sharing what she had learned about the list Lori was keeping, was that they would have found it themselves and come to the same conclusions, but now she wasn't so sure. It would be just like Lennox to miss everything important. She was happy to not be his top suspect anymore, but that just meant that someone else was, and there was a chance that person was just as innocent.

"About those boxes of Lori's, and Neil. I think he might have been looking for the list."

"What list?"

Claudia cringed at the sudden sound of accusation in his voice. Things had been going so well. But she had come this far, and there was no turning back now.

"I guess I have a confession to make," she said. "Those boxes that Lori had stored with me, that I turned over to you? I kind of had a look through them first. I didn't take anything, but I did see some stuff she was keeping, a list of names and a picture. I think it had to do with a friend of hers who committed suicide. I figured you had found them too?"

"I wouldn't know," Derek said, reproachfully. "The chief took all that stuff away and locked it up in the evidence room. If he found anything in it, he didn't tell me. You really should have said something about this sooner."

"I know, I'm sorry." Claudia didn't think this was the moment to explain that, at the time, she had not seen the police as particularly sympathetic. But since she was being helpful now, she tried to think of something she could do to make it up to him.

She cast her eyes around the marketplace, trying and failing to avoid the spot where Lori's body had been. Aside from the chairs having been pushed out of the way, the corner by the cheese shop looked exactly the way it always did, from the dark wood walls down to the wainscoting along the floor. That reminded her of something, and it took a moment for Claudia's brain to retrieve what it was.

"The fitness tracker," she said. Derek looked surprised, and she remembered that she had never confirmed to the police that it was hers. But it was too late now, so she pressed on. "It was under the body, right? So maybe it moved when Lori was killed."

"Could be," Derek said, still confused. "But what does that have to do with anything?"

"Because the whole point of it is it records movement. And that information gets uploaded to the computer." Claudia was already crossing the marketplace in quick strides, heading to her office in the corner. "The software wasn't compatible with my laptop, so I had to set it up in here. I can look at it and see the last time it moved before you found it, and that might help to narrow down exactly when Lori was killed. That would be a useful thing to know, right?"

"You can do that?"

"Sure. The whole reason I bought that brand was because they open-sourced a lot of their software. I thought I might be able to use it for something, but I never got around to it."

Her office was a cramped room tucked into a corner of the marketplace, between the storage closet and the bathroom. There was barely enough space for the desk that held the computer she had cobbled together from salvaged parts when they had cleaned out the offices at her old job. It didn't look like much, but it worked in exactly the way she liked, and she had long ago declared that she would do anything, up to and including black magic, to keep it running.

The comfort she felt just logging in was enough to relax her, and she clicked through to the application that controlled the fitness tracker practically on muscle memory. She was so sure of the outlines of what she was about to see, she barely paid attention to the details, until they were clear on the screen in front of her.

"That's weird." The words were out of Claudia's mouth before her brain finished processing the implications.

"What's weird?" Derek asked. The office was so small that he was left standing in the doorway, from where the screen wasn't visible.

"Um, the syncs stopped over two months ago. The battery must have died."

Claudia was lying. The battery was fine, and the syncs hadn't stopped. They had been happening at regular intervals, whenever the device was in range of her phone or the computer. Which made it pretty clear the tracker had been in her house since she stopped wearing it, talking to the phone when she was home. And it had still been working, and nowhere near the marketplace, on the night of Lori's death, when it was supposed to have been under the body. It had last connected from Claudia's house at three the following afternoon, right around the time Derek and Lennox had been there, telling her she was a suspect in the murder.

This was a problem.

There were exactly two people who could have taken the tracker then and later claimed it was found under the body, and one of them was there in the room with her.

"Sorry," Claudia said, just a shade too brightly. "I guess that was a dead end. Worth a try, right? Anyway, thanks for getting me my keys back. I should probably get to work, though, I've got a lot of cleaning up to do."

"I think that's going to have to wait." Derek was standing across the doorway, his broad shoulders blocking the exit, with his gun pointed at her chest. "I'm sorry, but I'm going to have to ask you to come with me."

CHAPTER TWENTY-FIVE

Time stopped, at least metaphorically. Claudia didn't know how long she sat staring at him, trying to process what was happening, but it was long enough that he narrowed those lovely blue eyes and waved the gun again.

"Come on, you don't have all day."

Frantically, Claudia tried to think of something she could do, some signal she could send with one or two taps she might get away with on the computer, but nothing was occurring to her. So, slowly and reluctantly, she willed herself out of her chair, toward the weapon that was pointed at her chest.

She kept her eyes focused on Derek's face, hoping he would give something away, but his expression was impassive and he said nothing, just stepped aside so she could pass and indicated that she should walk in front of him. Claudia knew that obeying wasn't in her best interests, that whatever he wanted for her was definitely not going to be what she wanted for herself, but her head was full of wool, and if there was a brilliant plan in there she couldn't get at it. So she went, and hoped she would think of something soon.

Derek walked her to the exit and had her turn off the lights and lock the door behind them. The fog was coming in, and the parking lot was cold and misty. Claudia tried to suppress her shivering and hoped it wouldn't be interpreted as a sudden movement.

The cold air had the additional effect of clearing her head, and after her initial freeze-up, her brain was working double-time now, making connections and spitting out theories faster than she could process them. Of course it was Derek—an attractive young man, newly arrived in town, who had every opportunity to frame her and suppress evidence. He was the person Lori was after, the subject of the list that Claudia had just so helpfully told him she had found.

And he was the angle that Neil had identified, either trying to avenge Lori or gain something from it himself, only he didn't get the chance. And Claudia, poor, dim, susceptible Claudia, hadn't given the possibility even a moment's thought.

She was all set for a good round of self-reproach, but this wasn't the time. Taking a hard look at her personal judgement was something she could do after she got herself out of this alive.

"The chief didn't tell you to give me back the keys, did he?" she said as Derek guided her out into the darkness. She was still thinking that in the long term it wasn't going to be a good idea to obey his orders, but for now she needed to keep the situation as calm as possible until she figured out what he was planning, and try to get as much information as she could in the meantime.

But Derek wasn't playing along.

"Don't worry about him, he doesn't know anything," he said. "Just keep walking."

"To where?"

"Your house. Now let's go."

It was the best news Claudia had gotten since she didn't think she was going to get good news again. If he had been taking her to his car, her only option would have been to bolt when they got to the road and hope Derek wasn't good at hitting a moving target. But the route back to her house gave her an idea, and that idea turned into a plan.

It wasn't a good plan, but it was a plan.

The fog rolled over them like sets of great waves on the rising wind. In the distance, Claudia could see the headlights of cars passing on the highway, too far for any hope that someone might hear her if she called out, even if for some reason they were driving with the windows down in fifty-degree weather. She was walking as slowly as she thought she could get away with, hoping against hope that someone would have misread the times for the outdoor market and a busload of badly-scheduled day-trippers was about to pull up to deliver her.

That didn't happen. Derek directed her across the parking lot, his gun held low enough not to be obvious from a distance, and Claudia tried to think of a suitable topic of conversation. But it was her captor who spoke first.

"I didn't want to do this," he said, sounding like a man making an unconvincing apology that he nonetheless expects to be accepted.

"You can quit any time you want," Claudia replied. "I'm not stopping you."

"It's not that simple." He was whining now, and Claudia wondered how she could have ever found this man remotely appealing. "You shouldn't have looked at that stuff, and now I don't have a choice."

"You shouldn't limit yourself like that," Claudia said encouragingly. "You don't have to do anything you don't want to."

She even managed a smile, but whatever sense of humor Derek had pretended to have wasn't in evidence now. In retrospect, trying to jolly a two-time murderer out of killing her probably wasn't going to work anyway, so she changed her approach.

"I've talked to Kara," she said. "She knows about the list. Are you going to fly across the country and shoot her too? I wouldn't say we were best friends, but if she hears about something happening to me, she might get in touch with someone, tell them her story about Steve Mann. In fact, I've already given a reporter her information, and asked him to send her pictures of people from local events. I know you're pretty careful about staying out of photos, but are you sure? If there's one picture with you in it, she'll spot you no problem. How do you think that's going to work out for you?"

That, at least, was something he wasn't expecting. Derek paused in marching Claudia across the parking lot and flared his nostrils in her general direction.

"Don't worry about me," he said, though from the unsteadiness in his voice it seemed like he might not be taking his own advice. "I can take care of myself."

"I can see that. But for how long? That reporter knows about Dana too. Whatever you do, this isn't going to end with me."

Claudia had hoped that might be enough to shake him, but no such luck. Derek just narrowed his eyes and pointed the gun at her a little more directly.

"That's not your problem, is it? Just keep walking."

They headed across the hillside toward her house, and if Derek noticed that Claudia was straying from the path, he didn't mention it. The fog was still swirling around them, making it hard to see more than a few feet ahead, and they both had to focus on not missing their footing on the uneven ground. Claudia was starting to worry she had misjudged her route, but they passed the rock that looked a little bit like a frog, and she knew they were still on track. Just a little farther, so she might as well start talking now.

"What do you think you're gaining by doing this?" she said. "If you leave right now, it's going to be hours before I can get anyone to listen to me, let alone go looking for you. Do you know how insane I'm going to sound, trying to convince Lennox that you killed both Lori and Neil, with absolutely no evidence? By the time I even got him to take my call, you could be halfway to Mexico. But if I'm dead, you're down one suspect, and you've got another body to explain."

"Not if you killed yourself because you were so worried about being caught. That should tie things up nicely." Derek sounded smug, like this terrible idea was something her silly little mind could never have thought of.

"How am I supposed to kill myself by being shot in a field? With your gun?" Claudia said.

"I'm not going to shoot you here." He explained it slowly, like he was talking to a small child. Clearly, he still hadn't seen the flaw in his plan, so Claudia helpfully illustrated it for him.

She stopped walking, at a spot just downhill from her goal, and turned to face her captor. It was now or never.

"Well, maybe you're going to have to. This is as far as I go. Shoot or get off the pot." She took a step backward, drawing Derek in that much closer and trying to keep in on a diagonal path. He was only about ten feet away now. She just hoped they were awake.

"Cute. But no, keep moving."

"Make me."

Derek stared at her, blank with confusion. It was clear that he believed that being person with the gun should earn him absolute obedience, and the failure of this basic principal had thrown him wildly off-balance. Claudia didn't expect that to last for long; she just hoped it would be long enough.

"Look," she tried reasoning. "If you pull that trigger you're going to be making a world of new problems for yourself. You know it and I know it, and I know you know it, and that's why there's no point waving that thing at me like you're going to get me to do anything. And you were going to have to leave anyway, right? Even if you succeed with me, it's only a matter of time until someone else makes the connections."

In the distance, she could hear the phone ringing in her house. It was probably just Betty, ready to say that she didn't care what Claudia thought, it wasn't safe for her to stay by herself, and expecting an argument. But Claudia decided to take a more optimistic approach.

"That's probably the reporter now, calling to tell me that Kara looked at the pictures and saw you. If he can't reach me, he's bound to have his next call be to the police station, to find out where you are. Or maybe he'll go straight to the county sheriff's office, hard to say. Either way, that's really going to cut into the time you have to make your getaway. Why not make it easier for yourself and go now?"

For half a moment she almost thought he was considering her proposal. But maybe that was just the time it took for him to work through her tortured syntax, because his only response was to point the gun at her more menacingly, if that was possible.

"You had better move or I am going to make you," he said. "Believe me, there's nothing I can do to you that I can't get Lennox to believe was your own fault."

Unfortunately, he was probably right about that. That left Claudia with exactly one option, and it was still about eight feet away. She took two more steps, and Derek advanced to match her. Claudia was starting to think this just might work when they were interrupted by a voice from up the hill.

"Put down the gun," it said. "I've got you covered."

The voice belonged to a man, tall and youngish, with an overgrown shock of black hair hanging into his eyes. He was dressed in pajama pants and a sweater, and holding a long-barreled gun, and Claudia had never seen him before.

"Who the hell are you?" Derek said.

"My name is Nathan Rodgers. I saw what you were doing, and I'm telling you to stop. It's all over now."

Of all the ways Claudia had envisioned meeting her cantankerous neighbor, this was not one of them. He looked nervous, despite being armed, and she suspected he was about as used to these kind of heroics as she was. She wasn't sure how this was going to affect her plans, but she certainly appreciated the help.

Derek, not so much.

"This is official police business, and this woman is a dangerous criminal" he said. "Now put that gun down, son, before I do something we all regret."

"Oh yeah? It's official police business to threaten to kill someone and make it look like a suicide? I heard you talking, and I've already called 911." He waved his gun in Derek's general direction. "Now put the gun down and step away slowly."

Derek hesitated, trying to decide between keeping his own gun on Claudia or turning it on the new arrival. That inspired Nathan to press his advantage by coming closer, which was a mistake. Claudia had thought from the start that there was something wrong about the weapon he was carrying, and when the patch of fog they were in suddenly lightened, she realized what it was.

You have got to be kidding me, Claudia thought.

Unfortunately, Derek saw it too. His face turned bright red and his expression went from uncertainty to fury.

"A BB gun? You thought you could threaten me with a goddamn BB gun? Do you know what happens to punks like you who try to pull something like that?" He was furious now, advancing toward the other man and ready to make good on his threat. Nathan, clearly unnerved that his plan had gone this badly, was looking for a way to make his escape, and only Claudia noticed the sound of ruffling feathers from inside the doghouse. She dodged out of the way as Derek took two more steps and crossed the invisible line and suddenly his life was a nightmare of feathers and honking.

The geese exploded out of their house, hissing and snapping at Derek and half-jumping, half-flying up at him. After a full day of being disturbed and harassed, this latest invasion of their private space was clearly too much for them, and they expressed their displeasure as only two very large geese can.

One of the birds was beating Derek around the arms and head with its powerful wings, while the other shot its beak out in the general direction of his inner thigh, landing several significant bites. They worked together in beautiful coordination, like they had been training for this moment all of their lives, the artistic free dance of the goose-attack Olympics.

Derek cried out like a man who had suddenly been attacked by geese and waved his arms in a hopeless attempt to drive them off. He tried firing his gun, but at that moment a beak found a very sensitive part of his anatomy and his arm shot up involuntarily, sending the bullet to vanish into the fog.

He probably would have kept firing but the pain had loosened his grip on the weapon, and the recoil knocked it out of his hand. Claudia and Nathan both lunged for it, with her getting there first.

"Okay," she said, pointing it at Derek as he extricated himself from his feathered attackers, bruised and bleeding, and stumbled down the hill with them waddling behind him, hissing like a pair of gas leaks. "Now do you believe me that this was a bad idea?"

Derek looked at her, then at the gun, then at the geese, then back at her. He started to say something, but changed his mind. Then, with one final, fearful glance back at the geese, he ran toward the road.

CHAPTER TWENTY-SIX

"And you just let him get away?"

"Well, I wasn't going to shoot him."

"I would have."

It was Monday, a full day and a half after the confrontation, and Betty and Claudia were sitting at Claudia's kitchen table. After spending all of Saturday night and most of Sunday at the sheriff's department headquarters in Santa Rosa, the last thing Claudia had wanted was to go out, or do anything other than lie in bed ever again, and that was what she had told Betty when she called at two in the afternoon. So, naturally, it had only been about fifteen minutes before Betty had showed up on her doorstep with a basket of scones, a freshly-made quiche, and a pot of hot coffee. Claudia had been about to declare this demonstration of competence too much to bear in her current state but, on the other hand, coffee.

And she had to admit, now that she had consumed half the contents of the basket and almost all of the coffee, it hadn't been a terrible idea. The quiche was fluffy, eggy perfection, enhanced with a generous quantity of chanterelle mushrooms from one of Roy's forager friends, and the scones were so rich and loaded with berries it almost seemed a shame to butter them. Ever vigilant, (except, apparently, when it mattered), Teddy stood by Claudia's chair, on high alert for any scraps that might escape, occasionally nosing her arm when she wasn't being clumsy enough.

"Okay, let's see if I've got it," Betty said, having taken a few minutes to digest Claudia's attempt at explaining what happened. "This guy, Derek, was some kind of scammer who had been cheating women out of their money, and Lori was trying to get revenge on him, because she was one of his victims?"

"No, her best friend was," Claudia corrected. "I had a call from the reporter I'd been working with, who talked to the friend's family this morning. Dana, that was the friend's name, she had hooked up with this guy she met online, thought he was the love of her life. None of her friends or family were really happy about him, but he got her to distance herself from them and she wouldn't listen to anything about him. I guess she and Lori got in a huge fight about it, and never talked again."

She took a sip of her coffee and went on.

"Dana's family wasn't quite sure what scam he used to get her to give him money, but his typical MO was to invent a health crisis for some fictional relative. Whatever it was, she fell for it, badly. She gave him everything she had, which was bad enough, but she embezzled some money from her employer too. So when Derek took the cash and vanished, she had nothing."

"And that's the woman who committed suicide," Betty finished for her.

Claudia nodded. "Yeah. I guess Lori must have just about lost it, and I've got to say, I don't blame her."

"But how did she end up here?"

"That part's less clear," Claudia admitted. "Things must have gotten a little too hot for Derek back East, so he moved out here to start over. Lori obviously tracked him down somehow, and decided that setting up a shop in the marketplace was a good cover for whatever she was planning. We'll never know exactly what that was, but from the looks of things, she didn't just want to get back at him, she wanted to ruin him."

"But how?"

"See that's where I think her plan had some problems. I think she had some sort of vague idea of using social media, and what she could learn about his previous victims, to make it turn into a viral story, but as far as I can tell she hadn't come up with anything more concrete than that. Or maybe she did, and Derek destroyed it when he got hold of her computer. Add that to the list of things we'll never know." She picked up a scone and stared at it like it might have one of those unobtainable answers hidden somewhere in it. But no, that was just a blueberry.

"One thing's for sure, he's not going to tell us. When I was in the station, I heard them talk about bringing him in, and the only thing he would say to anyone was that he wanted a lawyer," she said.

"Well, that's smart enough, but I don't understand why he thought a police car made a good getaway vehicle," Betty said, while she casually organized the paperwork that was scattered across the table. "He would have made it farther in pretty much anything else."

That was a sentiment that had been repeated more than once by the officers at the sheriff's department, once they had been convinced they really had a rogue cop on the run, and not just a couple of crazies who had taken their Saturday night a little too far. It had helped that one of them had recognized Nathan, though Claudia had never exactly figured out why.

Still, it had taken nearly two hours, over Lennox's loud protestations, from when Nathan's second 911 call had reached the county dispatcher with his extremely confusing message, until someone was finally willing to see if they could find Officer Derek Chambers to clear this whole thing up. From there, it didn't take long for it to become apparent that both the officer and his car had left the area, which was enough to enlist the help of some cooperating agencies to locate both, about twenty miles south of San Francisco.

"That's what's crazy to me; he didn't even think to go home and get his own car. Honestly, I'm almost more embarrassed than anything else, having been tricked by someone that dumb."

"It wasn't just you," Betty reminded her. "Tricking people was what he did. He just wasn't very smart at anything else."

"I guess that's the danger of overspecialization for you," Claudia said absently. "Anyway, I don't know what I'm thinking. I should be glad he wasn't any better at killing people and getting away with it. He certainly was good enough."

"Do you think he always planned to kill Lori?"

"Hard to say. It was definitely a departure from his previous behavior, but he seemed to take to it once he got started. My guess is that he didn't know she was here until pretty recently, maybe a week or so ago. She didn't get out much, and I wouldn't be surprised if she was intentionally avoiding him. I don't know why he didn't just leave when he did see her; maybe he wanted to figure out exactly how much she had on him. That would explain why he was hanging around outside her house when Brandon was there, and he followed her to the marketplace when she went to plant her stink bombs. After that, I don't know. He might have tried to charm her into giving up her plans, and when that failed he panicked and killed her."

"That's a possibility," Betty said. "Except . . ." She trailed off, looking thoughtful.

"What?"

"I don't suppose you remember, but when you mentioned that she was garroted, I was kind of taken aback by that."

Claudia admitted with some restraint, that she thought she had noticed something of the sort.

"Well, I didn't know how to bring it up without it being weird, but the crazy thing was, Roy and I had just been talking last week about garroting, and how it was different from strangulation. You know, just one of those strange conversations you have sometimes. Anyway, I didn't think anything about it until you told me that was how Lori died."

"But why? I mean, I don't know what you guys usually talk about, but that's a pretty crazy coincidence."

"I know. After you told me how she died, I asked Roy why he had thought of it in the first place, and he said there was a story in the paper about a lady who had been killed that way back in the twenties. So I have to wonder, maybe Derek got the idea from the same story."

"That could be," Claudia said, trying to hide her relief. "That doesn't prove premeditation, though. He might have just seen the cheese wire after he knocked her out and been reminded of the story. But that's a question for the lawyers."

"I guess so. And Neil?"

"He and Lori were together when she had her falling out with Dana, and he must have met Derek then. Derek probably found out he was in town when Neil went to ask about Lori's things. Once he spotted Derek, it wouldn't take him long to put two and two together, so he had to go."

"I have to say, I feel sort of responsible for Neil. He was our guest after all. We shouldn't have let him get himself murdered like that," Betty said.

"You should add that to your website," Claudia agreed solemnly. "We will try to keep you from getting murdered, but the Tyler Ranch cannot guarantee results."

Betty gave her a sideways look. "I'll consider it. Have they proved that Derek sent those texts yet?"

"I doubt it. That's going to take some time, though it'll probably be easier now that they know where to look. I talked to Helen yesterday, and she mentioned that a policeman had been talking to Brandon's friends. That probably explains where he got the information for the other fake text."

"Hedging his bets. It sounds like he had heard of the idea of framing people, but didn't really get the details. How did your fitness tracker get under Lori's body, anyway?" Betty asked.

"It didn't. Derek stole it from my house when he and Lennox came over to question me the first time, and then he snuck it into the evidence from the scene and claimed it was there all along. I guess one of the things Lennox wasn't doing very well was managing security in the evidence locker." Claudia had eaten all she could manage at this point, though she was eyeing the last scone and wondering if she had the strength to make an attempt. Betty, sensing that a bad decision was imminent, started packing up the leftovers.

"And another was doing background checks on his new hires," she said as she got the remainder of the quiche out of harm's way. "So he was planning on framing you the whole time? But why?"

Claudia shrugged. "Convenience, probably. Between my having argued with Lori and finding the body, Lennox already had me as a suspect. The sooner Derek could get me arrested, the less chance there was that the investigation would turn up his connection to Lori and her friend. That was also why he made sure to come out on his own to pick up her things from my storage. And of course, I didn't give any of it a second thought. He was just so attractive and charming, what could possibly be wrong? He was even nice to my dog."

Claudia looked down at Teddy, still cheerfully begging for crumbs and scratches.

"You, madam," she said, "Are a terrible judge of character. Almost as bad as me."

"Well, you've got plenty of company there," Betty said. "By the way, there's nothing official yet, but the town council had an emergency meeting last night on the subject of how soon they can get Lennox out. There was even some talk of getting rid of the department all together and going back to having the sheriff being in charge, after this."

Claudia agreed that there was something to that idea, and they might have elaborated on that subject for a while longer, but there was a knock on the door. Claudia and Betty looked at each other in mild confusion.

"Did you hear anyone drive up?" Claudia asked.

"No," said Betty. "Are you going to see who it is?"

"I don't know," Claudia said. "I haven't had a great record with guests lately."

But she went to answer the door anyway, since there didn't seem to be any reason not to. And there, on her doorstep, was Nathan Rodgers.

"Hi. I, um, just thought I'd stop by and see how you're doing? Are you doing okay?" He looked nervous, and slightly damp, like he had just taken a shower and not gotten his hair completely dry. He was dressed in a light sweater over a t-shirt and jeans, and carried himself with the abashed attitude of a college student who just realized he was late for dinner with his parents.

"Oh, uh, thanks. Yeah, I'm fine. I mean, as good as could be expected." Claudia was sure there was something else she was supposed to say at this point, but it took her a minute to think of it. "Would you like to come in?"

"Sure, thanks." He came through the door and took a look around, barely seeming to notice Betty.

"Wow," he said. "This place is small inside."

There wasn't much Claudia could say to that.

"Same as on the outside," she agreed. "You hadn't seen it before? I thought everyone in town had been through her while it was on the market." (The number of questions she had gotten about the bathroom tile after she had moved in had been frankly unnerving.)

"No, I was away traveling. I didn't even realize it was seriously on the market until the place sold. But, this is really small." He looked around like he couldn't believe such a place could actually support human habitation, which Claudia found annoying.

"Actually, I'd been thinking about applying for a permit to build an addition, but there seems to be some opposition on the local level to me doing anything with this property." Nathan might be friendly enough now, as well as absolutely not what Claudia had pictured, but she wasn't about to forget the amount of time her neighbor had spent treating her like public enemy number one.

He clearly hadn't forgotten either.

"Yeah, about that." He ran his fingers through his mop of black hair and looked to Betty for support, apparently seeing her for the first time. "I'm really sorry I gave you such a hard time. When I bought my house, obviously I knew these cottages and the market were there, but nothing seemed to be happening with them, and I figured it was all just abandoned. And then I was gone for a few months and suddenly there was all this going on and I, um, I didn't handle it well. I've kind of been going through some stuff," he added, as though that explained it.

It didn't, but Claudia was willing to give it a chance, considering their recent history. But it was Betty who asked the pertinent question.

"What are you doing living all the way out here, anyway?" she asked. "Do you work nearby?"

"No, well, not anymore. The thing is, a few years ago I got some cash together and opened a brewery, because I've always been kind of a beer nerd, and it ended up doing pretty well. So, eventually, this big conglomerate came along and offered me a bunch of money for it, and I'm like, that's a lot of money, and I could do whatever I want with it, so I took it, but then I couldn't figure out what I wanted. So that's what I was out here trying to do, and when all the people showed up it seemed like a lot."

Claudia thought that was the dumbest reason she had ever heard for blocking someone's permits to expand their parking lot, and she was about to say so, but Betty got there first.

"Waitaminute. You're that Nathan Rodgers? The reclusive boy wonder founder of Fog Heart Brewing Company?"

Nathan turned red, then faded to pink. "I really hated that magazine article. He was just mad I wouldn't be in their "eligible bachelors of beer" calendar. And the whole part about me sending back three shipments of hops for not being perfect was completely not true. There was only one, and it had weevils."

This was all very interesting, but Claudia thought there were some important points being ignored here.

"So you were mad at my business because you made too much money? And I'm supposed to feel sorry for you because of that?"

"No! I mean, yeah, but no. I've just been sort of in my own head for a while, and I wasn't dealing with it well. But when I saw what was happening the other night, with the guy and the gun and everything, it kind of snapped me out of it."

"About that. Not that I'm not grateful, but how did you know he had the gun on me in the first place? It's not that close to your house, and the fog was coming in." Claudia thought she knew, but she wanted to get it on the record. (From the looks Betty was giving her, she clearly didn't approve of taking this approach with Sonoma County's Boy Genius of Brewing, but that was her problem.)

Nathan at least had the decency to look uncomfortable.

"The thing is, I sometimes get kind of single-minded about stuff. And I couldn't always see what was going on down in the marketplace, so a couple weeks ago I ordered a telescope, and it just came. And when you guys came out with him pointing a gun at you, I figured that had to be bad news."

That was undeniably true, but Claudia wasn't going to let him off the hook that easily. "You were watching through a telescope to find something to be mad at me about?"

"Well, when you put it that way—Look, I was trying to save you."

"That doesn't make it any less creepy."

"Creepy or not, it's better than you being killed by that man," Betty interrupted, trying to calm the waters. "I think we can all agree on that."

"Okay, sure," Claudia said in what was possibly history's most grudging acceptance of someone trying to save your life. "But it's not like it was necessary. I had a plan."

That was too much for Nathan. "Your plan was geese!"

"Well yours was a BB gun!"

Neither of them had a further argument, so they reached a standoff, silently glaring at each other across Claudia's tiny living room. Once again it was up to Betty to play peacemaker, and this time she went with the direct approach.

"The important thing is that no one else died, and now that all this is settled, maybe we can finally have some peace around here." She looked from Claudia to Nathan and back again until she felt like she had achieved sufficient agreement. "Good. Now, Nathan, there are some blackberries growing next to your deck that look ripe, so why don't we all go and pick some and I'll make a cobbler."

Betty headed for the door and Claudia got up to find her shoes and a long-sleeved sweatshirt to protect her arms against the thorns, but Nathan just looked confused.

"Wait, what? Just like that, we're going to go pick my blackberries, because she says so?"

"Yep," said Claudia. "It's really good cobbler."

ACKNOWLEDGMENTS

This book could never have come into existence without the help of many people, who are to be praised or blamed as one sees fit. Personally, I'd like to thank them.

First, my husband Cameron, for supporting and believing in me, and serving as my expert reader for all matters computer-related, **and my parents, for a lifetime of support and encouragement.**

My agent, Abby Saul, who has been my guide and advocate through the ups and downs and sidewayses of publishing, and is always ready with an encouraging word and an on-point GIF.

My editor, Dan Meyer, and everyone at Seventh Street Books and Start SF, for all their work to take this collection of words and turn it into a real, live book.

The members of my writing group: Madeline Butler, Karen Catalona, Sharon Johnson, Kirsten Saxton, Karen Murphy and Cornelia Read, who read this book and all the others, and whose comments made them better.

All my family and friends for their encouragement, sympathy, and support.

And finally, everyone on the Alameda/Oakland to South San Francisco ferry, for putting up with a definitely-not-a-morning person trying to write a book on her commute.